Angela's Purse

Eileen Finn Loving

PAGE PUBLISHING, INC.
Conneaut Lake, PA

First originally published by Page Publishing 2021

ISBN 978-1-6624-3836-3 (pbk)
ISBN 978-1-6624-3837-0 (digital)

Printed in the United States of America

To My Husband Paul

New tresses now await you
Trimmed and styled with you in mind
No doubt your jaunty wearing will surely bring a smile
Your brightness and your spirit soaring to the sky
Inviting all who love you
Along this next short mile

Eileen Finn Loving

The Wicklow House

ANGELA COUGHLAN LOVED her house in County Wicklow from the first moment she saw it. She was ten years old then. The solarium stretching the width of the house facing the back gardens was her place of peace. It was where she sat on that first day in disbelief that it was hers, in disbelief that it had been given to her by the person she had come to cherish and love. Though the pain and grief of her loss still existed deep in her soul, she *was* at peace.

This morning, she awoke early in anticipation of the weekend off from her busy schedule as a paediatric oncologist at Park Edge Hospital in Dublin. The sun had just risen as she eased herself into her favourite chair, deep, warm, and big enough for two. The rim of the earth was on fire with spokes of red flame. The sun was high enough in the sky to allow Angela to look up at the miracle of colour. Beads of moisture from the night sparkled on the petals and leaves of the assorted flowers in the garden as they slid, dripped, and danced their way to the soil below. Without closing her eyes, Angela's thoughts drifted gently and silently, as if lubricated by the glistening dew, to her childhood house on Shadow Ridge Avenue in Baybridge. She was ten years old again.

Commitment

ANGELA AND HER sister Amy, two years her junior, were already in Mrs. Finnerty's driveway playing with her cat, Mrs. Miller. This is where they could be found most Sunday afternoons, expecting their neighbour's return from *Pepper*, the Indian restaurant where she ate lunch.

"She's here! She's here!" they squealed as they abandoned the cat and hurled themselves at her knees.

Holding her handbag aloft, she replied, mischief in every word, "Surprise, surprise!"

"You brought us laddu," echoed their reply, "our favourite!"

No surprise as the sugary pastries were part of their Sunday afternoon ritual. First, the treats then the discussion of last week's book and the choosing of the new one. Their very own book club! Since discovering, at an early age, that Mrs. Finnerty's downstairs was a library with books floor to ceiling, this ritual continued. Their relationship flourished but was never described. When they thought of each other, no words traveled along the pathways of their brain. It wasn't a thing that required language. It was a living sensation, like a breath or a heartbeat. It lived deep in their spirit and would shape what Angela and her sister would become. Mrs. Finnerty knew without a doubt that choosing to live next door to this family when she returned from India was no accident. This was where she was meant to be, and nothing present or yet to come would separate them.

Madge Costello, a neighbour with a gift for capturing precious moments with her camera, made an album tracking Angela's activities when Mrs. Finnerty had her stroke. She presented it to her while she was still in the hospital. Angela had an appointment that day to complete the plan for her *own* leg operation due to bone cancer and refused to leave without seeing her. Mrs. Finnerty showed her the album before replacing it under her pillow. "Will you always keep it under your pillow? she asked.

"I always will" came the reply.

"Will I always be with you then?" asked Angela.

"Always," whispered her friend.

Mrs. Finnerty kept that promise, cementing it by funding a foundation in Angela's name called *Angela's Tresses and Turbans* for children who lost their hair due to chemotherapy.

Barring a twist and a turn, the headquarters of the foundation was just across the street from where they lived as next-door neighbours in an old house they named the Bright House.

The Bright House

WEEKS EARLIER, MADGE Costello watched young Angela Coughlan and her wingman, Mrs. Finnerty, leave the Bright House together after their excursion there from the rehab centre. When the good news reached the people of Baybridge on the day of the operation that Angela's procedure to remove the cancer from the bone in her leg was successful, with no need for amputation, their hearts leaped, propelling them into a frenzied state to prepare the Bright House for their inevitable visit. The Bright House was chosen to fulfill a requirement as part of their rehabilitation program. Mrs. Finnerty's doctor admitted her for treatment following her stroke, and Angela went daily from home after a prosthesis replaced the cancerous bone in her lower limb. The purpose was to assess their functional capabilities in the real world and prepare them for discharge. This would be Angela's first visit. Mrs. Finnerty had not seen the inside of the Bright House since before its renovation due to her stroke. When she first saw it, on a rare visit to the nearby football fields, standing alone close to the Gaelic Football Club House, it impressed her so much it was the only premises she considered to house the headquarters of Angela's foundation. From first sight, she knew this was the right place.

It was meant to be, was the belief of all involved. The owner, a Mr. Jim Foley, was given the house by his uncle, and he promised himself he would not sell it. Indeed, he did not. For when it became known who was interested in this very special house with its wood floors, quaint-carved staircase, spectacular view of the mountain and surrounding farms, and what its intended use would be, he simply donated it.

The entire neighbourhood had joined forces to prepare this gem for that intended use. Madge, using her gift for telling a story with a camera, a gift she did not know she had, emerged as the publicity person. Fiona Hannon, the social worker at Angela's and Mrs. Finnerty's doctor's office, became director of social services. Mrs. Kitty Walsh, who, without any effort managed to fill a tote bag, now called Angela's Purse, with money at a mass said for Angela prior to her operation, was appointed treasurer. Angela's Purse continued being replenished without solicitation and no conflict of interest with the foundation. Two separate enterprises altogether. Gradually, those who at the start cleaned, brushed, polished, stained, and painted continued as members of the board, pooling their individual talents and training for the greater good. They were all here today to welcome their benefactor and Angela. Standing outside the Bright House now, when the festivities ended, Madge waved goodbye as the facility vehicle from the Baybridge rehab centre made its way to the main road.

As the white van, with its ornate logo proclaiming its destination, increased its distance from Madge, she turned back to the Bright House. A hesitation, a feeling of disquiet deep inside, caused her to sit a moment on the brightly painted bench on the porch by the main entrance. The unsettled feeling brewed like old tea in the pit of her stomach since Mrs. Finnerty's stroke a few weeks previously. Madge had great respect for this lady, not because of how she loved and helped Angela and her family, not because of her sharing her books with the local children, not because of the quiet, unassuming way she went about in Baybridge helping and befriending. She just knew and respected her for herself as a person, thinking of her as a kind human being with unique selflessness she had not met before now.

This whole stroke business had her disturbed.

The Twins Killfeather

MRS. FINNERTY ALIGHTED from the vehicle unassisted at the manor section of the premises. This was the original building to which a state-of-the-art rehabilitation facility had been added.

"She's back" came the voice from the weather-beaten white wicker chair on the portico. Shielding her eyes from the late-afternoon sun, she looked up to see the bejeweled hand of Harriet Killfeather waving. Her sister Eleanor, older by three minutes, tried to hush her.

"Harriet, please, a little decorum."

Though they were twins, now ninety-four years old, Harriet had enjoyed the role of the baby of the family and the giddiness it allowed all her life.

"Ring for the tea tray, Eleanor," Harriet pleaded. "I'm too excited to do a thing until I hear all the news."

Careful of her footing, Mrs. Finnerty climbed the semicircular stone steps reaching them in their usual afternoon spot and took both their bony hands in a gentle clasp. There was nothing gentle in the hearty handshake proffered by the Twins Killfeather. All three ladies waved to the rehab assistant who had been following Mrs. Finnerty at a distance. It was their signal she was safe and sound and in good hands now. No need to tarry. The aide could report to the physiotherapists of the uneventful return of the patient, confirming her ability to cope unassisted, a requirement for discharge. This success and the fact there were no stairs in the patients' home made it inevitable that she would return there. The stairs were replaced by a small lift years earlier when the entire ground floor of the house has been converted into a library.

"Ms. Harriet, Ms. Eleanor, what a welcome!" said Mrs. Finnerty, breaking loose from their tight handgrip.

"How was it? Is the Bright House beautiful? Did they change anything? Do you like it?" gushed Ms. Harriet.

"Now, Harriet, for pity's sake, let the woman catch her breath," interrupted Eleanor, trying to put manners on her baby sister. "Do sit down, Mrs. Finnerty, join us. Thelma is bringing out the tea tray," Eleanor spoke as Thelma, tray in hand, elbowed her way through the enormous ancient door.

"It was beyond words," reported their guest, accepting a seat in another of the ancient wicker chairs. "Love it. It's exactly as I imagined a space for Angela's foundation should be. The caring, sharing, welcoming atmosphere oozed from the very walls. More than that, it has an artistic aura inspiring Sammy and her team to create their beautiful maharaja turbans. The glass-walled studio, once used as the kitchen overlooking the pastures and the mountain, is inspirational."

After taking a deep satisfying breath, she took a mouthful of tea. Harriet stifled a chuckle at the gulping sound.

Eleanor gave no sign that she noticed, instead, asking, "What was Angela's reaction? Was she overwhelmed at all?"

"She was quiet. She paid attention, taking it all in, but did not ask any questions. I sometimes wonder if she has difficulty with the foundation bearing her name. When the idea first arose, it was a remark from her sister Amy that was the trigger. She was admiring a piece of fabric I brought from India years ago and made the comment it would make a nice hat or scarf. I thought of the hair loss Angela would have to endure as a result of the chemo and things took off after that. Of course, that may not be true. Angela loves what the turbans do for others whose self-esteem takes such a battering due to hair loss at their lowest time. There is no doubt about that. But she takes no credit for any of it. She does, in her generous kind way, get the big picture and would, even if she herself were not in the same condition. You've met her here at the centre and know her ways," concluded Mrs. Finnerty.

They sat in silence for a while. The Twins Killfeather were beginning to get the big picture too.

"Is there anything to be done about Angela's feelings? Where is she now in her treatment?" asked Eleanor.

"She is recovering from the leg operation and doing so well. Very soon, it will be time to go back to Park Edge for the first of the chemo cycles after surgery. She is a trooper with the treatment. It's being away from her own bed and Amy that distresses her," explained Mrs. Finnerty.

"Oh, the poor child," said Harriet.

"It seems they have a great love for each other," offered Eleanor.

"None of the squabbling you sometimes get among sisters."

Harriet shot her sister a questioning look. "Not us, Harriet dear, aren't we practically one, though I am your elder?" teased the first-born twin. Harriet did not seem bothered by the *elder* reference.

All good relations restored they patted the back of each other's veiny hand. While the sisters' exchange was going on, Mrs. Finnerty recalled Amy's earlier refusal to go to the main production factory in Haymarket until Angela was well enough to go with her, she was adamant about this. She wondered aloud now to the twins if such a visit before Angela's return to Dublin might be possible.

"Oh, it sounds just right," declared Harriet. "It's on the way, and it's a lovely town on the Shannon. As they will be making the trip together, neither one will have an advantage over the other, an equal experience."

"What a wonderful way to put it," beamed her sister.

Hill Hands

SAMMY AND KITSY crouched over a piece of fabric. The sunlight was streaming in through the enormous glass windows that formed the back of the Bright House and their workspace. One only had to raise the eyes to be transported to a rural paradise of fields and mountains. Artistic inspiration at the lifting of the head.

It was a busy day today. Fiona Hannon called moments before, "We have four orders for your maharaja turbans ladies, one local boy, one in Galway and two in Dublin." The Haymarket factory was closer to Galway but only supplied girls' turbans. Orders for boys' turbans were filled from the Baybridge site with Sammy at the helm. Kitsy designed the logos, a small disk with a duckling whose wing had the letters *ATT for Angela's Tresses and Turbans* expertly embroidered on each. Angela referred to her favourite book, *Make Way for the Ducklings*, using a line from it to let the doctors know when she was ready to return home following her treatment. That is why Angela and Amy chose a duckling for the logo. Then off they went to Haymarket and attached to each turban, supervised by their designer, Mrs. Shiva.

"Thanks, Mrs. Hannon, four in all, right on it," Sammy replied. She sauntered back to where Kitsy was sitting.

"I don't know," Kitsy was saying. "Does this look off-center to you? Or dull or something? It's just not right."

As she spoke, Sammy lifted the swatch she was examining towards the light. Kitsy abandoned her stool and stood looking over Sammy's shoulder. Without the backing, now left on the workbench, the light streaming through the window transformed the piece. What seemed crooked, off-center and dull before now in response to the light looked like it had movement, a dance giving life and vibrancy to the pattern. Smiles lit their faces as they nodded at the discovery. They were true artists indeed, born and raised in an area of Baybridge known as the Hill. Some might consider it the wrong side of the tracks, but those who thought that way failed to notice the talented, hardworking, generous contribution made by those people to the commercial and artistic success of Baybridge. The studio at the Bright House where the amazing turbans were made bore the title *Hill Hands* in recognition of those on the wrong side of the tracks.

"That's it!" Kitsy announced. "No backing." It was to become the signature design feature of the Baybridge product.

"Hello, anybody doing any work here today?" asked the voice as it approached.

"Not if we can help it," Sammy replied as the voice neared them.

"And there I was, Samantha Garvey, thinking that you were full of dedication," teased Mrs. Kitty Walsh, owner of the voice and treasurer of the foundation.

"Oh no, Mrs. Walsh, we're just gazing out the window, hoping some kind person would drop in with something tasty to go with the tea."

"Well, as luck would have it, I happen to…" started Mrs. Walsh.

"What? Did you really bring us something to go with the tea? You did, didn't you?" continued Kitsy as she eyed the bag from Quigley's in Mrs. Walsh's hand.

"Now, now, calm down, you'd think you hadn't had a bite to eat in months."

"We haven't, have we, Sammy?" asked Kitsy.

"We are all on a fast around here. It's worse than Lent," answered Sammy with big mournful eyes.

"Ah, go on with ye," Mrs. Walsh said. She opened a bag, releasing the glorious smell of warm bread mingled with jam, honey, fruit, and much more into the already-fabric-smelling room. Bliss!

"Just one apiece," she instructed, going to visit Mrs. Finnerty with the rest.

"She's doing well I hear, so well, it seems she will go home soon," said Sammy.

She and Mrs. Walsh were with Mrs. Finnerty when she had her stroke in the car on their way back from Haymarket. They took her straight to the hospital and stayed with her, beside themselves with worry all the time.

"Today actually, thus the treats for the last hurrah."

"Hurrah indeed," both artists said in unison. "Well done, Mrs. Finnerty."

"It's great news really. Her excitement at being home next door to Angela and her family is palpable. She missed Amy's company. She loved having her stay at her house when Caroline and Tony took Angela to Park Edge. It eased the burden on those young parents having her next door. It's good times ahead now, at least before Angela returns to Dublin for the next round of chemo. Isn't it wonderful that Una is staying with her, though? I'll never get over the way she needed a new job and a place to stay when her university assignment at the girls' school ended. Amy and Ms. Flynn, or Ms. Una as they now call her, are the best of friends since she helped Mrs. Finnerty launch the foundation on sport's day by having Angela's class and some of the teachers wear turbans. Then as you know, she accepted a position here with us at the Bright House now that she has graduated. Her skills as a social worker will be invaluable to the organization going forward. In true Mrs. Finnerty's style, when she learned Una needed a new place to stay, she invited her to mind the house while she was in hospital and rehab following her stroke. Then she suggested Una stay on as she could do with the company. She must return to the university, of course, sometime in the next few weeks to officially graduate and receive her diploma." After a brief pause, she begged, "Any chance of a quick cup in my hand before I go pick up her ladyship from the centre? I'm parched after that long speech."

Kitsy and Sammy had to shake themselves back to the present so engrossed were they in Mrs. Walsh's account of how this all came about. Unbeknownst to each other, the same notion began to germinate in their brain.

Jumping up to show an eagerness that was surely exaggerated, Kitsy said, "Coming right up."

As soon as Mrs. Walsh was out of earshot on her way to pick up Mrs. Finnerty, the two artists crouched together as if examining a piece of fabric.

This time, they were hatching a plot.

Uplift

UNA FLYNN LEFT her post in the administration office just inside the main door of the Bright House after one o'clock to go home to ready the house for Mrs. Finnerty's homecoming. This was not your typical house. The entire ground floor apart from the mini kitchen was a library. She had kept the books dusted, so no work was needed there. She was standing in the kitchen, wondering how often she would need to wipe the spotless tiny counter and the spotless tiny table when the doorbell rang. *It's way too early for Mrs. Finnerty*, she thought as she opened the door.

"Ms. Una," said Amy, standing beside her sister Angela. "We brought flowers. Mammy is coming in a minute with the dinner."

"I'm so glad you both are here. I need you to walk around and tell me if anything needs wiping or polishing or sweeping," Ms. Una said.

"Are we to do a house inspection for you, Ms. Una?" Angela asked.

"Exactly" came the reply.

"Okay, so you take the flowers, and we'll inspect. Come on, Angela."

Ms. Una, as the girls had taken to calling her, American style, was in her element as she stood back watching their seriousness in the task at hand. At one point, though, it crossed her mind that they really might find fault. All was well until they went upstairs.

"Ms. Una, you missed the tray in Mrs. Finnerty's room for when she brings her tea up in the morning," said Amy.

"Oh, I didn't know about the tray. Where do you think it might be?" asked Ms. Una.

Amy went straight to its spot on the kitchen counter. She knew this since she stayed here with Mrs. Finnerty while Angela went to Dublin for her first chemo treatment. Even at eight years old, she had a sense of responsibility for Mrs. Finnerty and this house. Now satisfied with their work, the sisters settled at the front of the library just inside the door, where the children's books were on the lower shelves of the bookcase.

"We can't really say *upstairs* in Mrs. Finnerty's, can we, as there are no stairs?" whispered Amy.

"I suppose we can't because of the lift. We could say *uplift,*" offered Angela.

Short pause, and soon the contagious laughter of the two filled the room. No matter the situation, they always managed to dwell on the comical, eventually bringing others along and lightening the mood.

The girl's mother, Mrs. Coughlan, finished putting the food in disposable containers, took her cup of tea to the large circular table in her big family-size kitchen, and sat down. She surveyed the fruits of her afternoon labours. The containers did not look too flimsy, she decided—better those than Pyrex dishes when taking food to someone's house. From her own experience, it was no help at all if that someone spent days scrubbing the dishes before returning them, sometimes to remove stains that were years old. If they had that much time and energy, it would be better if they just cooked themselves. No, her disposable ones looked just fine. The phone rang.

"Caroline, oh, good, you're still there," Caroline recognized Mrs. Walsh's voice.

"Mrs. Walsh, how are you? Everything all right? No delays or..."

"No, no," assured Mrs. Walsh, "we're making a good time. Mrs. Finnerty just popped down to let the Twins Killfeather know she was leaving but would be back to see them soon. The three of them have become great friends since Mrs. Finnerty was well enough to move over to the independent rooms in the manor from the rehab centre. They are quite quaint together. I am glad for them. In fact, it turns out they have been helping her with a little dilemma, and it appears your input will be needed. All in good time."

"Intrigued," said Caroline, "and glad someone else is giving help to Mrs. Finnerty. It's usually the other way around. Knowing her, it won't remain a dilemma for long."

"Too true," replied Mrs. Walsh. Going down now to meet her on the veranda, and we will be right over."

"I'd better get a move on with the food then. Bye for now," said Caroline.

Gathering up her things, she made her way from her driveway to the next-door driveway, a path well-trodden over the last few months. As she turned up Mrs. Finnerty's path, she startled Mrs. Miller, her cat, sitting on the windowsill in her usual spot, or so she thought. In fact, Mrs. Miller was getting used the all the goings and comings of late and was coincidentally stretching at that precise moment, not in the least bit startled.

"It's just me, Mrs. Miller," said Caroline, mistaking the stretch for an attack stance. She probably would not have given her the usual irresistible pet today, even if her hands were not full. Mrs. Finnerty's front door was ajar in anticipation of the arrivals, so she merely announced herself. Immediately, her two daughters appeared in the doorway. It was clear something was amusing them as they were laughing while their mother squeezed her way into the house.

"Mammy, Mammy, Ms. Una said *upstairs*, but I said it couldn't be in this house with no stairs, so Angela said it has to be *uplift*."

Having said this, Amy ran back to her book. Angela followed more slowly. Both continued to laugh without shame. Since birth, Angela's laugh was infectious. Caroline remembered an outburst once in front of Dr. Owens, their family doctor, when they took a fit of the giggles over a mix up between funny bone doctor and a funny bone. Mrs. Finnerty got the blame for that one.

"You two will have some explaining to do to Mrs. Finnerty about renaming her house parts behind her back," Caroline said, failing miserably to look cross as she made her way back to the tiny kitchen. The once-large kitchen was sacrificed to make room for the lift while the stairs had to be sacrificed to make room for books. Mrs. Finnerty's arrival was quiet, no rushing forward to embrace, no leaping up and down and clapping of hands. She stood inside her front door in silence and looked around her. Amy and Angela understood at once the reason for the pause.

Mrs. Finnerty stepping towards them, arms outstretched, borrowed a line from Angela's book, and simply said, "*And when night falls, they swim to their little island and go to sleep.*"

No Dilemma

MRS. WALSH NODDED to Caroline when the time was right to distract the girls after the commotion of greeting and feeding everyone was over. It wasn't difficult as there was not the usual grouping of chairs and sofas in this house. Inside the door on the right, a low table with a lamp and one chair had evolved over time into the children's reading nook. That's where the girls always settled. On the other side of the front door stood a large carved desk in the same wood as the bookcases. This was Mrs. Finnerty's usual spot. It afforded her a view of the avenue through the large bay window.

As the adults gradually gathered around the desk, the separation of the girls became stark and bothered Mrs. Finnerty. With a questioning look towards Caroline and a similar nod in the girl's direction, she got the solution.

"Girls," called Caroline, "if you two want to be part of this, it's standing room only. Otherwise, we can let you know when we get to the good part."

"Okay" came the reply. Neither raised their eyes from the books they were reading.

"Okay," replied Caroline, not sure if the girls really heard her, but what did not escape her was the gentle pat Una Flynn gave Mrs. Finnerty's hand resting on the table between their two teacups.

Mrs. Finnerty spoke in her usual voice, not resorting to a whisper though she was aware that the girls were within earshot, "I'm afraid it looks like a formal meeting here. No need for that. If any-one wants to wander around or break into a dance, it's fine. I just wanted to bring up something that's been on my mind since Angela and I went to the Bright House together. She seemed quiet to me, disconnected from the work being done there in her name. I am not concerned about that so much, as she's a ten-year child. Caroline, do you remember when Amy chose not to visit Haymarket until she and Angela could go together? I think Angela might be holding back a bit because it was Amy's chance remark that started the whole thing." Mrs. Finnerty paused.

All eyes were on the speaker up to this point. Now Caroline looked at her husband, Tony, the steady, dependable police sergeant, and wondered if they might have missed something, something big between the girls. Before either of them could respond to that look, even with a thought, their attention went at once back to Mrs. Finnerty. Silently, the girls had taken up their standing-room-only invitation and stood on either side of Mrs. Finnerty like sentries.

Amy spoke, addressing her mother sitting opposite, "Mammy, I know I saw the shiny cloth first, and I said it would make a nice hat or scarf. That's all I said. I didn't know anything about turbans, not ever before. Angela knows why the turbans started to be made. They had to be called Angela's, not Amy's 'cos they're not. So, can we go to see where they make them? Can we Mammy?"

As if rehearsed, they simultaneously planted a big kiss on each of their beloved neighbour's cheeks.

That was that. Mrs. Coughlan said she would ask Dr. Owens tomorrow at the afternoon appointment.

Angela asked, "Can we go visit the Killfeather ladies when I finish therapy in the morning? We'll get them scones at Quigley's on the way."

That was that too. The sisters returned to their books.

If the assembled adults had anything to say on the matter, it was not shared. These little girls had quietened them in the past with their simple, wise solutions. Enough said. They would find out more tomorrow.

When Una closed the door behind the last visitor, she quietly suggested, "Mrs. Finnerty, you should get some rest now."

"Una," came the reply, "I am saturated in rest. Won the lotto jackpot of rest. Now I am itching to do something. I will come to the Bright House with you in the morning and pester Sammy for that early cup of tea. Oh! Can we do what Angela suggested and bring scones from Mrs. Quigley's?"

Una would not have been surprised if Mrs. Finnerty clapped her hands with joy like a small child. Instead, sporting a broad smile and a glint of mischief in her eyes she rose from the impressive carved desk, declaring, "Onwards and upwards."

As she made her way to the lift off the mini kitchen, Una Flynn distinctly heard a series of muted claps and a single whoop as her *house friend* entered the lift. Amazed as always by Mrs. Finnerty, Una sat a while in the now-fading light. As she reflected on her time in Baybridge, she found her thoughts wandering and eventually settling on the first time she learned of her assignment to St. Paul's primary school in this amazing place.

She had no idea what this first assignment as a social worker had in store for her and others as she sat there, remembering.

Una's Assignment

ANTICIPATION BUILT IN the corridor of the university as they awaited the posting of their final assignments. Diverse options included but were not limited to hospitals, doctors' offices, a community centre, public health facility, and schools. The tiptoeing and huddling began as soon the secretary locked the glass display case, outside the dean's office, now holding the assignments. Though Una Flynn was the tallest, she could not see from where she stood behind the other five because of the tiptoeing and the huddling. Soon, she was alone standing there, the others to the side gasping and shrieking and peering over one another's shoulders. Una stepped closer to the display case and scrolled down to her name. *Ms. Una Flynn, Saint Paul's Primary School, Baybridge.*

Taken aback a little, she pondered what experience she would get there. If her assignment was to a school, she expected it to be at a secondary school or university. Now there would be a challenge! She did not know any children of primary school age having been born and raised in a rural area without any immediate neighbours, and she was an only child. Still, she liked the little ones she saw about town or in church, in their oversize uniforms and their whispering, telling of secrets behind their adorable little cupped hands.

The five scattered, all seemly happy with their lot. Una dawdled a while longer, reread the notice in the glass case then made her way to the dorm.

Little did Ms. Una Marie Flynn know how her own life was going to change and how she was going to change the lives of many. No such thoughts entered her mind as she plopped down on her bed. Her large duvet and the small dorm bed never really worked, so long ago she had given up trying to make them match. They would have to stay at odds. The excess bedding, however, made for a comfy plop on the bed that she took advantage of almost every time she entered the small cell size space. Looking up at the bland, uninspiring ceiling above her head, she found it easy to project herself forward and ponder the new assignment. It wasn't hard as the dorm ceiling offered no distraction. Her eyes had grown accustomed to the one damp stain in the corner. It took on the appearance of a failed art project overtime. Prior to today's announcement, they were aware suitable accommodation was arranged for them at their new locations. Some would be in dorms in various colleges, some in small flats, some boarding with local families, and still others in hospital quarters. The type of assignment dictated where they would live. Her thoughts continued to stray as she imagined herself living with the family of one of the pupils in a quaint cottage on the outskirts of town. She knew Baybridge was in the west of Ireland near the ocean. Maybe she would get a bike!

Now as she was entering into the spirit of things, excitement filled her though she could not imagine her skills as a social worker getting much of a workout in the picture now forming in her mind. A uniformed sea of little people hopping, skipping, and jumping on a playground. The noise, the giggles, the squabbles, the weeping, the joy all real to her now as she watched with her mind's eye. What possible need could they have for her in such a place?

As she roused herself from her wandering, she became aware of her current surroundings. She stood up and walked towards the little lift. As she pressed the button to take her to her room, vague images floated lightly like clouds across her mind. Amy, Angela, hospitals, St Paul's, stroke, chemo, turbans.

Without realizing it, she was answering her own questions. She did not know yet—this was just the beginning.

Sticky Buns

MADGE WAS IN Mrs. Quigley's corner shop. Mrs. Finnerty was already there. It was just after seven o'clock in the morning. Mrs. Finnerty showed neighbourly delight at seeing Madge. Madge Costello stopped dead in her tracks at the sight of Mrs. Finnerty. She went into a fidgety sort of panic that Mrs. Finnerty was having a relapse or another stroke and somehow made her own way to Quigley's, enticed by the aroma of her baking.

"Mrs. Costello, good morning," greeted Mrs. Finnerty. "You haven't snagged all the fresh scones, have you?"

"You're looking for fresh scones then, is that it?" Madge stuttered. *Oh god*, she said to herself as a rebuke for how she must have sounded. Faking an early morning smile, though still worried, she managed to explain, "No, no, there's loads left. I actually came in for eggs and washing powder."

Apart from Mrs. Quigley's scones, running out of those two items was good enough reason for any mother to be in her shop at this ungodly hour. Running out of milk and toilet paper was reason enough too. She was okay for these—she had already checked.

"What are you two up to?" asked a familiar voice.

Soon, Mrs. Walsh was in their midst. She too was in search of the first batch of the famous scones.

"Ladies, ladies, if our foundation meetings have been relocated to Quigley's, I am all for it," Mrs. Finnerty declared as all three embraced.

Madge was still in need of reassurance that Mrs. Finnerty was well enough and hadn't just wandered out unbeknownst to Una. She now took solace in the fact that Mrs. Walsh showed no alarm at her presence at the pastry counter.

That was all well and good for them, but Una was on her third trip out as if to feed the cat while, in truth, she was hoping to catch a glimpse of Mrs. Finnerty on the street somewhere. Soon enough, she caught sight of her elegant landlady, dressed to the nines. She scolded her once for calling her *landlady*. Mrs. Finnerty preferred the term *house friend*. Una could never be comfortable with that, choosing instead to navigate all references in such a way as to avoid using either. Una watched her approach, struck as always by her stately gait. Bag of Mrs. Quigley's goodies swinging at her hip, she rounded the corner to the driveway. Una clearly heard her sing, "*Off to work we go.*"

"Ah! There you are, Una, all set?" she said. "I've got the goodies."

She raised the bag aloft as in a salute, petted Mrs. Miller, her cat, and stood waiting for Una. It was early, but apparently, there was no time to waste. Realizing this, Una ran into the house, grabbed her bag, and played catch up to Mrs. Finnerty as they headed to the Bright House.

Madge Costello rushed home with the shopping. She fed the washing powder to the idle machine. The first load of the day was on its way. No doubt it would rain later. Now time to feed the children, a rushed and haphazard affair at best.

"No buns?" complained Kieran.

He was stuffing odd food items into a backpack and obviously thought a bun was essential to round things off. At seventeen, he believed without this huge doughy, sugary, icy, sticky addition it was hardly worth going out at all. He'd never last the day. His summer job consisted of helping his father, a civil engineer, in the office, with the occasional trip out to measure a new road or bridge or other. Not hard graft to the average person. To a seventeen-year-old boy on his break from school, it was torture. He needed that bun.

"Look behind you!" said his mother. She loved to play tricks on the boys. His brother Justin, age fifteen, and Michael, age twelve, knew the game.

"Where?" asked Kieran, seemingly, as always, missing the tease. He leaned back in the chair, twisting his body to look over his shoulder without falling. A miracle!

"Aw, Mam," he groaned as he snatched the familiar Quigley's bag, badly hidden behind the tea caddy from the counter, and dropped it into the backpack. He took one long stride towards Madge, slobbered a kiss on her cheek, and sent a clear message to his siblings.

"None for ye, ha!"

They listened to hear his bicycle tires grind on the gravel driveway. His absence left a void. They loved it when he was in the house. They loved *him*.

Charlotte, seven years old, the youngest and only girl, sat among them silently observing this one-act play. She liked it when they were all together. Unaware of her natural beauty and the effect she had on her brothers, separation from them always caused a tiny crack in her shell. She was not frail or needy in their company and played her own part in their boisterous shenanigans. The last time they called her Charlotte was the day she was christened. She was six weeks old. Her name since then was Charly. Her big brothers would not have it any other way. She loved that bit the most. Hearing them call out her name when they came home restored her shell.

Madge shouted to the boys from the laundry room.

"You'll be late," but they were already on the move, gathering their things for a football camp. It was a short walk to the Gaelic football fields behind the Bright House. With noisy goodbyes and door banging, they were gone. On her return to the kitchen, Madge stopped in the doorway to drink in the beauty of her daughter. She was breathtaking, sitting there in the sunlit kitchen, unaware of her mother's presence. When Madge Costello had the time to look at herself in a mirror, she failed to recognize the older version of her stunning daughter looking back at her. Not unlike Charly, Madge too had no idea how her own beauty affected others.

Neither did she know the effect she would have on the community, far beyond her unassuming beauty in the not-too-distant future.

Break of Day

FIONA'S PATIENTS FOR today were located close to each other and her home. She walked every day, usually setting out from her house on Shadow Ridge Avenue, covering an average of four miles. Today, she had time before her first visit to do something different. She drove towards the beach while it was still dark, parked, and walked the remaining two miles, hoping to reach the dunes to watch the sunrise over the Atlantic.

Although the tourist season was well on its way, she was surprised at the number of people already there. She made her way down to the beach and walked parallel to the shore. Darkness still reigned, her eyes alert for the change that was inevitable. The collective focus was now on the ocean, awaiting the moment when the earth and sky would separate, the moment the horizon could be identified. The mood changed, silence prevailed, broken only by the crash of a wave or the cry of a seagull. The walkers slowed their pace, and the joggers walked. Those sitting on blankets or chairs looked up, not yet shielding their eyes. It was time. A multicoloured fan of light gradually spread before them, announcing the imminent coming of day. Absolute stillness. The lace remnants of night hung in the sky as the first rim of the sun teased the day. Breathy gasps from the onlookers as gradually, then suddenly, a spectacular orange ball set fire to the sky, so spectacular it was not possible to look. The day arrived when the orange ball of fire rose higher in the sky, bidding farewell to the night. The sun rose this morning and would rise again tomorrow morning. Those who witnessed it felt they had attended a onetime performance beyond description, and they were one of the lucky few who got a ticket. It took several minutes for any attempt at activity to resume as people were reluctant to stir from their spot. Each sunrise was unique, its arrival heralded by its own pace, its own unveiling, and its own burst of light. The encore was guaranteed to elicit the same stunning response.   Sated in inner peace, Fiona floated back to her car. An orange glow from her mobile phone lying on the front seat indicated an incoming call.

"Hi, good morning," she said to the orange glow now in her hand. "You're up early. Shouldn't you be sound asleep with no school children to cause you agony?" Fiona was speaking to her middle sister Keelynn, who was headmistress of a primary school in Dublin.

"An enjoyable and worthwhile agony. Now Fiona doesn't be mean to the little children," teased her sister.

"Keely, you know how I feel about these little children. I have a few of them in and out of here all the time," soothed Fiona.

"Enjoyable and adorable they are too," said her sister Keelynn, who loved her pet name Keely. "It's time to come see them and taste the salty air. Do you have anything on this weekend?"

"Salty air? I'm on my way home from a sunrise walk on the beach. There's one waiting for you. Are you really coming down?"

"You're at the beach? Can't stand it. Have to come," oozed Keely.

"That's great. Do you need a bed? Is Philip coming? Or are you staying at your usual haunt nearer the beach?"

"Yes, Philip is feeling deprived again, so we have booked into the room with a view. Oh! I can hardly wait. We'll set out early and come straight to ye."

Fiona's ride home was so smooth, she wondered if her car really had wheels or was it floating.

A Visitor

KEELY SAT FOR a while when she got off the phone. She was in her front-sitting room when she called her sister. Looking around now at this early hour, the room seemed dark. She moved to her sprawling, well-equipped kitchen at the other end of the house. Sun streamed in through the high windows. Of course, the sun rose in Dublin too, she thought, and although there was a coastline somewhere, it was not in her backyard. Still, sunshine was sunshine, and she was happy there with her steaming mug of fresh tea in her hand.

She did not feel deprived. Philip didn't either. It was code for "Let's go somewhere." A few weekends ago on a whim, he suggested they drive to the west of Ireland, choose a different county, and play it by ear. They had a wonderful time exploring a small town, eating great pub food, and even rented bikes. They rode for God knows how many miles along a canal. Everyone who saw her photo on social media declared it suited her, with her helmet and matching shirt. Maybe she herself should get a bike, if only for the outfit! All the same, when you were born and raised in Baybridge, it was hard to beat as a destination with its river, its swans, its mountains and proximity to several beaches. She loved those swans. When she returned from a visit, telling her city friends about its beauty was a bonus.

She was alone in the house, which was quite nice. Phillip was at the hospital, where he worked in pathology. Their youngest son, Leo, who lived at home was off out early to fuss over his horse, the be-all and end-all. Understandably so, as she was a true beauty. Might he leave her and come with them to Baybridge? Probably not. She would ask anyway.

Time to start the washing if she intended to have anything to pack later in the day. It was gearing up to be a good drying day. Usually, the choice of clothes was simple, but this trip a dressier outfit was called for. She was determined to take Fiona and her husband Mark to dinner at *Pepper*. Though they had been there before, it was ages ago. Each time since then, something always prevented their return. She decided to take a chance. When they opened at eleven this morning, she would call and make the reservations for Saturday evening.

She left her house and crossed the street to see Mrs. Peterson. When they spoke the day before, she announced with great excitement that her daughter would be visiting this weekend. She lived in London and worked as a hospital administrator. This delightful lady was in her eighties, and though elegant, articulate, and witty, a painful hip made it difficult to get around. Keely, aware of the woman's need to be independent, was cautious when offering to help.

Answering the door, she said, "Keely, how nice to see you, come in, come in."

"Good morning, Mrs. Peterson, you look hale and hearty on this lovely day," greeted Keely.

"I slept so well despite my excitement at Rose coming this evening," she replied. "It's short notice, I know. Some last-minute conference at one of the hospitals in town. I forget which one. Anyway, I love these kinds of visits. No wondering or waiting, it's on top of you before you know it."

By now, they had migrated to the kitchen. While they were still standing, Keely saw an opportunity.

"Maybe you can help me out then? Philip has declared we are going to Baybridge for the weekend. Great as that is, it's left me with a bit of a problem. Mulligan's butchers in the village had the best free-range chickens yesterday. Of course, I got one, not knowing about the trip. Could I impose on you and Rose to have it for your tea this evening? You know those are never as good once you freeze them. Would that be a bit of an imposition?" Keely used her soft pleading tone in tandem with her soft pleading eyes. It worked.

Mrs. Peterson accepted graciously, saying she hadn't given the evening meal any thought. Keely said she would be off home now to get it in the oven. She returned later with the cooked chicken, a mixed salad, and a fresh loaf of French bread from Connelly's bakery. At that time, having accepted the food, Mrs. Peterson extended an invitation to join Rose and herself for sherry at six o'clock and bring Phillip.

Keely understood it would be *one* sherry, and they *had* to accept the invitation. She also understood that Mrs. Peterson took no offence at the offer of help, and their good relationship was maintained. As a child, she had watched her mother perfect this skill in their shop at the foot of the *Hill*.

Rose answered the door at exactly six o'clock. "Hello you two," she greeted, "right on time. Come on in."

It would be hard to miss the twinkle in Rose's eye as she said this. A reciprocating smile from Keely conveyed they knew her mother's ways and enjoyed them.

"Welcome Rose, an unexpected visit I hear. Those can be a nuisance or a gift, I know, but we are glad to see you," said Keely.

"It's not so bad really," Rose replied. "The conference is at Park Edge as far as I know, which means I don't have to travel down the country and can spend more time with Mam. Of course, that could change as it was put together at the last minute. How are you, Philip? Keeping you busy at work like the rest of us I'm sure."

"Good to see you, Rose," he replied. "Lab keeps ticking away at a fair clip as all hospital labs seem to do."

By now, they were each holding a crystal sherry glass older than their hostess. The dark amber liquid enhanced the cut, adding dimension to the ancient glass. Neither Philip nor Keely cared much for sherry, but the elegance of the crystals made it quite palatable. Soon, their *one sherry* visit came to a gentle conclusion with promises of seeing each other after the weekend.

Rose Peterson came to Dublin with a clear agenda and high hopes for a positive outcome. A lighthearted encounter across the street would elevate that expectation beyond her wildest dreams.

Summer Homework

CAROLINE AND ANGELA stopped at Quigley's to choose pastries for the Twins Killfeather. Mrs. Quigley was at the door of the shop as they arrived. It was the first time she had seen Angela since the whole disturbing business of the leg had started. The tall thin quiet lady stared at the young girl and, without losing her composure, allowed a smile as broad as the moon to light her face. Unsure of her next move, she stood still until Angela stepped forward and threw herself at her long legs in a tight embrace. Control now ebbing, Mrs. Quigley bent and kissed the top of the colourful turban bobbing just above her knees. Only Caroline was aware of the tears landing silently on the silky fabric. A sniffle and a shuffle later, they were at the bakery counter, making their selections.

Just before reaching the shop door on their way out, Angela stopped and said, "Mammy, wait a minute."

With that, she headed back into the shop to where they had just left Mrs. Quigley.

She looked up at the tall lady and said, "I know you help Mammy and Amy and Ms. Una. I have to go back to Dublin next week, so thank you." She rejoined her mother, leaving Mrs. Quigley in such an emotional state she had to excuse herself and return to her adjoining house in search of a handkerchief and a cup of strong tea.

The rehabilitation department was in full swing. Caroline sat to the side as usual while Angela got set up.

When things were settled, she approached the reception desk and said, "Anya, when you have a minute, would you call over to the Twins Killfeather and tell them Angela wants to visit after therapy, just to make sure it's okay?"

"Oh! I am sure they will be delighted, but I'll tell them anyway," replied Anya.

A nod and a smile exchanged as Caroline sat back down. She wondered what had transpired between Mrs. Quigley and Angela earlier. She knew if Angela had anything to tell, she would do so without questions or prompts.

After Angela's rest and hydration period, they slowly made their way over to the manor. The walk along the tree-lined path was pleasant and soothing. Of course, it had rained earlier, which gave the foliage a gloss as if polished to perfection just for them. A gentle tap on the door to the Killfeather rooms resulted in the immediate appearance of Eleanor in the doorway.

"Come in and let us have a good look at you, Angela," she invited as mother and daughter tentatively advanced into the room and back in time.

When the government purchased the property seventeen years earlier for the purpose of building a state-of-the-art rehabilitation centre, the deal included the manor house. With it came the Twins Killfeather, who occupied the home since they were born. Though renovations took place to equip the top floor of the Victorian house for its new purpose, Harriet and Eleanor chose to keep their rooms as they had always been. Over time, they had agreed to the odd update and the installation of the occasional electrical gadget to help Thelma. Thelma's parents worked for the Killfeather family, and she just sort of grew into that role over the years. Their relationship had long ago changed from employee to a lifelong friend.

Harriet, who, with unexpected agility, stood up from the gate-legged table where she sat and with surprising athleticism strode towards Caroline and Angela with outstretched arms. Her attire was as elegant as it was unexpected. Her skirt, ankle-length, draped around her legs in pinks and reds and purples, gave the illusion of floating as she walked. Her blouse was cream linen with a high-laced collar. Long loosely fitted sleeves nipped at the wrists with matching laced cuffs added elegance. It was an authentic Victorian piece. Very fine lace knuckle-length gloves, perhaps more proper for afternoon tea in days of yore, completed the look. This ensemble would surely be the envy of any self-respecting hippie, if any still existed. Tara Doherty, the manager at the Haymarket branch, also a keen dealer in retro fashion, would surely need restraining to prevent her from pillaging their wardrobe should she ever find herself in their rooms. Caroline and Angela responded in kind to their welcome as they were shown to the chairs at the already-set table.

"Thank you," said Caroline calmly as if this was how she spent all her mornings.

Given Angela's age, it might have surprised some to hear the ease with which she said, "Your skirt is lovely, and your gloves are different. I like the fingers short like that so you can feel things better."

"Exactly, someone was very clever to think of that. I like your turban today too," Harriet replied. "I see we have the same taste in colours."

She gave her skirt a little shake, revealing similar muted tones of rose and pink lurking in the folds. By now, Eleanor had joined them. Unlike her sister, she was wearing a pale-yellow linen dress with fitted elbow-length sleeves, cinched at the waist with a stiff matching belt and fabric-covered buckle. This garment had a youthful modern look carried off well by Eleanor. The dress was first worn by her on her fiftieth birthday. Whether it was due to good tailoring or choice of fabric or good care over these years, it looked as if she had bought it yesterday.

"Angela, your turban is catching the sun as you sit there. I agree it is lovely, Harriet," commented Eleanor.

"Mammy is going to ask Dr. Owens if we can go and see where they are made," Angela explained. "Amy didn't want to go with Mrs. Finnerty when she went before, so she waited for me." She shuffled a bit in the high-back chair and readjusted her leg. Eleanor noticed.

"We hope to get the all clear today for the trip," said Caroline. "There may be a few tests before going back to Park Edge. I must give credit where credit is due to Dr. Owens and Dr. Allen. They have made every effort to do what is possible here rather than in Dublin."

"That's what you wanted right from the start," said Eleanor directly to Angela.

"I just show them my duckling book when it's time to come home," Angela said as she repositioned herself again.

"Harriet, where did we put that velvet bound journal, we found the other day?" asked her sister. "We lamented how neither of us ever wrote in it. It just seemed to have tucked itself away for all these years. Caroline, can Angela come over to the armchair by the bookcase and see if her younger eyes can do better than ours in finding where we put it this time?"

Caroline had noticed Angela's discomfort and was grateful to Eleanor for this solution. The journal when found really was very special. The burgundy cover favoured the colour hues in Harriet's skirt, and the aged paper echoed the cream of her blouse. Angela stroked the velvet cover, causing the shifting pile to change its hue. Caroline and Harriet exchanged a knowing glance. The older lady then suggested,

"What about recording your trip to Haymarket, like a record of what you learned from the experience? For instance, the transportation by road to get there, then seeing the boats travel on the Shannon, what about how a factory works?"

In minutes, topic after topic came tumbling out.

"Textile industry," said Eleanor.

"Distribution," added Harriet.

"Oh, we forgot the design," cut in Eleanor, "and art and business management."

This went on for several minutes while Caroline just sat in silence. The journal had taken on a life of its own by now. Finally, Angela said, "It will be my summer homework project. Ms. Una and Mrs. Finnerty will help. I'll hand it in when school reopens."

"Genius," the Twins Killfeather said in unison.

A door creaked open.

"Are you ready for your tea yet?" asked Thelma.

41

Two More Cups

AS UNA AND Mrs. Finnerty arrived at the Bright House, the mischief in the older woman intensified. Instead of accepting Una's invitation to enter first, she nudged the younger woman to go ahead and hid behind her as they made their way down the long hallway that led to the Hill Hands studio. Kitsy was the first to notice Una in the doorway.

"The early bird catches the worm," she said casually, raising her head from her work. Just how early, she had no idea.

"Good morning Kitsy," Una replied, the uncertainty in her demeanor also lost on Kitsy. Quite honestly, Una did not know what to do next or where exactly Mrs. Finnerty was. The answer came just then when she jumped out from behind her, revealing herself and the Quigley's bag.

"Surprise!" came the yelp, causing Kitsy to stab herself with a pin.

At precisely that moment, Sammy appeared from the nearby kitchen and discovered how adept she was at avoiding spilling scalding cups of tea all over herself.

"Mrs. Finnerty!" They both gasped at the same time.

"Yes, the one and only," replied the seventy-something-year-old prankster waving a bag of Mr. Quigley's best as she advanced into the studio. Kitsy licked a drop of blood from her finger as Sammy placed the cups on the nearest surface. She was the first to speak.

"What in the world are you doing here and at this hour? We didn't expect you for days yet."

"You should take it easy for a while at home," urged Kitsy.

Mrs. Finnerty, who did not subscribe to that idea at all, said, "Nonsense. I have never felt more rested in my life, and I have been to Quigley's this morning. First batch."

With dramatic effect, she opened the pastry bag teasingly, allowing the tantalizing aroma to stifle any further objections.

"We'll be needing two more cups then, Sammy," conceded Kitsy.

The ice now broken, they all set about their usual routine. Mrs. Finnerty did not have an office at the Bright House. When she was there, she made rounds, resembling a matron or a head nurse in a small cottage hospital but with less formality. Watching and learning in the studio with Sammy and Kitsy took up a lot of her time. Their attention to detail impressed her. She made it a point of being with them all day when the fabrics from India arrived. She wallowed in their scent and elegance finding herself transported with wonderful memories. She worked hard on those days, unpacking, sorting, and stacking under the guidance of Sammy. Kitsy pitched in to hasten the sorting of the supplies to avoid any delay when the skilled work of making the actual maharaja turbans began.

An onlooker would be forgiven for mistaking this diligent woman as a beloved, resolute supporter of the cause. Unless you knew otherwise her role as founder, benefactor, mentor, and principal writer of cheques would totally escape you.

That is exactly how Mrs. Finnerty liked it.

The List

ORDINARILY, AMY WOULD not accompany Angela to her doctors' appointments. Today, however Mrs. Coughlan, Angela, and Amy set out for Dr. Owens's office together. It was a bit of an adventure. Their dad, Tony, a Garda sergeant in Baybridge, was escorted to the door with orders to quell any illegal activity that may be afoot hereabouts. Their voices trailed behind him, lilting, "Go get 'em, Daddy."

As soon as he backed out of the driveway in his own car, his family boarded the luxurious minivan known as the Chariot. Mr. Hennessey, the owner of a local upscale car showroom, made a gift of this ultramodern vehicle to the family when his equally generous wife mentioned Angela's numerous visits to Park Edge Hospital in Dublin. Amy named it when she first saw it in their driveway, and to this day, nobody asked how they came to own it. The donor had been adamant about this when he first broached the subject with their dad.

Both girls sat together in the third row of seats with enough space for Angela to prop up her leg if needed. Angela brought the beautiful book bag given to her by Mrs. Finnerty when she first went to the Dublin hospital. She loved its soft silky Indian fabric, studded with all manner of glittery stones. It was never far from her side. Today, it also held the velvet-covered journal given to her by the Twins Killfeather. Tucked away discreetly in a small compartment, a neatly folded piece of paper awaited its reveal. The heading read "Things to ask Dr. Owens." The largest compartment housed the beloved book given to her by Dr. Allen, the bone doctor. This book, *Make Way for the Ducklings*, was her means of communication with the medical staff. A quote from the book made her wishes about her treatment known, and it served them all well.

The sisters spent the previous evening going over the questions they had. By morning, they had reached an agreement to call it "The List."

"Mrs. Coughlan and the girls are here," beamed Brenda from behind the reception desk as they appeared. If ever there was a person suited to be a doctor's receptionist, it was Brenda. It was often said you could be doubled over in pain until you caught sight of Brenda's smiling face. Pain seemed to diminish in her presence. Today, nobody appeared to be doubled over in pain as the trio approached the desk. "Good timing," declared Brenda, nodding towards an open-door, framing Dr. Owens and his broad smile.

"Good to see all of you, lovely ladies," he said as he stepped aside to allow them to enter. "I see you brought reinforcements Angela, I had better watch my Ps and Qs today with Amy looking over my shoulder. That's an interesting bag you have there Amy."

By now, they had reached his exam room. Caroline helped Angela onto the exam couch. Amy hovered in silence nearby, clutching the book bag protectively. I wasn't time yet for "The List."

The first few questions were general in nature—any pain, coughs, or temperature, anything new to report. Nothing to report. It was time to move to the next phase.

"Angela, do you have anything to ask me at this point?" the doctor asked. Was now the time for the questions?

Amy stepped closer to Angela, presenting her with the now open book bag. The most encouraging smile ever passed between the two of them.

Reaching into the bag, Angela removed the list from its hiding place and simply said, "I have a few, Dr. Owens."

Their mother looked on in astonishment and heartbreaking pride. The girls were taking charge once again.

Fiona Hannon was not surprised when the intercom buzzed in her little social service nook behind Brenda's reception desk. Neither was she surprised at how early it was. Dr. Owens was skilled at tailoring time spent with each patient according to their current needs. He saw Angela at once. Fiona made her way along the corridor to the exam room. Her light tap on the door was answered by Amy.

"We've got help today Mrs. Hannon. Amy is keeping things moving along," spoken by the doctor as Fiona followed Amy further into the room.

"Good thing too. Stop us from dillydallying about the place," offered Fiona.

She returned Caroline's glance with a reassuring smile as she continued to where Angela was now sitting in a comfortable chair. The physical exam was now over.

"No dillydallying here Mrs. Hannon, no indeed. We have a lot of business to take care of, right girls? It's all here on Angela's list," explained the doctor.

"What a grand idea, a list," exclaimed Fiona. "I don't remember the last time a patient brought a list to us."

"It's a helpful thing to have and has made our work here today easier. Angela, is it okay for me to share the list with Mrs. Hannon?"

She responded with a slight nod. Fiona sensed uncertainty in her demeanor and noticed her mom had abandoned her chair in favour of the footstool by Angela's chair. They were holding hands. Amy, still guarding the book bag, noticed the change in her sister and understood it meant something.

Dr. Owens continued, "As you see Mrs. Hannon, these are very serious questions. The first two we already touched on but could do with a bit more attention. Angela wants to know if the lump was bad and will she have to go back to Dublin."

"Very serious questions," agreed Fiona.

Dr. Owens walked to where Angela was sitting and took up his position on another stool at Angela's feet.

Looking directly at her with a soft gentle smile, he said, "Can you please tell Mrs. Hannon what we said earlier."

Fiona understood that feedback was essential to ensure information was imparted and understood correctly by the patient and, in this case, the parent also. Whatever hesitation Angela exhibited earlier was no longer evident.

She sat upright in her chair while still holding on to her mother's hand and spoke clearly, "Dr. Myers called Dr. Owens yesterday from Dublin and told him all these lumps like mine are bad. She said even though she gave me that strong medicine before the operation and the lump was small in one place only and Dr. Allan took out that part of the bone and put in a new part, she doesn't trust the lump. She said they are very sneaky, and mine was a high grade and could not be trusted at all, not ever. I'm going back to Park Edge Hospital to my old room on Happy Street on Monday so Dr. Myers can make sure not a smidgen of that sneaky lump is left behind. Dr. Owens said I might have my labs and my hearing test done here. Oh, Dr. Myers said to be sure to bring my duckling book so I can let her know when I feel well enough to come home. I probably will have to go back for more medicine in a while." Then she sat back in her chair, slowly releasing her mother's hand. Under any other circumstances, there would not have been a dry eye in the house, but Angela's command of the situation didn't allow for it. Instead, Amy produced the favourite book from the bag and placed it on her sister's lap.

"Well done, Angela. I couldn't have explained it better myself," congratulated the doctor, rising from the stool. Turning to Fiona, he added, "We need your expertise in answering the last two questions."

He was standing over the Coughlan family now as they formed a tight group around Angela's chair and mischievously asked them, "Do you think Mrs. Hannon can handle this?"

Rapid nodding and conspiratorial grins were all he got from the Coughlan camp. With an equally conspiratorial grin and an exaggerated shrug of the shoulders, he said, "Here goes. They want to go to Haymarket to see how the turbans are made. Angela wants to record the trip in an antique journal for school, and they want Mrs. Finnerty to see Happy Street. Oh, and Angela needs to be in Park Edge by teatime on Monday."

All that was left of the doctor as he made good his escape was the hem of his lab coat.

Brenda could attest to the laughter following him from the room.

Haircuts

IT DID NOT take long for news of Angela's pending return to the Dublin hospital to travel the length and breadth of Shadow Ridge Avenue and beyond. Grainne first heard of it from Mrs. O'Hara as she was rolling the last curler of her new perm. "I hear Angela Coughlan is heading back to the Dublin hospital in a day or two, poor wee thing." Grainne looked up from the curler, catching a glimpse of her client in the ornate mirror. She studied her own reflection.

Satisfied it revealed no reaction to what was said, she returned her attention to the aforementioned curler, saying, "I just noticed what good condition your hair is in today, Mrs. O'Hara. Had you noticed it yourself? I think you were right to stop using the blue rinse."

So taken was the lady in the mirror with a compliment coming from Grainne, she reached up to pat her new curls, completely forgetting what she had just told her esteemed hairstylist. Skill in this type of situation was as much a part of the job as was the styling of hair.

That tidbit of information did however prompt her to pay a visit to the Coughlan family, who lived just across the street from the salon, later in the day.

"Grainne, the very person we need to see, come in, come in," beamed Caroline, who led her down the long corridor to the large welcoming kitchen.

"Anyone home? Anyone at all?" she called out as she neared where she knew the girls would be.

A chorus of "*Grainne!*" assailed her ears.

"I had a few spare minutes and thought to myself I'll go across and see the girls."

"And just in time too," their mother explained. "We got our marching orders for Park Edge Hospital, so we will need to look presentable. I don't want the big-city folks thinking we are all unkempt out here on the coast."

"Oh, as if the big-city folks didn't ever have to get their hair cut. Nonsense, we can out style them anytime. We in Baybridge are the trendsetters of this country. I'm sure it's not every day they see such beautiful heads adorned in Indian silk," offered Grainne.

By this time, she was sitting between the girls, her arms draped over the back of their chairs. Neither were wearing their turbans. She liked that. Ease and comfort passed between them as she made a quick silent assessment of Angela's hair, noting the expected changes since she styled it previously.

"What say you Angela about this hair business?"

"I want mine all gone. I would like a buzz if you please."

Silence followed by more silence.

"Is it a rock star you are now?" teased her mother.

"We should call ourselves *The Turban Girls*," announced Amy.

"*Yeah! Yeah! Yeah!*" sang Angela, accompanying herself on a phantom guitar.

Amy grabbed two wooden spoons from a nearby drawer and drummed on a wooden chair. An almost-empty roll of kitchen paper made a perfect microphone as Caroline boomed, "Three buzz haircuts please, Grainne!"

No sooner said than done.

"I will be back in a jiffy. Angela, get your styling set from upstairs. I need a few things from the salon, and then we will show the world what real style looks like." All this said as she sprinted towards the front door.

The others, full of excitement, transformed a section of the large kitchen for the task at hand. Angela retrieved her personal hair kit given to her by Grainne during the last round of chemo. To avoid the risk of infection, she did not share with others or go to the salon. Caroline spread a sheet under the chair they would use and piled a mountain of towels nearby. They cleared the table and covered it with an outdoor vinyl tablecloth. Grainne returned at lightning speed and placed her equipment on the table.

"Well done. It's perfect. Angela, if you please take your seat and let's show them how it's done."

"No mirrors until we are all done," said Angela.

"We agreed we would all look together," explained Caroline.

"Of course," offered Grainne. "See, I brought a mirror for each of you in honour of this momentous occasion. Amy, I have a job for you. I need you to gently gather the locks into that special box there, and we will send it to the wig-making project. What an amazing contribution that will be and a surprise to those volunteers."

Snip, snip, buzz, buzz. Done! She presented all three with their mirrors, and all three whooped and hollered at the same time. Just about then, their dad was putting his key in the front door lock. He paused for a moment, wondering what they were up to now. Still wearing his Garda uniform head to toe, he quietly advanced towards the noise as if staking out a criminal. He stood statue still when he saw his wife and daughters. He ceremoniously removed his police uniform hat revealing a bald head.

"Daddy, Daddy, who told you? Who told you?" squealed Amy and Angela together, running to him.

"Love told me, my pets. Love told me."

When Mrs. Finnerty heard her doorbell ring, she knew the visitor would either put her out of her misery or plunge her further into it. Una was at the Bright House, leaving her without distraction in the afternoon. She spent some time recalling the joy she felt, surprising Sammy and Kitsy by her unexpected early return. Now that was replaced by uncertainty about Angela's visit to Dr. Owens today and whether there was a time in the schedule for a detour. She believed going to Haymarket with Amy would make a difference to both girls. As she approached the door, she paused on hearing the commotion.

She could see through the stained-glass paneling that she had more than one visitor on her doorstep.

Fiona Hannon's voice was the first to reach her ears. "There I was, minding my own business when I was accosted by these two scalawags."

"We were just bursting to show Mrs. Finnerty" were the next words, this time spoken by Amy, linking her sister's arm in solidarity as they made their way into the house.

"Well, come on in and show me," invited their confused but less miserable neighbour.

The girls were wearing their turbans as they moved further into the library, ignoring the books on this occasion.

"We didn't know you were going to be here, Mrs. Hannon, so now we can show you too," said Amy.

"Mammy and Daddy will be here in a minute, but we wanted to come first, and we didn't mean to bump you, honest," explained Angela.

Without waiting for the apology acceptance, both adults were ordered to close their eyes. The girls removed their turbans and, in unison, declared, "Ta-da! Open your eyes!"

No comment from either for what seemed like an age. The girls held their pose.

"I have never seen such beauty," whispered Mrs. Finnerty.

"Perfection," uttered a stunned Fiona.

"Grainne did it. She said we were the trendsetters," Amy explained.

"She is very good at doing hair, and she gave us each a mirror, and we gathered our hair in a special box to surprise the wig makers," added Angela.

"We did not look until we were all finished. Then we looked at the same time. Daddy didn't get a mirror. He came after we got ours." These details were carefully explained by Amy.

"Mammy got one, though," further clarified Angela.

As if on cue, the doorbell rang again. Fiona answered, allowing Caroline and Tony to make their entrance. It seems the Coughlan family was gifted with perfect skulls.

"Caroline, you look absolutely stunning, you really do," said Fiona.

"And what about me?" inquired Tony with a mock pout.

"No worries if you lose your hair as you grow old then, eh?" she answered.

"You look stunning too, Tony," consoled his wife, casting a phony rebuke scowl in Fiona's direction.

Tony exchanged his pout for an exaggerated fluttering of the eyelashes. After much commentary and exchange of compliments, the significant business at hand was broached by Caroline.

"We saw Dr. Owens today as you know, Mrs. Finnerty. Dr. Myers in Dublin and himself had already conferred, deciding to readmit Angela to Park Edge. Angela and Amy put forward their request to visit Haymarket and that you go with them to see where Angela stays on Happy Street and see the Pirate Ship. But Angela needs to be on Happy Street no later than four o'clock on Monday."

These words fell heavily on Mrs. Finnerty as she feared it was not possible for her to go.

"I see" was all she could muster by way of reply.

"Fiona was brought in to see what could be done and still meet that deadline," continued Caroline. "As expected, she collaborated with the team and did her magic. Tell us the plan, Fiona."

"No magic. Just a little teamwork. The audiology department can do the pre-chemo hearing test tomorrow, and the labs can be done after that. Mrs. Finnerty, if you can arrange a stopover at the Haymarket site early on Monday morning on the way to Dublin, Angela will be in plenty of time for her admission. In fact, if you feel up to it, Dr. Owens said you could go on to Park Edge with her and share that experience."

One might wonder how it's possible to smile from ear to ear and cry like a baby at the same time. Mrs. Finnerty had no problem doing just that.

Sisters

FIONA APPROACHED HER house with increasing excitement. She was feeling good now that Angela's audiogram and labs were completed. Her sister and her wonderful husband, Philip, should be here shortly from Dublin. Apart from checking in with Caroline and Mrs. Finnerty to finalize the plan for Monday, she was free for the weekend. They arrived in the driveway within seconds of each other, Fiona pulling in behind them as if in a convoy. Keely jumped out, not waiting for her husband to turn off the engine, and gathered her sister in a mighty bear hug, declaring, "Such timing!"

"Gifted, the pair of us, simply gifted," replied the squeezed Fiona.

Philip appeared and greeted his sister-in-law in a more gentlemanly manner. Nevertheless, his pleasure at seeing her was evident in his smile.

"Come in, come in. Are you starving?"

"No, could murder a cup of tea, though. Keely don't forget the pastries," he added.

"Pastries," echoed Fiona, "did you stop in Carrick?"

"Do you think we would dare pass the next best bakery to Mrs. Quigley's in the country and leave those scrumptious goodies behind? Not a chance. We have an assortment to share with everyone. They had to start another bake by the time we left," said Keely, her voice betraying mischief. So much for *healthy eating.*

"We had better snatch ours then before the rest of them turn up and scoff the lot," warned Fiona.

They were in the large welcoming kitchen by now, kettle already on the stove. Keely, very much at home here, rummaged in the cupboard for cups and saucers and plates in an effort to set the table however rough and ready it turned out to be. No need for grandeur. The sight of the confections and the aromas they emitted from the mismatched platter was quite enough thank you.

They sat in comfort. Fiona poured the tea. Punctuated by sounds of tea slurping, lip-smacking, and fingertip licking, Keely said, "Fiona, I went ahead and made a decision without consultation. Brazen of me, I know."

Fiona didn't even look up from her plate, taking that announcement in her stride, knowing it was bound to be good. She knew her sister well and had complete confidence in whatever she had decided.

"Well, I took the liberty of making a reservation for the four of us for dinner at *Pepper* this evening."

That got Fiona's attention.

"*Pepper*? *Pepper*? Oh, you are brazen!" she squealed and paused. "Stop eating this minute," she ordered.

"Not me," said the quiet, smiling Philip.

Angela was excited about this trip. She was finally going to see the Haymarket studio and how the turbans were made. She and Amy would enjoy sharing this experience together. Amy had been generous enough to wait until she was well enough to go. She would never forget that generosity. Then Mrs. Finnerty had agreed to go with them to the hospital after Haymarket. This was very important to Angela. The doctors had told her that this next round of chemo would be harder than before. She needed her good friend and special neighbour to see where she would be while she was going through this. She wanted her to see her room on Happy Street, its yellow door displaying number four, the curtained window on either side, its mini blue chaise where she would spend most of her bad times, the bench that was a hidden bed where her mother would pretend to be sleeping while watching her at every moment. On the windowsill above the hidden bed, the penguin would also keep watch, guarding the nicely decorated IV pump that would quietly deliver the medicine that at first would make her deathly sick and eventually make her whole. She wanted her to see how she kept her turban near at hand and where the duckling book would be. She did not want Mrs. Finnerty to imagine any of it, to try to conjure the space. She needed her to see it and feel it for herself.

Amy and Angela found themselves in Angela's room after they returned from the preadmission tests in Baybridge Medical Centre. Caroline remained in the kitchen, contemplating the next move. There were many things yet to be done before Monday, and it was good to have a quiet time. Angela lay on her bed while Amy sat cross-legged at her feet. They were passing one of their new mirrors back and forth between them.

"I really like how we look now," mused Angela. "I might leave the turban off sometimes."

"I do too," agreed Amy. "But I also like wearing my turban."

They continued to pass the mirror back and forth, looking this way and that, examining their heads from all angles. On with the turban, off with the turban, this way and that until Angela finally said, "I know who will advise us the best. Come on, we'll ask Mammy to take us to the manor."

"The Twins Killfeather. Can we call them that?" Amy wondered. "Can we call them by miss whatever their first name is like we do to Ms. Una?"

"We will ask" was all Angela had to offer as they both made their way down the stairs.

Their mother's quiet time was short-lived.

No sooner had Caroline knocked on the door, which was mere minutes after she called to see if they could come, when the door was opened. It was impossible to know which one had opened the door so closely they stood together.

"Is it true you girls wanted to see us about something important?" Harriet almost whispered. "We love important things, don't we, Eleanor? Especially clever girls' important things."

"We hope we can be of help," answered Eleanor. "Come in and let us see. Angela, why don't you sit by the books in case we need you to find a long-lost treasure for us like last time. Caroline, Amy, sit where you feel comfy."

"Are you sure this is convenient at such short notice? These two insisted only you ladies would have the answer," explained Caroline.

"By all means it's convenient. Let's hope we have an answer," said Eleanor.

Harriet had settled herself deep in the velvet of what must be the oldest and largest armchair in the country. She patted the space beside her thin body, inviting Amy to sit. Amy seemed hesitant, but the second patting and shuffling reassured her, and soon, she nestled beside Harriet. Caroline sat in the nearest chair at the small dining table. Angela spoke with such confidence. Caroline was startled, but not the ladies.

"Is it proper to call you Miss in front of your first name like we do to Ms. Una? She likes it, but she is younger. It's so you know which one we are talking to because that might be rude too."

Eleanor sat randomly on the nearest chair while exchanging amused glances with her sister.

"Well, if you want to talk to me, you can say Ms. Eleanor and Ms. Harriet if you want to say something to my sister. Would that help, do you think?"

Angela thanked her, saying it would help.

"Ms. Harriet," she continued, turning towards the armchair, "Grainne gave us all new haircuts, and we love them, but as you can see, we are still wearing our turbans. I must go back to Dublin on Monday after we stop at Haymarket to see them being made. Amy and I always wanted to go together. Dr. Owens said we could, and Mrs. Finnerty is coming all the way to the hospital with us. We don't know now since we got our haircut what to choose, and we came to ask you and Ms. Eleanor too."

Amy stood up and removed her turban, revealing her chic hairstyle. She took a bow. The others followed suit, minus the bow.

"That's by far the most difficult question I have ever been asked," said Eleanor. "Both are equally stunning."

"Oh my!" said Harriet. "I wish I had a choice between two trendsetting styles. In our day, we sometimes wore turbans to avoid doing our hair. Not so in this case. The choice is yours. I suggest wearing your turban when you might otherwise wear a hat or want to really dress up. Otherwise, show off your beautiful heads. Of course, the mood on any given day could change your mind. That's the beauty of good style. You can show it off anytime or anywhere you like."

"We didn't think of anything like that, did we, Mammy?" said Amy.

She had remained in the armchair, listening to Harriet, wide-eyed.

"No, we did not, my pet, not at all" answered Caroline. Addressing the ladies, she added, "Thank you so very much. Now we know how to be stylish. Angela was very pleased about being stylish," she told them.

"Your bag is way beyond stylish, Angela. Tell us about it," asked Eleanor.

"It's a book bag from India. Mrs. Finnerty gave it to me to carry my books to Park Edge. I brought my duckling book to show you. My velvet journal is in here too. I'm starting to write in it tomorrow as we will be getting ready to start the trip.

"Would you mind if Harriet and I wrote a little something to start you off?" she continued.

Angela handed them both the books. In the velvet journal, as it was now known, the inscription read,

> *I know you'll be kind and clever and bold*
> *And the bigger your heart the more it will hold*
> *Then you will discover all there is to see*
> *And become anybody that you'd like to be.*

The signature read "The Twins Killfeather."

Angela recognized the quote from *The Wonderful Things You Will Be.*

As they left, the vision of the elderly sisters clinging to each other, unaware of the tears streaming down their furrowed cheeks tore Caroline's heart apart. Sensing something but not sure what, the young Coughlan sisters returned to the old sisters, burying themselves in their ancient skirts for just one moment longer.

The Send-Off

MRS. WALSH WAS barely out the front door of the Bright House when Sammy said, "What do you think about my lemon cream cake? Would it suit this occasion?"

"That's a lovely cake Sammy," said Kitsy, "and I will make Mam's trifle. She's bound to be looking over my shoulder, so there is no need to look so worried."

"I'm not worried about the trifle. I was just wondering if the two of us can manage to do this and keep it a secret," explained Sammy.

"Do you mean the food or what?" asked Kitsy.

She was surprised to hear Sammy hesitate over such things as she came from a very big family, and feeding the masses was her norm.

"I'm not sure if we should mention to someone that we would like to do a Sunday afternoon tea for those going to Dublin on Monday and Una following in a few days. I know we have the run of the place during the week when we are working. Stepping outside that on a Sunday afternoon probably needs some sort of permission, don't you think?"

Kitsy contemplated that for a second, then nodded sagely. They both agreed Mrs. Hannon would be the best person to ask.

Now that the legality of the matter was in hand, they threw themselves wholeheartedly into the planning. Still hoping to keep the secret and knowing all would be safe in Mrs. Quigley's hands, they decided to ask her to make her famous scones.

"We must make sure she understands this is a business transaction like with any other customer. Otherwise, we just won't get any. She has done so much already," announced Sammy.

"What?" exclaimed Kitsy, feigning shock. "No Quigley's scones. Are you mad, woman? That would surely be a short tea party with everyone going to the shop to get their own and continuing the party in the park."

"I've eaten in worse places," offered Sammy, "but how would they manage your trifle?"

Kitty's response consisted of a wallop on Sammy's arm.

They continued to plot and plan, and later the next day, Fiona Hannon gave the go-ahead, saying it was a great idea. She also informed them Mrs. Finnerty would be heading to Dublin with Angela after the visit to Haymarket, which surprised and delighted them. An area of disagreement arose between them when Fiona offered to help with the cost and bring some food.

"Mrs. Hannon, thank you very much, but no thank you. You have done more than your share up till now. This is a Hill Hands project and in a way an acknowledgment of how all of you have made us welcome from the very beginning. It's such a little thing, but we want to do this," explained Sammy.

"Oh, Sammy, you and Kitsy are part of us, have been as you say, from the very beginning. It's a lovely thing you are doing and by no means *little*. It's going to be brilliant and such a surprise. Oh, I nearly forgot, can I bring my sister Keely? She is here from Dublin for the weekend and like the others heading back in that direction later. Seems everyone is Dublin bound, except us. Girls, we'll have to fix that someday soon," suggested Fiona.

"When? When?" whined Kitsy. Despite her very convincing plead, they ignored her. *So much for my acting skills!* More pressing at this moment was how and when to invite everyone. They settled at two o'clock on Sunday afternoon.

"I almost called Mrs. Finnerty to ask permission," confessed Sammy. "Good job I didn't as she is counted as one of the travelers. She wouldn't have breathed a word, though."

"Soul of discretion is our Mrs. Finnerty," replied Fiona. "You work your magic with the party and I will take care of the rest. By the way, can we stop with "The Mrs. Hannon", I'm Fiona."

Now the real work started with only one day to prepare. When the Hill ladies, all as discreet as Mrs. Finnerty, heard of the *event*, they sprang into action. Mrs. Harte at number fourteen had two tea sets to offer, and although they were a different pattern, they complimented each other she said. The "only for best" tablecloth was sent up to Sammy's house forthwith from number ten. The lady of the house at number fifteen went next door to number sixteen and joined that lady of the house in a mammoth-baking undertaking. Their joint children were very agreeable in the tasting process. The rich aroma of rising dough wafting in the gentle breeze enticed the neighbours outdoors. There would be tasty offerings for them later. So, it continued.

Kitsy's mother, Masie, said gently to her daughter, "Ah, pet, sure I'll make the trifle. You have enough to do." What she really meant was "I can't have Kitsy's effort going down to the Bright House for that little girl and her family. No sir. She better stick to making the turbans." *Secretly*, her daughter was relieved.

When Sammy's brother arrived to transport the supplies on Sunday morning, he wondered aloud if his sister had made a change from sewing to baking. Her reply was to give him a sturdy wallop on his arm. *He was a big man and deserved it*, she told him. There seemed to be a lot of arms walloping these days. Isn't love grand!

Fiona never disclosed how she managed to do it, but at two o'clock on Sunday afternoon, a procession of finely turned-out people of various genders and ages were seen entering the Bright House. A special occasion thought the onlookers. Mark, Fiona's husband, was the last to arrive and with him the Twins Killfeather.

A special occasion indeed.

Insomnia

TARA DOHERTY, DIRECTOR of the Haymarket branch of Angela's Tresses and Turban, decided it was futile to lie there any longer, expecting sleep. She allowed her elegant silk-clad legs to dangle over the side of the bed, as her brain registered how unusual it was for her to be awake. Her reputation as a sound sleeper was a legend. Descriptions of that event ranged from *like a baby* or *like a log* or *like the dead* to *sleep on a clothesline* or *wake the dead*. Once, her young son said she *sounded like a passed-out drunk*. She wondered for a long time how he knew what a passed-out drunk sounded like. She was always afraid to ask.

None of that tonight. Sleep evaded her for the first time in her life. No doubt tomorrow was a big day for the Haymarket studio. Visitors were coming from Baybridge. True. Sleep had nothing to do with that.

Her feet touched the plush area rug placed on the wood floor beside her bed as she reached for the matching dressing gown on the nearby antique chair. Sliding her toned arms easily into its soft folds, she made her way to the kitchen. She needed a cup of tea. While the kettle boiled, she stood with her back against the fridge door. Though it was obviously not cold, it calmed her as she gathered her thoughts.

The Haymarket studio ran like clockwork. The smell of the delicate fabrics, mingled with the legacy of canvas and paint from the previous owner, an artist, enhanced the creative atmosphere. Mrs. Shiva, the design manager, was top-notch, using only the finest of materials from her native India. With the help of two of the best local seamstresses and, on occasion, Mrs. Shiva's thirteen-year-old son Previn, they produced custom-made turbans at short notice.

It was a mere accident she and Mrs. Finnerty even met. Her late husband's brother, Nathaniel Doherty, had befriended her in Baybridge and talked about her often when he visited home. Unfortunately, he died very suddenly, just as her husband, his brother, had done earlier. The task of tending to his house and business affairs in Baybridge fell to Tara. During that time, Mrs. Finnerty was in hospital following an operation. Tara went there to thank her for her friendship with her brother in law. She also wanted her to know she could not even imagine how traumatic it must have been for her to discover he had died outside while waiting to drive her home from her hospital appointment. Mrs. Finnerty was taken aback at her presence. Her chic, fashionable appearance, coupled with a forthright approach, was impressive. Added to this was the fact Mr. Doherty had never mentioned *her* or any family. Despite the surprising nature of the visit, they spent a pleasant time together during which Angela's name and the intention for the foundation came up.

Tara listened intently to all Mrs. Finnerty had to say and was all set to leave when she paused and said, "I'm in the fashion business myself with two shops in Haymarket, a modern boutique and one specializing in vintage garments. In my line of work, I come across all manner of interesting fabrics and the like from all over the place. I'd like to collaborate with you if you think it would help."

Mrs. Finnerty gave the Haymarket project to Tara within minutes of her expressing an interest. As soon as she sat in her car outside the hospital, she started making calls to her numerous contacts. One call generated another and another and another until she had to resist the temptation to drive while talking on the phone. Turning it off completely, she eased her way out to the busy street and headed for home. The response was such that, within days, she located Mrs. Shiva at her market booth surrounded by fabulous material. Together, they made a trip to a hat factory in Dublin and on their return came across the most suitable premises ever for their artistic endeavors with a perfect view of the River Shannon. None of this was any surprise to Tara Doherty. The forthrightness noticed by Mrs. Finnerty reaped rewards.

Seated now with her cup of tea, staring at the black of night, she knew her insomnia had little to do with any of that. Angela had affected her deeply the day she saw her, and Mrs. Finnerty helping each other get off the rehab bus at the official opening of the Bright House. At that moment, her spirit shifted. It wasn't overwhelming or debilitating, rather a subtle awareness of a deep change inside herself.

The impending meeting with this extraordinary child brought those feelings into focus. Angela, a ten-year-old child, was making a visit to the studio named after her, where they made turbans from vibrantly coloured fabric, bearing her logo. Their intended purpose to brighten the lives of young chemotherapy patients who lose their hair as a result of the treatment. Her visit will be short because she is on her way to an oncology unit in Dublin, where she will continue *her own course of chemotherapy*.

Tara Doherty put her heart into everything she did. She put her *soul* into the foundation.

The Cake Cutting

MADGE COSTELLO WAS pleasantly surprised when she realized they were all trooping to the Bright House in their Sunday best. They must have been quite the sight strolling up the same path that led to the football fields, tottering in their high heels. Grainne was bringing up the rear with Mrs. Walsh, carefully avoiding the muddy spots. Kieran Costello was mumbling a verse of "Blue Suede Shoes" as he sidestepped the pitfalls left by the earlier rain. His mother wondered later if any of the fans felt the need to rush home and dress up in case they had missed an announcement about a dignitary or other celebrity expected at today's game.

"Hope you are all on that side," Fiona said over her shoulder when the roar of the crowd reached their ears.

"One for all and all for one," answered Kieran on behalf of the others.

The presence of the Chariot parked outside the Bright House was a dead giveaway. The Coughlan family was already inside.

"We are all on *that* team," he added, nodding towards the parked vehicle.

"Never a doubt about that, young man," Fiona said, placing her arm across his broad shoulders as they made their way to the front door.

Audible gasps escaped from them as their eyes first met the transformation. The large wooden workbench (formerly a massive kitchen table) usually used for cutting fabric was now draped in linen tablecloths and laden down with platters of food. The centerpiece consisted of three identical cake stands nestled in folds of shimmering fabric, each supporting an elaborately decorated cake, the center offering bore Angela's name expertly inscribed in pink icing. Mrs. Finnerty's name, in silver icing, and Ms. Una's name in gold adorned the two on either side. Kitsy may not have been as good as her mother in the trifle making department, which now took pride of place on the table, but she would be hard to beat at cake decorating.

"Let's walk around and see all the lovely food, pet," Madge said to her young daughter Charly.

"There's such a lot to eat, Mammy, and it all looks lovely," her daughter said. "Who made it all? It must have taken ages."

"A lot of very kind and generous people helped to put this together. Sammy and Kitsy live in an area of town called the Hill. It's around the corner and up the street from the big bank," her mother explained.

"I know. It's near the bridge," offered Charly.

"Exactly. So, all those ladies came together to help put this on for Angela, Mrs. Finnerty, and Una as they are heading to Dublin soon for a wee while."

"That's very nice of them," Charly answered.

Then she went very quiet and seemed deep in thought. Madge recognized the Hill Hands and the Hill Women in every item of food on that table. Many of those ladies were employed in bakeries, cafés or hotels in Baybridge and the surrounding districts. Some were seamstresses who worked out of their homes or in large shops offering alterations. She knew their talent and generosity. Although only Sammy and Kitsy were present today, Madge could vouch that anyone who had a cup of sugar, a pinch of salt, or a drop of milk had offered it for today's send-off, and their hearts ached when they remembered what lay ahead for Angela.

Sammy insisted people stop looking and start eating. She went as far as putting sandwiches on some of the kids' plates. She enlisted Grainne's help, knowing how persuasive she could be. Mrs. Walsh was only too happy to lead the charge. Everything looked so good. Then the clamoring and the chatting started in earnest, recommendations to try this and taste that abounded. There was a bit of a lull when the Twins Killfeather made their entrance, sporting their ancient elegance with *turbans* from the twenties adorning their heads. Sammy and Kitsy were intrigued by the artistry from that time period. The others, however, continued to be intrigued by the food.

Soon, it was time to cut the cakes, causing the whole thing to grind to a halt.

Charly was the first to voice an objection by saying, "We can't cut them. It wouldn't be right, Mammy. They are so lovely!"

It seemed everyone agreed with the little girl, so nobody made a move, leaving Sammy standing with the cake knife in midair—not a good look at such an event!

Ms. Una took a tentative step forward close to where Angela was sitting and said, "What if we cut my cake and save your cake until all the trips to Park Edge are over and—"

She was interrupted midsentence by the sound of a door opening and heavy footsteps coming towards them. All heads turned in time to see Dr. Owens, Angela's family doctor, and Dr. Allen, her orthopaedic surgeon approach. With the brightest smile on her face, Angela got to them before her parents. She reached up while they crouched down to accommodate a hug and a whisper. The whisper did not go unnoticed, and they knew Angela was up to something. Taking the doctors by the hand, she led them to the cakes. She had one more thing to whisper to Sammy. Then everything was ready.

"Excellent. Good timing. Now if you would be so kind, Dr. Allen, Angela would like you to cut her cake as you are such a good cutter," said Sammy. "Mrs. Finnerty, shall we give Dr. Owens the honour of cutting yours as he was right about your recent operation only needing a small cut?"

With whoops and hollers and whistles from the young lads, the cake cutting got underway. Ms. Una and Angela were holding hands when Angela asked her if she could keep her cake until after the last visit to Park Edge. A squeeze of the soft hand said *yes*. Ms. Una's cake could wait for a special moment in the future.

The other cakes tasted as good as they looked.

Hijacked

"I'VE GOT YOUR book bag, Angela," called Amy over her shoulder as they made their way down the driveway to the Chariot.

It puzzled Tony at times that none of them ever questioned how in an instant they became the owners of this luxurious vehicle. At those times, he offered up a silent prayer of thanks for Mr. Hennessy, the owner of the car dealership, responsible for its generous anonymous donation. Unlike Angela's first trip to Park Edge Hospital, there were no well-wishers to wave them off. Una had arranged to meet with a concerned mother in town to discuss her son. She suggested Kelly's, where Grainne used to work saving every penny before opening her own hair salon, thinking the proximity to the river and its bevy of stately swans might ease the pain of her little boy undergoing tests to check for cancer. As if anything would, except finding out he didn't.

"Thanks, Amy," Angela said as she made her own way independently to the back seat and accepted her usual spot surrounded by her accoutrements.

Caroline and Mrs. Finnerty boarded then, settling themselves next to each other in the middle row, which was unusual, all the while talking.

Tony Coughlan knew talk of the tea party would dominate the conversation, at least as far as Haymarket. No doubt about it. In fact, it had already started. Though his good wife, Caroline, and his elegant extraordinary neighbour Mrs. Finnerty did not engage in idle chatter, they were certainly chatting now. It started the previous evening on the walk home from the Bright House. Then there was a phone call or two later in the evening. Still, they continued to talk. When Amy sat in beside him in the front passenger seat, he knew his suspicion was confirmed. This conversation was just getting going. *Did they plan this seating arrangement, or did the female instinct dictate it?* he wondered. He would never know.

"How ya, Daddy," said Amy, flashing her youngest daughter's smile. He took her in with raised questioning eyebrows and amusement, and it pleased him on this otherwise worrisome morning. Reaching into the pink bag at her feet, she deftly retrieved a Disney clipboard with a glittering pencil attached.

"I'm making notes on the trip for Angela's homework, Daddy, so I have to keep an eye out," she explained.

He smiled at her, his heart softly melting and cracking at the same time.

"Right so. Where to, ladies?" he demanded while tipping his imaginary chauffeur's hat to the rearview mirror.

"To the Turbans! To the Turbans!" came the resounding reply with one voice while they tilted their turbaned heads coyly. A passerby would be hard-pressed to determine who these people were and where were they going.

"The Twins Killfeather, can you believe it?" Caroline said, picking up where she left off in an earlier conversation.

"Indeed, I can," replied Mrs. Finnerty. "It's more active and livelier they seem to be getting."

"But those turbans," gushed Caroline, "they had them from when they were in their twenties. They are the genuine article, the real McCoy. Did you see Kitsy's face when they first walked in? I don't think they ever met before."

"Now *that* look would have been hard to miss," replied Mrs. Finnerty. "When Harriet took her turban off to allow Kitsy and Sammy to take a closer look and *then* suggested the Haymarket crew might appreciate a look too, I felt sure they would both pass out. Though the ladies' turbans are not made at the Bright House, they were so keen to learn how these original ones were constructed and so add to their skill. So talented those two." She paused for a moment to recall how she first met Sammy and how the relationship with Angela's Tresses and Turbans was natural from the beginning. "She just walked into Dr Owens' office, asked for Fiona, told her how she saw the difference the maharaja turban made in the life of her little neighbour Marty, and offered her services there and then." She continued, "Without meeting, I invited her to join Mrs. Walsh and myself on our first visit to Haymarket the next day. Kitsy, her friend from the Hill, was an unexpected bonus when she later joined Sammy. Now they are Hill Hands, increasing that community's contribution to others even further. It is well-known a lot of talented people on the Hill lend a hand with many project, all done without fanfare. We learned yesterday just how deep this quiet relationship runs with Sammy when she credited half the Hill for the party."

The Chariot made its way out of Baybridge, up the hill, passing the larger houses on the outskirts, along the outer wall of the racecourse, and past an old church. Soon, the mountain came into view, still wearing its smoky hat of early fog with the promise of a fine day to follow.

Amy found herself losing interest in the summer homework project as she was drawn more and more into the conversation behind her. Voices drifted towards her, bearing snippets of a conversation between her mother and her neighbour.

"The food, oh my goodness, and I thought I made a good trifle. Oh, and those ham sandwiches! They baked that bread you know. So much delicious food." Her mother just couldn't praise it enough.

Amy lost control of the pencil as words appeared on her clipboard—*Hill Hands, Ms. Harriet and old turban, take to Haymarket, baked bread, skill.* She overheard Mrs. Finnerty say how Fiona's sister Keely lived near Park Edge. They talked about school teaching, and though they both had vastly different experiences, they found they had much in common.

Amy heard Mrs. Finnerty ask her mother, "What do you make of Keely's generous offer of an overnight stay with her, if needs be?"

Her mother said, "Very generous for sure and it might work out very well."

She heard the reply "Oh, what a blessing to be near as Angela has her worst few days ahead."

Amy's pencil wrote, *school talk, Keely, near hospital, invitation, settled, worst days.*

Was the summer school project hijacked?

Magic Pencil

AS THEY LEFT Baybridge in the rearview mirror and just before the motorway, Amy said to nobody in particular, "I need to stop."

Ordinarily, this would cause a chorus of whys and what's, but the driver, aware his passengers were female, one wife, two daughters, and an elderly neighbour, located the next suitable ladies' room and did as he was bid.

"Mrs. Finnerty, Mrs. Finnerty, I have to talk to you," cried Amy as she caught up with her on the path to the ladies.

She stopped and turned to find a disheveled and distraught little girl trailing after her with a glittering clipboard in her hand."

My pencil is just writing like a mad thing. Nothing to do with Angela's school report at all."

As intrigued as she was at the notion of a pencil writing, years of teaching taught her to *wait* and *listen.* After a suitable pause, she asked, "What is your pencil saying instead?"

Without answering, Amy thrust her clipboard, almost rudely, in Mrs. Finnerty's face, evidence that this was real. Exhibit A was given a careful examination, noting the scrawled collection of words on the page. Amy's wide eyes and pained expression showed she was clearly waiting for an explanation. To put it another way, her face read "Help." Further scrutiny of the proffered words brought a smile to Mrs. Finnerty's spirit, if not to her face. She knew maintaining an aura of seriousness was called for right now. Continuing, she gently asked, "Why do you think the pencil choose those words, Amy?"

"I heard bits of what you and Mammy were saying, and the words just appeared. I was trying to see things along the way to write for Angela's report on the trip, but those words didn't come."

By now, they had reached a wooden bench surrounded by late-summer flowers and sat down. The others were still rummaging in the Chariot. Mrs. Finnerty glanced over the seemingly random words as it became clear to her she was reading a story, the text consisting of key words only. Though quite a few of those words were spoken earlier by herself, the story was clear and told on the page by an eight-year-old child. Extraordinary!

"I love these words, Amy, but they were not the ones you meant to write."

"No, not at all. I was supposed to write things for Angela's school report to put in the velvet journal."

Amy's distress and confusion did not seem to be any less than earlier. It occurred to Mrs. Finnerty that maybe it was time to clear this up and put the poor child out of her misery, as she said, "Ah, was that something you thought Angela wanted you to do? Maybe a thing that might take some weight off *her* shoulders."

"I thought if I let you and Mammy sit together and talk, I could keep an eye out for things to put in the journal. How is Angela supposed to do homework and get sick at the same time?"

A short gaze at the flowers nestled by their feet gave her a moment to think. Finally, the experienced teacher in Mrs. Finnerty urged her to say, "Amy, you are the best sister to Angela, but this is not a thing *you* need to worry about. When school children are unable to attend for a certain length of time, particularly for illness, they get their own home tutor who makes sure they don't fall behind. When the time is right, the school will send someone to talk to your parents, make a homework plan, and all will be well."

A look of relief just for a second crossed the child's face until she remembered and said, "What about the Twins Killfeather?"

"Oh, those two are so old and wise. You do not ever need to be concerned about them. They wanted Angela more than anyone to have that journal, so they just made that up in case she refused to take it. Anyway, once they wrote that beautiful inscription, it had a different use entirely. They changed it into a diary where Angela can record her own private thoughts and whatever else she chooses. It's a velvet journal all right, not a homework copybook. Way too special, wouldn't you say? However, you, my darling, will make a great journalist."

Amy stared at her, still wide-eyed but now with a hint of a smile stealing its way across her beautiful young face.

Caroline caught up with them, explaining she couldn't find the snacks, which was the reason for all the rummaging in the Chariot earlier. Mrs. Finnerty, realizing they had not yet made their way to the ladies, took all the blame and shooed Amy in that direction.

"Was she in need of a bit of a chat?" Caroline asked, nodding in her daughter's direction, who was now skipping over all manner of foliage to catch up with her sister.

"A mix up about the velvet journal."

They linked arms in solidarity as they walked towards the ladies' room, and Mrs. Finnerty gave an account to the mother of all the goings-on and just how lucky she was to have two such gifted daughters. Tony was in earshot by now, hoping there might be a snack in it for him too.

Coming alongside Mrs. Finnerty, he whispered, "The gifted part is from my side of the family, just so you know," as all chances of him getting a snack now went down the drain according to his wife.

Without any discussion about seating arrangements, Amy gathered up her belongings from the passenger seat and settled herself beside Mrs. Finnerty on the opposite side to Angela so that she could turn around and see her when they spoke. Caroline took her usual spot beside her husband, who took this to mean the tea party topic had exhausted itself.

"Miss you," he said to the rearview mirror, catching Amy's eye.

"I'm just back here, Daddy, with Angela and Mrs. Finnerty," she reassured him.

"I see, and a good thing too. You need to keep your eye on those two."

"Oh, Daddy, that's so silly." She chuckled.

"Well you never know. I'm here if you need me." He was aware something was amiss before the break, but now everyone seemed fine. He was glad of that.

The journey continued as they made their way out of the built-up areas and reached the beautiful countryside. Small thatched roof cottages were to be seen here and there, but mostly, they passed modern houses with huge backyards and sculpted lawns, flowing impressively towards the main roads. Flowers and vegetable gardens were everywhere, and many had a cow or two grazing in the nearby pasture. Here and there, they caught a glimpse of a farmer tending to his crops, usually accompanied by the working dog, most often a collie. Sparsely, fluffy clouds quilted the sky, their shape forming anything or anyone the imagination could conjure. Small towns, their streets dotted with shoppers and the early lunch crowd, sailed by.

Amy spent her time in a lazy fashion, looking out the window now that she was relieved of the homework responsibility. Gradually, the landscape changed from rural to more densely populated areas when, suddenly, the River Shannon came into view, meandering like a silk ribbon between its banks. As if by command, a palpable air of anticipation caused the hitherto listless passengers to sit bolt upright.

"We're here, ladies. Hold onto your hollyhocks," announced Tony.

Within seconds, the silk ribbon was almost obscured with all manner of boats. A variety of cabin vessels, all shapes and sizes, accommodating families on holiday, stretched out before them. Barges and yachts bobbed about as far as the eye could see, and what a sight it was. The Chariot had taken them to Haymarket to witness the last week of river revelry before school started.

"Look at all those boats!" cried Angela "Daddy, do people live on them?"

"For some people, it's their home, but most of these are rented to holidaymakers. Next week, all but a few of them will be gone. Work and school will take them all back to reality. Lucky for us, we are not staying as I can assure you there is no room at the inn.

"But Daddy, Swan River at home is not like that. Is that because we have all the beaches?" asked Amy.

"Exactly, and lucky for us we do," said their dad. "It's hard enough to get through town as it is."

"I like it," declared Angela.

Mrs. Finnerty remembered her last visit here in the off-season. She liked that better—no crowd, space to walk side by side along the promenade, and seating for all at the best bakery in the country. In contrast this time, the place was jumping with excitement and colour. Memories of the stroke she had on her way home from that trip remained buried deep within her.

Caroline had the address and directions in her hand as the Chariot slowly and carefully navigated the throngs. "There it is! Look! Over there! Everyone see the sign?"

Welcome to Angela's Tresses and Turbans, Amy proudly recited, as she read the hand-painted plaque above a brightly painted door.

On the top step beneath the ornate sign stood thirteen-year-old Previn Shiva, his maharaja turban catching the sunlight. His poise transported Mrs. Finnerty back to Tamil Nadu and the village she taught in for all those wonderful years. She turned to see Angela's expression as she saw him too, and her heart soared at what she saw.

Previn

TONY WAS NOT sure about the parking situation, so he left the Chariot engine running as he skipped up the steps. Previn met him halfway and said he was fine where he had parked. Tony went to complete the job of parking. Previn approached the now-open sliding door as Amy and Mrs. Finnerty stepped towards him on the footpath.

"You made it okay, I see," he said.

"Previn," said Mrs. Finnerty. "This is Amy, Angela's sister."

"Welcome, Mrs. Finnerty, and you, Amy," he replied with confidence and without familiarity. His eyes drifted over her shoulder. "Excuse me," he said as he left them in time to reach Angela as she started her exit from the vehicle. It took just a step or two to reach her, steps full of purpose and anticipation. Angela's body continued to uncoil itself until her turban-framed face appeared before the young boy, and the world stood still.

Tony came rushing, full of apologies. "Did we all abandon you, pet? Just as well there was one gentleman to the rescue."

"I was checking around, wondering if I should bring anything with me," she explained.

"No, darling, nothing but yourself," her mother answered, having just reached them.

Without a hesitation, Previn reached in, took her hand, and eased her forward and eventually to the pavement. Words fail to describe the look that passed between Caroline and Tony. Mrs. Finnerty, on the other hand, wasn't at all surprised.

"I'm Angela," she said as she took her first step alongside him.

"I know," he said. "I'm Previn Shiva."

"I know" was her answer.

They led the party up the steps to the front door. Then Angela stopped, smiled at him, and dropped his hand. She sought Amy in the group behind her and called, "Amy, we're here."

Her sister knew what she meant and, breaking free from Mrs. Finnerty's hand, sprang forward to join her. Previn Shiva stepped aside, knowing the sisters should be together, a mature point of view for a thirteen-year-old, some might think. This, however, was no ordinary thirteen-year-old. The door opened to reveal Tara Doherty, and a sea of eyes behind her all fixed on the entrance. Nobody spoke. There was no need. In the broadest embrace ever, Angela and her sister were scooped up by Tara such that they felt encircled by her but yet not trapped. Somehow Angela felt *secure in that space.*

"Welcome, welcome, come in," Tara managed to say, releasing the girls. "It's a big day here for us, isn't it, ladies?" she added to the rest of her crew without taking her eyes off Angela.

Completely at odds with her usual confident place in the world, she now found herself floundering and somewhat at a loss for words. The thoughts and feelings she held before about Angela were in an instant diluted with no relationship to what she was feeling now. Seeing her and holding her in the flesh floored her. Remembering what she had already endured and what was yet to come when she left them in a little more than an hour, well, she just couldn't say how it made her feel. *This is a ten-year-old kid*, she repeated to herself over and over as she watched her meet and greet the others. Her young sister Amy walked beside her with such poise.

"Oh, for the love of Mike, where are my manners? My mother would be mortified. Mrs. Finnerty, you look great. Very happy to see both of you again," she continued as she shook hands with Caroline and Tony in welcome. Apart from the intense embrace on arrival and the thoughts nobody knew were racing through her head, Tara Doherty seemed to be in complete control. Amy and Angela barely got space to see what the place was like. Their welcome was a bit overwhelming. Watching the girls across the impressive expanse of the studio, Caroline had a quiet word with Tony on behalf of their daughter—intervention alert! He made his way unobtrusively to where they stood among the other workers.

"Hi, ladies, any chance of a wee sit down for Angela?" he said rather sheepishly.

"Oh, what are we thinking," said Mary, one of the earlier wide-eyed seamstresses. "We have a bit of a spread for you all over here. The girls are so beautiful in their turbans we almost forgot. It's the first time any of us have seen them worn in real life. We were overcome, weren't we, Dymphna?"

Nods, but no words followed.

The studio had a carved-out alcove overlooking the River Shannon with its array of colourful boats as far as the eye could see. A simple table of home-cooked food from locally produced ingredients spread out before them. Angela took the nearest chair. Dymphna, the logo seamstress who was about to direct her to the special place allotted to her at the far end of the table, thought better of it, deciding instead to let her rest where she was.

The others began to drift towards the food where Angela could be heard telling Dymphna, "I didn't realize the people who make the beautiful turbans never get to see who wears them. That's what matters. It's not what we call the place or whose name is on the door. It's the child who wears them that matters. It's their turban. My friend at Park Edge, her name is Amelia, wears a turban that you made for her and sent to her in the hospital. She loves it, so it's Amelia's Turban really, not Angela's."

Such relief came over Dymphna when she realized Mrs. Finnerty was standing behind Angela's chair and overheard the conversation. This was way out of her league. Little did she know she was not the only one relieved. Mrs. Finnerty finally found the root of Angela's hesitancy at the Bright House that first day, and it had nothing to do with her sister.

"That's a very interesting way to look at things I must say, Angela. It did not cross my mind that the ladies who make these beautiful turbans do not get to see the joy they bring to the children, but they know what a difference they make. Dymphna and the others here love what they do because they know and care and use their talent to show that. You have your name on the turbans because when a child gets one with your logo on it, it's a chance to tell that child that *ATT* stands for Angela's Tresses and Turbans and what the duckling means. The Mammy or Daddy or nurse or doctor will tell them that you are going through the same tough treatments as they are and that you want them to know you are thinking about them. When you and Amy asked Kitsy to design the logo, you wanted it to have the duckling from your special book and *ATT* embroidered on each one. Sammy sends the logos over here after Kitsy makes them. Dymphna, I believe you oversee that side of things," said Mrs. Finnerty.

"Indeed, I am, and very proud of it too," answered the seamstress. That pride reflected in her tone. "We were all amazed when we found out who did the design. It makes the turbans very special, like a little personal note from you, Angela, with each one. So, it wouldn't make sense if Angela's name were not on them."

Mrs. Finnerty sat next to Angela and looked into her eyes. She saw the glistening of the tears as for the first time, this young girl grasped the depth of the foundation, *her* foundation. Without realizing it, Dymphna had nailed it with her simple honest explanation.

"Where's Amy?" Angela whispered.

"I'm here beside you, and I'm starving," she said.

Angela looked at her sister, and if Amy noticed any sign of tears, she did not comment. Instead, she said, "I told you it was a good logo, and I'm getting more starving."

The tears dried, the smile appeared, and their contagious laughter took over. Case closed.

Mrs. Finnerty caught up with Caroline and Tara at the other end of the studio. Tara was in the middle of a conversation with Caroline.

"Oh, she's adorable and bright as a button. I couldn't help hearing her conversation with Dymphna, such selflessness and insight. I just can't get over her. I sense a great bond between your two girls, Mrs. Coughlan, and that laugh of theirs just drew us all in."

"Oh, they can go from cry to laugh and profound to ridiculous in the blink of an eye. Despite everything, we tend not to dwell on the downside for very long, not with those two," Caroline was saying as Mrs. Finnerty reached them.

"The very two people I need to see," she said. "Caroline, it's a relief to know that Angela's reluctance with her name being on the turbans was due to a much deeper reason and had nothing to do with Amy. Thanks to Dymphna's straightforward approach and Amy's *starvation*, everyone is back on track. As I have said in the past, leave it to the children to sort things out."

"You're all amazing is all I have to say," said Tara.

"That may be. Nevertheless, we do need your help with another small matter," said Mrs. Finnerty.

"We do, we do," echoed Caroline as she proceeded to tell the convoluted saga of Angela's velvet journal and who had given it to her. "If you could share some info on how things work here with Angela, it would be a great help. For example, sourcing the fabric, getting the orders for the turbans, how you transport the finished product, the cost, and whatever you could put together suitable for a school report. She wants to do it because the Twins Killfeather suggested she write a report in the journal they gave her, but it is ancient and no doubt valuable. We will get a school copybook more suitable to hand in for a report." Mrs. Finnerty added,

"It might prove to be a great distraction during the days ahead. I'm staying on in Dublin till the end of the week so we can spend time on it together."

"Like I said, you are all amazing," said Tara." "Dymphna, I need you. We have a *project*. Bring the girls. Give us half an hour."

With that, she was off at her usual pace and *no time like the present* attitude.

The *project* entourage moved from station to station in the studio in a serious, businesslike manner. However, every now and then, the girls slowed to admire something, make a remark, and more than once to giggle. The entire staff was enjoying their antics, forgetting what their destination was today. Caroline and Mrs. Finnerty went back to partake of the delicious food. Before joining Tara in her quest, Ame Shiva went in search of her son. She found him with Tony Coughlan outside on the narrow balcony just off the alcove, overlooking the colourful expanse of boats littering the river.

"That one there, see, with the orange canopy, has been here all summer," he was saying to Tony, pointing just below. "It's a bit dilapidated, but it's the most interesting, all sorts of people in and out with musical instruments."

"There you are, telling Mr. Coughlan all about the orange boat, I bet. He tells us he's going to get one when they move and park it right there," said his mother.

"Well, at least you'd have a bird's-eye view of the shenanigans, Mrs. Shiva," offered Tony. No sign of his police Sargent skepticism coming through.

"Well, for now, it's terra firma for you," she informed Previn. "Meanwhile, Mrs. Doherty and the girls need your help. They are in her office gathering things to help Angela's with a school project."

Without a word, he bolted from them. Tony was still leaning on the railing, looking down at the boat.

Ame Shiva joined him, saying, "How rude!"

They turned to face each other, still bent over the railing. Some smiles can be very contagious. Some conveying a clear understanding.

Phone Home

BEFORE LEAVING HAYMARKET, Mrs. Finnerty asked to use the office phone. She conducted no business there today. That was not the purpose of the visit. She did not see her role as having any direct involvement in those affairs at all. She had full confidence in the people who did have that responsibility, knowing they would inform her if anything came up that needed her attention. Trusting, one might say, which was true. Her interests lay elsewhere.

"Una," she said when she heard her voice on the other end of the phone, "it's me. I hope things are good at home. I called for two reasons. First, Angela and Amy are getting along like stars here, and the situation about Angela's turban naming is no more. I'll tell you all when I see you. Be happy to know it did not involve Amy. Well, she did help to solve the problem, but I will explain it all later. Now how did the meeting with the young mother go at Kelly's this morning?"

"Kelly's was an excellent choice. The smell of freshly made tea infused with the tantalizing aroma of hot scones and muffins wafting out from the kitchen was enough to distract anyone, even a distraught mother. Though Grainne is not there anymore since she opened her own hair salon, the morning waitress was perfect. Of course, she did not know our business, but she seemed to sense something, just like Grainne. Maybe Mrs. Kavanagh, the manager, discusses this awareness with the employees, as so many of their customers are on their way to or from the hospital. Anyway, it put this young mother at ease if only for a moment. Her son Liam is seven years old. He has been ill for a while, and blood tests are abnormal. Though no diagnosis has yet been reached, the word leukemia has been mentioned. She heard about the foundation and wanted to just talk freely without constraint. The family is solid with good support mechanisms. She wanted a place where she could speak as herself without burdening anyone. A friend or neighbour, I'm not sure who, suggested she call us." Una took a breather.

"God bless that friend. How did she seem afterwards? How are you?" Mrs. Finnerty always asked how the staff were feeling about any interaction.

"I feel good. She was somewhat reassured when we decided to cross the bridge when we come to it. We had doubt on our side without a definitive diagnosis. Taking a leaf out of your not *Crossing Bridges* book seemed apt in this situation," Una said.

"It has worked in many instances. Then you discover there is no need for a bridge at all. In this case, it has played up the hope that it might well be something else entirely. That is our prayer. For now, you did well with that approach. We are setting out for Park Edge here shortly. That is one huge bridge yet to be crossed. Be well, Una," last words as she finished the call.

The Coughlan's farewell was as dramatic as their welcome. A box of turbans bound for Park Edge Oncology Department found its way into the boot of the Chariot. Caroline was laden down with Angela's homework box, which led her to believe there was more inside than receipts and bills. Tony's burden surely consisted of edible items if the inviting mixture of aromas emanating from his package was anything to go by. No telling at this time what additional items Amy's Disney bag contained. Mrs. Finnerty seemed to have gotten off lightly as she was still carrying the handbag she came in with. It wouldn't look good to be bribing the boss! Waves and blown kisses from everyone. Previn escorted Angela and helped her into the back seat of the Chariot, the others standing aside as if it was the most natural thing in the world for them both. It was.

Tony once more found himself wondering if the seating arrangements in the vehicle were previously planned or instinct dictated where they should sit. Caroline, as was sometimes her habit, sat beside Angela in the bed-like back seat, inviting her to prop her leg up on her lap if she felt the need. The homework box fitted perfectly on the floor between them. Amy slid her Disney bag in next, spreading herself and assorted items along the seat occupied on the first leg of the journey by her mother. Mrs. Finnerty and her handbag took their seat beside Tony.

"I didn't see a bus stop anywhere," she teased. "Mind if I hitch a lift?"

The matter-of-fact tone of the question matched by Tony as he answered, "Aren't I going that way, anyway. No bother."

"You're so funny," said Amy from behind them, prompting Angela to ask what was so funny, which, in turn, required Amy to explain. In true Coughlan style, it started with a stifled giggle and very quickly erupted into contagious laughter as the imagination of the young went wild. The tone was set as the Chariot wound its way uphill and down dale towards the capitol. When they left the treacherous Curlew Mountains, well behind them a more relaxed atmosphere descended on them. Shortly before the sights of Dublin came into view, a rare thing happened. A cell phone rang. It was Mrs. Finnerty's. None of them could recall her having such a thing, but here she was now, answering it.

Keely went to a spinning class in the morning. She had not been all through the summer choosing instead to walk, hike, or bike. When she could, she managed a swim. On her return from Baybridge, she decided to return to her reliable work routine a week early, knowing the chances of doing any of the could not be guaranteed once school started. In addition to this, she needed to allow time for Mrs. Finnerty and Angela's family during the daytime. She had no idea what help she could offer or in what way she could relieve them of some of this burden. She did know she was ready to give them anything they needed within her power.

She was feeling good about her return to the gym this morning, the raucous welcome from those who had continued through the summer was not kind but very welcome.

"Would ya look whose back? Thought we'd seen the back of you riding off into the sunset. I don't think there's a spare bike, do you, Ann?"

"None, I'm sure, all taken by the regulars." The teasing continued while she was being hugged and helped setting up her bike. She was back among her friends, known collectively as the Five Thirty Club, due to the unearthly hour they choose to work out prior to heading off to their respective places of work or home to let a spouse do so.

Before leaving Baybridge the day before, she and Mrs. Finnerty arranged to speak on the phone when they neared Dublin. Checking the time after class, Keely made an educated guess as to where they were on the road by now as she picked up her phone. Mrs. Finnerty raised her phone, indicating to Caroline, now leaning forward in the back seat, it was the expected call. Caroline nodded, a reassuring smile lighting her face.

"Hello, Keely, you estimated well. We are getting close. How are things at your end?"

As she spoke, she shifted in her seat so she could get a glimpse of the others behind her. Though the girls were aware of offers of help from Mrs. Hannon's sister because she lived near the hospital, nothing more was known yet. Their parents, however, had a tentative plan, which could not be ironed out until Angela's treatment schedule was announced later.

"I'm getting a little giddy now as we get closer. Excitement at seeing all the things I've only imagined, especially Angela's own room at number ten Happy Street. Oh! let's not forget the Pirate Ship."

"Well, I have everything ready here. No bother at all. Give Tony and Caroline my best wishes and tell them whatever they decide is just fine. They need to be at ease. Call me when you know."

Switching off her phone, Mrs. Finnerty said, "Mrs. Fitzpatrick sends her best to you girls, and she hopes to see you for a bit while you are so close. She has a grand house too and a garden I hear. Amy, maybe you and I could take a peek at it later while Angela is settling in. What do you think?"

Amy, turning in an exaggerated bounce to face her mother, asked, "Can I Mammy?"

Step one complete!

Brief Fantasy

THE ENTRANCE TO Park Edge Hospital was nothing less than stately. Suddenly, Amy squealed, "Look up, Mrs. Finnerty, see the top of the gate with the huge Goldie letters!"

Craning their necks, they all looked up to see the banner bearing the hospital's name and crest. It was a fixed structure spanning the driveway, not affected by the opening and closing of the gates below.

"Oh, Amy, it's so high, and the letters are indeed huge. I don't recall ever seeing such a gate before," replied Mrs. Finnerty.

She was genuinely impressed. The Coughlan family knew from being here before what to expect. A uniformed porter approached them, the gold rim of his peaked cap and the gilded edge of his name tag catching the last of the day's sun. His beaming smile outshone all that glitter, including the gold hospital crest on the cap proudly perched atop his head.

On this occasion, the bright yellow golf cart he was driving was much bigger than those they rode in before, thus capable of transporting more passengers. The girls noticed this.

Amy whispered to her sister, "How did he know to bring a big cart, Angela?"

"It's because of Mrs. Finnerty, but who told him? He didn't see inside the Chariot because of the tinted windows. See, she was meant to come. I told her that," Angela whispered back.

"Good job she came. It must be very important," Amy said, continuing the conspiratorial banter between them.

"There you are, the Baybridge Party. Welcome to Park Edge," exclaimed the porter without any hint of conspiracy.

With all this formality, Mrs. Finnerty wasn't sure where she had landed. She thought her destination was a children's hospital, the outline of which was visible from where they stood. A line from Yeats's poem referring to Lisadell House came to mind,

> The light of the evening, Lisadell.
> Great windows open to the south.

"Did you pack your gown?" she quietly asked Caroline.

Without missing a beat, she answered, "The maid did *and* the jewels."

Not as much as a smirk passed between the two. Way too good at the character acting those two! Tony took Angela's Indian book bag and Amy's Disney bag out of the Chariot, oblivious to any of the notions swirling around the others. Caroline shared a bag with Angela. They boarded the cart, Mrs. Finnerty beside the driver, whose name tag proclaimed him as Sean, Amy and Angela in the next row, their possessions stowed in a compartment somewhere under the vehicle, and their parents like royalty behind them. The girls felt sure something special was happening. They sat up straight in their seats as if they *were* royalty, all thoughts of where they were going momentarily abandoned. For one moment, Caroline and Mrs. Finnerty succumbed to the fantasy as they all sat there in their golden carriage. Tony Coughlan found his throat tighten and his chest squeeze as the golf cart made a slight turn, bringing the entrance to the hospital into view.

It was time now for Sean to hand over his charges to Fergal, an equally well-turned-out young man who was waiting for them inside the main foyer. It reminded them of the entrance to the manor, where the Twins Killfeather lived. It too was an old building, to which the new modern hospital had been added. Amy and Angela took their place on the indoor version of the golf cart and followed by the others walking behind, made their way to the oncology unit. The girls remained resolute believing Mrs. Finnerty's presence was essential for this round of treatment. Angela needed her there. Amy needed her there to be with her sister.

The true wonder of this place descended as soon as they entered Happy Street. Mrs. Finnerty stood inside the electronic door, unable to take the next step. Fergal had already departed with his fancy yellow wheelchair once he announced their arrival. Nurse Ellen was on her way from the nurses' station, cleverly concealed as a pirate ship, to greet them. Everything she had been told and imagined about this space faded in comparison to what now lay before her. It wasn't so much the decor, the numbered little houses with their curtained windows, behind which powerful medication dripped into tiny veins, the miniature chaises used more often than the hospital bed or the convertible furniture needed to rest a weary family member who refused to leave the room. It was the children. As she looked around, she saw several sitting in varying groups, one or two with a staff member, others with family, and some alone. It was those little ones who stopped her in her tracks. She was no stranger to the joy of children. This was something else entirely—not a glum face in sight, not a complaint or moan to be heard. Smiles and happiness wafted towards her. She reminded herself signs of pain, nausea, vomiting, cramps, and sore mouths had already been endured by some, for others, it would soon be upon them. The sound of the space would change blanketed by the soothing softness of a caring voice.

Nurse Ellen reached them, unaware of the temporary paralysis suffered by Mrs. Finnerty.

Her voice brought her back as she said, "Angela, you did it, you brought her with you. What a clever girl. I think this *must* be Mrs. Finnerty." Taking her hand in greeting, she added, "You are most welcome to Happy Street. We have been expecting you."

If anyone saw the exchange between Angela and her sister, they did not remark on it. One thing was for certain, the large yellow golf cart *was* for Mrs. Finnerty, and it was a good job she came.

Guest of Honour

IT SHOULD HAVE come as no surprise to any of them when they realized Mrs. Finnerty was being fussed over. She was, after all, the founder and benefactor of Angela's Tresses and Turbans, responsible for the turbans adorning the heads of many at this very moment, including Dr. Myers, Angela's oncologist. Hers was a special order rushed to Park Edge Hospital at Amy's request. They first met when Amy's fascination with how the doctor washed her hands, resulted in her getting a private lesson on the dos and don'ts and the appointment of the enforcer of the rules whenever anybody was around her sister. Woe betide the person who deviated.

Standing here now amid all this, oblivious to the fuss being made of her, was testimony to Mrs. Finnerty's generosity, humility, and dedication to the bigger picture.

"Let's go see the Pirate Ship," said Amy, looking at Nurse Ellen for permission to advance further up the unit as a few of the children were out of their rooms.

Amy always had her infection control hat on. The go-ahead was happily given with a nod and a smile. The girls, one on either side, holding her hand, led the way. The nurse took the opportunity to guide their parents to the admission office across the corridor.

Dr. Myers was a sight to behold. Amy saw her first as they turned from the Pirate Ship. This elegant tall woman wearing her vibrant turban was standing closer to Angela's room, looking through a file. As always, wisps of her untamable mop of red curls peeped out here and there from under her beautiful headdress. Long before the era of Angela's turbans, this paediatric oncologist covered her hair while on duty, a note of solidarity with her young patients. It was the highlight of their morning and the subject of much speculation as to which one she would be wearing. Amy tugged at Mrs. Finnerty, propelling her forward as only a child can.

"Come on, Angela," she urged as her sister lagged behind.

The older woman had no choice but to keep up as she was attached to the almost-sprinting child in a firm handgrip.

"Hello, girls," greeted Dr. Myers nonchalantly as she continued randomly flipping through the chart.

As Mrs. Finnerty became aware of the intended mischief in the doctor's attitude, a warm feeling spread through her. She knew this was a good match for the Coughlan family whose motto was not to dwell on the downside for very long.

Instead, she greeted their escort, "You must be Mrs. Finnerty. Welcome to Happy Street."

"How did she know?" Amy said to the air around her.

Dr. Myers took it upon herself to answer. "A little bird from the west coast told us to expect a guest today. We all wondered *who it could be.* So, while I was getting the report from the lovely Dr. Owens this morning, I mentioned the matter. Without naming names, he said we all should be on our best behavior, and I should wear my best turban today."

"Dr. Myers, you guessed it right," said Angela.

"I did, didn't I?" she answered. "I'm wearing my very best turban. Thank you. The bit about behaving myself, well, I'm not so sure."

"We have trouble with the best behaving bit ourselves, don't we girls?" replied the guest of honour.

"Fair warning. Anyway, you are welcome. Thank you again on behalf of us all. Now, Angela, you and I have to get down to business. Let's get you settled in number 4. I know you brought your duckling book to help us make our plan."

As they walked ahead of the other two, the ease and confidence between them reminded Mrs. Finnerty of the relationship she had with the doctors at home in Baybridge. How lucky for Angela to have such a team. As they all caught up with each other just inside the yellow door of number 4, the good doctor stopped, saying, "Oops, I forgot something. Be right back."

It was no accident that Mrs. Finnerty found herself alone with the girls in the pretty curtained room, where Angela received chemotherapy. Her feet stuck to the floor once again, making the next step impossible. She could see the intravenous pole beside the hospital bed, the mini chaise where Angela's little body would battle the debilitating fatigue, nausea, and sore mouth, the convertible window seat where she and Caroline would sit and endure their inability to alleviate what their precious little girl was going through.

Then the penguin perched on the pillow of the hospital bed saved her.

"Girls, look, the penguin is waiting for you just like you said."

Her outburst seemed to melt the glue under her feet. Amy danced the penguin around the room while explaining everything. Soon, Angela plopped onto the mini chaise, sought Mrs. Finnerty's eyes, saying, "*You will always be with me. Always.*"

Amy opened the decorative book bag, the permanent home to the special books. She took out *Make Way for the Ducklings*. She placed it beneath the pillow, its home for the next week or so under the penguin's watchful eye.

"Mammy, Daddy," said Amy as Caroline and Tony entered the room. "I showed her everything like we promised. I put the duckling book under the pillow, and the penguin is going to mind it. Dr. Myers went out, and Mrs. Finnerty is taking me to Mrs. Fitzpatrick's house."

"Good girl, Amy. You have Angela all settled then," said Tony. It was all he could do, not to run to her and scoop her up.

"She has, Daddy," replied Angela. A light tap on the open door heralded the return of Dr. Myers.

Amy, on cue, went to Angela, now lying back on the mini chaise. Soon, she would transfer to the hospital bed before going down to radiology for her scans prior to treatment. She lay beside her sister long enough to kiss her on the side of her turban closest to her ear and whisper to her. Angela smiled broadly. The doctor remained framed in the colourful doorway.

"We're off now to visit Mrs. Fitzpatrick," she said.

Taking Mrs. Finnerty's hand, she propelled her towards Dr. Myers as she had done previously.

"I know *you* will beat the bad lump, and *I* promise to keep all the hands clean."

They departed, leaving the adults staring after them and Angela's smile fast becoming a giggle.

Just Chatting

KEELY JUMPED WHEN her phone chirped. She had been on pins and needles since the earlier call from Mrs. Finnerty while they were still on the road. Tentatively, she put it to her ear.

"Mrs. Fitzpatrick, good news, great news in fact. Can you come and get us? We are sitting here on the bench outside the main door."

Keely snatched car keys and handbag and was on her way to the car when the conversation ended.

The young girl sat, swinging her legs, black patent leather shoes and ankle socks trimmed in lace rhythmically moving in the air. The Disney princess on the cuff of her socks appeared to be dancing. Though it was early evening, the sun shone bright and warm. Summer sunset in Ireland came late and sudden, a spectacular show, but not yet today. The older woman sat beside her in no hurry to do anything. Her closed-toe Indian leather sandals were firmly placed on the brick path beneath. The hem of her lightweight beige linen pants brushed the metal buckle adorning her footwear. A splash of colour caught the sun about the knees, revealing a vibrant tunic bought in India too long ago to remember when exactly. Haphazardly across her shoulders, lay a silk scarf vaguely picking up the tones in her tunic. Another relic from India, its silk so fine it could pass through a wedding ring. As a sort of joke, her late husband put it to the test on the day he gave it to her. They giggled like schoolchildren when it slid easily through. The girls loved the scarf but were unaware of the backstory.

"Oh, it's so peaceful," she said to her dancing bench mate. "Look, you can see the big gate from here."

"And the yellow golf carts parked over there. Can you see your big one?" asked the child.

"No, they must be fussing over somebody else by now" came the reply.

"It's not that. Sean got the loan of it today just for you. He's away now to give it back. They won't be fussing over anyone else now you are here," mused the young girl.

"I suppose not. It's getting late now for fussing," said the older woman.

"Way too late," reassured the child, thus bringing *that* conversation to an acceptable conclusion as only she and her sister could so skillfully do.

"I find myself imagining what Mrs. Fitzpatrick's house is like. It's in a village but not out in the country. I imagine it will be bright with a lovely flower garden. Probably a kitchen with a big table like you have at home. I'm sure it's not like mine." Mrs. Finnerty paused then.

"Well, not if she has stairs. Does she have stairs?" asked Amy after considering the possibilities.

"I don't know." Another pause.

"Some houses don't have stairs, but there isn't a lift taking up space in the kitchen," Amy explained.

"That's true."

"Or a library. I think it's an ordinary house like ours. Mrs. Fitzpatrick is very nice, so her house will be nice too," said Amy.

"It was good of her to invite us over no matter what kind of house it is. It must be big though because she said if we liked, she would love it if we stayed with her tonight so your Mammy and Daddy could talk with Dr. Myers about Angela's treatment. We can think about that after we get there, no rush." Longer pause now to let that sink in.

"Daddy wants to stay for that. I stayed with you when he did that before. That was nice. We can stay with Mrs. Fitzpatrick. I'll miss the lift, though." Skillfully done as always.

Keely spotted them sitting, chatting away on the bench, and resisted the temptation to honk the horn, not wishing to intrude on what seemed, even from afar, a personal exchange between the two. She also remembered she was on the grounds of a children's hospital, so no honking!

"Is that Mrs. Fitzpatrick's car?" Amy asked as a sparkling BMW approached.

"I hope so," Mrs. Finnerty said, playfully nudging the little girl. "Otherwise, she has stolen it because that's her driving."

Amy abruptly looked at her and allowed a gasp to escape before saying, "Well, it's a nice one."

She popped down from the bench, slithering into the straps of her pink Disney backpack. Her partner retrieved her handbag, which really wasn't a handbag, from where it had been hanging over the back of the bench. She hoisted it over her head as it came to rest on her shoulder. This bag was another relic from India, capable of expansion according to the need. Today, it was at full capacity. She ran her fingers through her chic short curls to undo any possible damage done by the strap. Her naturally grey hair sported sparse highlights today styled by Grainne in honour of the occasion.

As Keely pulled in alongside the manicured grass verge, Amy took Mrs. Finnerty by the hand and led the way to the next step in their adventure.

Many more would follow. Today, neither of them knew where those steps would lead.

A Penny in a Basket

THE DRIVE TO Keely's house was beautiful and short. They passed along the impressive wrought-iron fence separating the hospital grounds from the outside world. It was not hard to imagine its past as a public park, the locals strolling carrying picnic baskets, mothers and hired nannies pushing prams, and children boisterously chasing a stray ball. They could still do all that in many areas of the city, including the world-famous Phoenix Park, but not here. Patients, visitors, and staff had this gem all to themselves. For those children well enough to venture outside, it was the best of therapy, and not one person begrudged them that joy.

"It's a lovely car," said Amy.

"Do you think so, Amy? It's new, and I'm trying to get the hang of it," replied Keely.

"Mrs. Finnerty thought you might have stolen it," added Amy. She continued to take in the sights as she gazed out the window from her luxurious seat behind them.

Without missing a beat, the driver caught a glimpse of her in the rearview mirror, saying, "I stole a penny from our shop when I was about your age. Actually, I found it in the onion basket and kept it. I bought sweets in the shop on the corner with it. Nevertheless, my father pointed out that was stealing. I got into a lot of trouble then, so I gave up stealing. Instead, my husband bought this very nice car for me on my birthday because my other one was an old clunker."

Silence.

"Much safer," concluded the child.

The teachers in front shared a silent but well-known joy brought about by a rare pupil like Amy, who saw the world and its conundrums differently. The endgame was clear to them from the outset. The convolutions, twists, and turns inserted by most would never occur to them. It was all straightforward, no need to climb Mount Kilimanjaro!

The assortment of vehicles deftly parked in the wide driveway informed Keely her husband, Phillip, and youngest son, Leo, were home. Taking their bags with them, they zigzagged their way to the front door which was ajar. Immediately, the smell of breakfast food assailed their nostrils. Without a doubt, somebody was cooking rashers of bacon, which suddenly reminded the guests of how hungry they were. Could it be because they hadn't eaten since Haymarket?

"You *do* have stairs," said Amy as a flight of stairs came into view.

"I do," replied Keely.

It was a true statement as there it was, inside the door on the left, narrow and quaint. Directly across a small sitting room, with a marble fireplace briefly caught the eye, as they made their way down an equally narrow quaint hall.

"It's another Bright House. See, it has the big wooden table and the lovely huge window looking out on the backyard," Amy exclaimed in a throaty whisper, which was not loud but had the potential to be had she not caught herself.

Phillip to the rescue, saying, "Amy, it is like your Bright House. We didn't notice that before I suppose because of the view you have of that mountain in Baybridge. Anyway, you are welcome, and it's so nice to have you here, Mrs. Finnerty. This is Leo, who missed the goings-on when we came to the party because he had a horse to look after."

"I know that mountain well, Amy. I see it every time we come to Auntie Fiona's. The Bright House is on the way to the Gaelic football pitches. See, I know it, Dad."

"Ah, but you missed the cake," replied his Dad.

"Did your dad just have the last word?" asked his mother.

"Nothing new in that" was all Leo had to say on that matter.

"I heard that" was all his father had to say, again having the last word.

Philip went back to flipping the bacon. Leo announced tea was made, and without further ado, a sumptuous platter of breakfast food was laid before them. Amy sat opposite Leo, and automatically, the tall handsome twenty-two-year-old and the eight-year-old were deep in conversation. Amy's gaze fell on a giant wicker basket of eggs on the kitchen counter.

"Where did you get all those different coloured eggs?" she asked.

"At the farm where I keep my horse. They have loads of various kinds of chickens clucking around all over the place. That's why they look like that, even five or six with speckles," explained Leo.

"It's like a painting, especially the way they nestle in that basket," said Amy. A discreet glance passed between the grown-ups at the sophistication of the little girl's remark.

"They have vegetables and meat there too. I get all the good stuff for Mam when she needs it," explained Leo.

"We get ours in Quigley's. I suppose she gets them from a farm too because they taste so good, but I don't know if they have any horses there," said Amy.

"Maybe one or two just for themselves, not other peoples," offered Leo.

"Is it far to your horse?" she asked.

Leo glanced at his mother for a clue as to how he should continue. He was not sure if it was a quick visit or more. He searched her face, a face he knew well and understood the signal to go ahead when it came.

"It's about half an hour in the truck, not far at all. Would ye have the time in the morning for a quick trip out, Mrs. Finnerty?" he asked.

"Leo, there's always time to visit the horses. Can I come too, Amy? asked Mrs. Finnerty

Now that was an unexpected distraction!

"Oh, can she? Mrs. Fitzpatrick too if she wants," pleaded Amy.

"I want," replied Keely.

"Well, that's a fine state of affairs. Make the best evening breakfast for you lot, then you send me to work tomorrow as ye go off galivanting," pouted Phillip.

"Too bad, but somebody has to bring home the bacon," said his wife. This friendly banter seemed to be the way of it around here and Mrs. Finnerty found it quite comical.

It did not go unnoticed that at precisely that moment, Keely speared a juicy piece of bacon and popped it in her mouth. Amy giggled as only Amy could, and in no time, they were all laughing. The doorbell interrupted their joking.

Pushing his chair away from the table, Philip said, "I'll get it."

He returned with Mrs. Peterson's daughter from across the road.

"Rose, nice to see you," Keely said. She stood up and relieved the newcomer of the platter she was returning.

"Thank you for the delicious chicken. We polished it off for the tea this evening."

"Phillip treated us to breakfast for *our* tea this evening as we had visitors from Baybridge. You'll have a cup of tea with us. Leo, bring another cup like a good lad."

Soon, Rose was seated at the table like one of the family and, in true Irish fashion, did not decline the cup of tea.

"This is Mrs. Finnerty, and she is here with Amy, whose sister is getting settled in at Park Edge before her treatment starts in the morning."

If Rose's eyes widened at that announcement, it went unnoticed.

Rose spoke to Amy, "Park Edge is the best hospital *ever* for that kind of treatment. I came all the way from London where my hospital is to see how they do things there. Many people from all over the world were at our first meeting today, even from America, to meet the experts. I love the yellow golf carts too. I'm going to see if

I can get some for Hillgate Hospital where I work when I get back," explained Rose.

"They used the big yellow cart for Mrs. Finnerty so they could make a fuss over her because she was the special guest Dr. Owens told them was coming," said Amy.

"It's always best to make a fuss over a special guest. I see you are wearing a beautiful turban. We saw a few people at the meeting today wearing turbans," said Rose.

"Oh yes, they do because Mrs. Finnerty has them made in Baybridge and Haymarket for Angela Tresses and Turbans. They made a special one for Dr. Myers too. That's why Mrs. Finnerty is a special guest. Angela is my sister, and she is going to stay with her while she takes the *fierce* medicine. I promised Dr. Myers I would make sure everybody washed their hands when she comes home." Amy finished her milk and took Leo up on his offer to look at the back garden before it got too dark.

"That's about the size of it," said Mrs. Finnerty.

"My tea is stone cold," said Keely, rising to get the teapot.

She placed a gentle hand on the stunned Rose's shoulder as she passed. Rose had moved way beyond the temperature of her tea as her mind churned with the realization her agenda for the Park Edge conference was now on a whole new path.

God Bless Leo

BY THE TIME Angela returned to number 4 Happy Street, Dr. Myers had already looked at her scans. Tony and Caroline thought about getting something to eat while they had a chance but instead stayed close, sipping something from the vending machine that bore a vague resemblance to tea. That fact escaped them both due to their minds being in turmoil awaiting the results. The appearance of the doctor did nothing to alleviate their anxiety. She always looked relaxed and at ease. Her bright smile crowned by her turban and stray curl gave no indication as to what news she was about to deliver.

Angela, now back in her room, wrapped in her penguin-patterned hospital gown, wriggled up on her pillows as she slid her fingertips under just far enough to touch her duckling book.

"Ducklings tucked in tight?" asked the doctor as she approached. Angela's reply was a knowing smile. "Well, I have good news for them. Your scans are good. No sign of that nasty lump or any of its friends prowling around." Audible escape of held breath from both parents, acknowledged by Dr. Myers with a nod and her assuring smile. "As we talked about before, this lump is sneaky and so is well-practiced at fooling people. Not us. No, sir. We are going ahead with the plan to start treatment at nine tomorrow morning."

Angela looked at her mother without speaking. Caroline had been desperately trying to give the doctor space. The look brought her rushing to the bedside.

"It's great news, pet. You are so strong and the toughest wee fighter. That lump never had a chance. Now you can make sure not the tiniest bit is hiding," her mother had spoken with outward confidence while inside she was bawling like a baby.

Dr. Myers left them, her insides in total conflict with her outward appearance. Tony sat on the window seat; his long legs stretched before him. As he watched his wife and little daughter lie entwined on a hospital bed, his intense love for them saved him from total collapse.

Time to call Mrs. Finnerty. "We have good news at this end," he told her after the initial greeting. "The scans were clear. We are breathing normally again. Thank God. Caroline lay down with Angela, and they both dozed off. It's a lovely sight before the chemo starts at nine in the morning. How is Amy doing over there?"

"Remarkable and knocking the socks off everybody with her way of telling things. She has hit it off with Leo who has asked her to go see his horse in the morning. Apparently, it's an early activity, crack of dawn I believe. That will be good timing for you two to get on the road. Caroline and I will look after things here. How are *you* doing, Tony?" Mrs. Finnerty asked.

"If it wasn't for the goings and comings, I would be in a right heap," he replied.

"You would be forgiven for that, so don't expect too much from yourself," reassured his friend and neighbour. "Amy and Angela are very much in tune with each other and have their own way of dealing with things. They are amazing to watch. Keely and Phillip are enjoying Amy as she stuns them on a regular basis. As I mentioned before, she and Leo are the best of friends. Sometimes like a big brother and others young uncle. The rest of us are like amused spectators. Rose, the daughter of the neighbour across the street, popped in at teatime. She is visiting Park Edge Hospital for an oncology conference. Imagine our surprise! Amy engaged her in a lengthy conversation, but I will let her tell you herself as only she can. Brace yourself. Now Keely is all set to take me to the hospital in the morning after we see the horse as Amy is not expecting to go back to see Angela before going home. What if you come to the horse farm, spend a little light-hearted time with herself and Leo, and then head out?"

"God bless Leo. It's perfect."

Horse Whisperer

UNLIKE MOST YOUNG lads, Leo was first up. Amy, not too far behind, found him scalding the teapot for the first and best brew of the day.

"Up before the milkman I see," Leo said, catching a glimpse of her in the doorway. Tea now made, he moved to the window overlooking the backyard. He maneuvered a kitchen stool close to where he stood and helped his new young friend to kneel on the top, giving her a better view of the outdoors. As yet, she had not spoken, not because she was shy, she didn't have anything to say until now.

"Leo, look at those birds on the fence." She shuffled forward, placing her elbows on the granite counter so she could get a better view. "There's two of them. See, right there." As she pointed, they flew away. She almost crawled onto the counter to see where they went.

"Oh, that's Janie and Mac. Don't worry, they will be back soon. Those two loves to perch right there above that flowering bush. It's their favourite spot. They strut back and forth on the wooden fence where the bush is low. They're a couple of doves and have become quite famous with the neighbours," explained Leo.

Mrs. Finnerty watched them from the kitchen doorway, the little girl in her fancy leggings, ankles outlined by frilly socks. The young man wearing riding gear, already anticipating the sensation he would feel later as he urged his beloved April into the air and over the jumps. They posed in such contrast to each other, yet their heads touched as they searched for Janie and Mac.

Within minutes, the kitchen was bustling.

"Good morning," Keely said as she sneaked past Mr. Finnerty. Spotting Amy and Leo straining themselves to find the birds, she continued, "Any sign of them yet?"

"Been and gone," he answered. He helped Amy down from the stool.

"It won't be long before they are back, Amy," reassured his mother. "Thanks for making the tea, Leo."

Phillip appeared stowing his briefcase on an empty chair, and out of nowhere, a spread of brown bread, butter, jam, eggs, and cheese appeared on the table. Leo produced a smorgasbord of cereal and a glass of milk for Amy. Mrs. Finnerty resisted the temptation to compare the brown bread to that of her local baker, Mrs. Quigley's. No need to worry as Keely and Phillip were also fans of that bread from their frequent visits to her sister Fiona's in Baybridge. As miraculously as it appeared, the leftover food made its way to the fridge, and the day began in earnest. Time was of the essence on *this particular* day.

"Do you want to come in the van with me?" Leo asked Amy as they all assembled in the driveway.

She waited for someone else to answer. A brief questioning look passed between the adults before he got the okay nod. Buckled in safely, Leo jumped in beside her. She could not immediately name the strong odour emanating from not only the contents, but also the fabric of the seats. Living on the west coast of Ireland, she was never far from a farm and soon identified the familiar smell of horses. For reasons she could not explain, it made her feel sophisticated and grown-up.

The road to Oaklawn Farm and Riding School resembled roads leading to farms all over the country. Well-worn gravel tracks on either side of a grassy strip bore witness to the vehicles that passed along its surface for years. Horses and carts in days of yore started the first imprints, followed by tractors, lorries, horse trailers, vans, and cars in modern times. The bicycle remained the one constant through it all.

"How are we for time?" asked Mrs. Finnerty as she and Keely bumped along behind Leo's van.

"I was wondering about that myself. It's going to be tight. Even though we are travelling towards the hospital, traffic can be brutal at this time of the morning," Keely replied.

"I didn't realize Park Edge was in this direction. That's something at least," said her passenger.

"All the same, I don't want you to be on edge and anxious. You have to be there before they start the treatment You need to be your usual calm and reassuring self at this time," Keely continued.

"You are so right, Keely. This is no time for a chink in the armour," said her friend.

"Might I suggest you and I make this a flying visit. Amy and Leo are getting along so well they won't even miss us. April is a beautiful, gentle horse. I expect Amy will get a little jaunt around the paddock on her before she leaves. If Tony agrees, we should set out for the hospital before he gets here," said the driver who knew these roads better than anyone.

"That would give us loads of time. Are you sure Leo will be okay with that?" asked Mrs. Finnerty.

"Are you kidding me? Sure haven't we been mere spectators since the two of them met? We could turn around now and not be missed," replied Keely.

"I'm calling Tony this minute."

She did, and he said, "That's a great idea. We can take our time with the horses. Amy will love that."

Keely was right about not being missed. By the time they caught up with Amy and Leo, they were already leading April out of the stable. Mrs. Finnerty took a deep breath as she stepped out of the car. She stood still, absorbing her surroundings. The light rain falling did nothing to detract from the beauty of where she found herself. All but one or two of the horses were already out and about, their hooves playing a clip-clop tune on the cobbles. A mountain range, whose name she did not know, rose in the mist contrasting the white fences and jumps in the foreground. An assortment of outhouses bearing the name *Oakland Farm* or *Oakland Riding School* outlined the perimeter of the farm. Keely watched her friend, still but not frozen, as she scanned the scene before her. She wondered if Angela was the cause of her stillness. She was not. Her friend found herself transported to India where she and her late husband shared a scene such as this with their fellow teachers on Saturday afternoons. She recalled telling Mr. Daugherty in Baybridge all about it when they first met. She confessed having a *little flutter* from time to time at these events, and the excitement they shared when any of them won. He confessed to being a betting man himself, and every Saturday since then, he placed a bet for her at the bookies in Baybridge. He came to her house in the afternoon with news of how well they did, handing over the winnings if there were any. The bet placed was always his treat, and he enjoyed her excitement when she won. Since his sudden death, a few short weeks ago, she had not grieved. She did now as long-stored tears rolled down her cheeks. She told Keely the story.

Suddenly, a loud noise penetrated the atmosphere.

"Was that a horse, Leo?" asked Amy.

"That's Custard calling me," he explained.

"Which horse is talking to you?" she asked.

"The creamy-blond mare up there in the far corner, the tall one." Custard continued the whinnying. "I'm coming, Custard, just hold your horses," instructed Leo.

"That's funny," said Amy, climbing on the fence to get a better look at Custard.

"Custard thinks so too, that's why I say it." April made it clear she was ok with him going to see Custard with a loud nicker sound. "Ah, thanks, April, I won't be long," replied Leo.

"What did April say?" asked Amy.

"Go see to Custard. For pity's sake, I can't take much more of that racket."

"Did she really say that?" asked Amy.

"No. April is much nicer than that," he explained.

Keely found Leo and told him the plan. He told his mother his plan was to settle Custard and borrow a riding helmet for Amy from the tack shed.

The two ladies set off for Park Edge Hospital. Keely explained how Leo and horses talked to each other since he was a little boy. Mrs. Finnerty marveled at that, adding how she felt all the better for her cry among such beautiful animals.

Secret Project

"IS THAT YOU, Mrs. Costello?" said the voice of an unseen person on the other side of the tins of peas. Clicking footsteps heralded the arrival of the owner of the voice.

"Mrs. Brown," said Mrs. Costello. "How are you?"

"Fine really, thanks. I'm so glad I ran into you. I wasn't sure how to do this. A few of us pitched in when we realized Angela was back in Dublin. She's such a lovely wee girl, lovely family too. This is for Angela's Purse."

As she spoke, she thrust a bulging envelope into Madge's hand. Charly, Madge's young daughter, watched the transaction with unusual interest. Her mother was often accosted by people, most she knew, a few she did not, with donations since Angela's Purse first launched itself. Charly was a bystander in those instances, not understanding what it was all about. For reasons she could not explain, today's encounter triggered something in her. Since the send-off party at the Bright House, she felt a growing need to do something for Angela. The idea lurked at the edges of her mind ever since. At that party, she would have preferred the guests to admire the wonderful array of food instead of eating it. She did voice her protest at the cutting of the cakes. She saw the handcrafted food as a painting, a tribute that should last. Eating it evoked in her, a feeling akin to defacement, simply she didn't think they should be tucking into it.

"Does Angela have a purse?" she asked her mother on the way home.

"Well, I don't know," replied her mother. "Why do you ask?"

"When people give you money, they always say it's for Angela's Purse."

"That's true. They do say that, but it's not an actual purse. It first started when the school had a mass for Angela before she went to the Dublin hospital. The people attending the mass wanted to give, even a small amount of money, to her parents to pay for the extra things they were sure to need. It really wasn't necessary, but their kind neighbours wanted to help. Mrs. Walsh had a shopping bag, and everyone put the money in there. One man in the crowd seeing the tote bag called it a purse, and that's where the name came from," explained Madge.

"Oh" was all Charly had to say. By the time they reached home, it was clear to her what she would do, and she would need help. She knew exactly where that help lay.

Sammy and Kitsy were delighted to see Charly come bouncing in ahead of her mother.

"Charly, slow down, you're scaring the people," she called after her. Neither Sammy nor Kitsy paid her any mind as they scooped the beautiful youngster up in a hug. "She has a secret project and needs some guidance with it," added her mother.

"Oh! We *love* secret projects, don't we, Kitsy?" said Sammy.

"Nothing better," added Kitsy. Casting an exclusionary glance at Madge, they huddled in a conspirator's pack. The whispering and the oohs lasted until they came to a consensus whereupon the pack broke up, announcing all was in good order with no need to worry.

"Good to know," acknowledged Madge. "Are we to go now and come back another day?"

"No, no, we can start now. We have research to do, and we need Charly's help with that. Right Charly? She'll be okay with us for a while."

"Can I Mammy, please?" pleaded her young daughter.

113

"I suppose if it's a secret, I can't stay." The crestfallen tone in her voice bought her no sympathy. "Will I come back at dinnertime, around one?" asked Madge.

"Thereabouts," both adults answered at once.

It was getting harder to keep up the facade, so Madge took her leave without further ado, missing out on the kiss her daughter was about to place on her cheek. She shook her head in amusement as she made her way down the lane from the Bright House.

The research started in earnest as soon as Madge left. Questions galore, leather or fabric, large or small, bright or dark colour, ornate or plain. Charly had a clear vision of what she wanted.

"I like a customer who knows what she wants. It makes the project much easier," said Sammy.

Kitsy started to sketch. The other two ransacked the storeroom in the hopes of finding something suitable. Simple excitement infected them as they identified each item they could use. Sammy announced just before one o'clock she had a major component of the project at home and could they adjourn till tomorrow. Hunger had them all in agreement as Madge arrived.

Quiet Visit

WHEN MRS. FINNERTY heard a noise at the door to number 4 *Happy Street*, she assumed it was Caroline returning from the snack room provided by the hospital for families. Angela dozed off as she read to her. Still, she continued to remain seated by the mini chaise and lowered her tone as she read. She found the quiet drone soothed Angela. She looked up, expecting to greet Caroline, discovering it was someone else entirely. It took all her self-control not to jump up and cry out when she realized who the visitor was. He crept towards her almost apologetically. She did not really know him but knew all about him. It was Dr. Alan Moran, Angela's orthopaedic surgeon, who stood before her. She got up from her chair, urging him to take her place. She hoped against hope Angela would notice a change in the atmosphere and wake up to see this special visitor. She did. A broad smile lit her face. He sat beside her and gently reached for her hand. Moments passed before Angela asked,

"Are you going to see Dr. Myers?"

"I saw her already. She told me you are doing well and might be up for a quiet little visit. She said today is day two, so I thought I'd take a chance. I'm glad I did."

"So am I," she replied.

Before she could say more, her mother returned. Dr. Moran stood and took a step towards Caroline who became emotional at the sight of him. This was the kindest and most sincere of men, the one who saved her young daughter's leg and known affectionally to Angela and her sister as the *bone doctor*.

"Dr. Moran is it really you?" she whispered. Angela, can you believe this, Dr. Alan on *Happy Street*?

"In the flesh, back to where it all began. I'm here for the big conference going on this week and look who just happens to be here too. Did you plan this, missy?"

She acknowledged the *missy* with a smile.

"How are you holding up, Caroline?" asked the doctor.

"Good really. Angela too. She had a bout of nausea this morning, and that mouth is sure to give her trouble as before. She's a brave wee soul and knows what to expect."

"I'm okay," Angela said from her semi sitting position on the chaise. "Mrs. Finnerty is here with us. She reads to me."

"Oh, my goodness, Mrs. Finnerty, where are my manners!" gasped Caroline. "Dr. Moran, this—"

"Yes, we crossed paths briefly at the cake cutting. It's great you are here." He reached to shake her hand before noticing she was still holding the book she had been reading to Angela when he arrived.

"I believe you are familiar with this story," she said, smiling as she turned the cover towards him. He was the rightful owner of this book, before giving it to Angela at one of her appointments at the start of this arduous journey.

"Angela, are you still letting the ducklings talk to the doctors?" Mrs. Finnerty handed him the book, and he sat back down on the chair beside Angela. He started to read as she and Caroline receded into the background.

And when night falls, they swim to their little island and go to sleep.

Mrs. Finnerty reached into her overstuffed bag for tissues. The child's mother took one.

The child slept. The doctor quietly stole from the room.

Mrs. Finnerty was first to hear the whimper. She reached the mini chaise just in time to save the penguin from Angela's retching droplets. Caroline raced to the other side of the chaise. As was her habit, Mrs. Finnerty gently withdrew at such times. This was a mother's place.

"Mrs. Finnerty press the call bell," said Caroline, the only words needed right now. If the nurse had been standing by the door, she could not have been there faster.

"Angela, I need you to roll onto your side towards me. Good girl. I'm going to dab your lips with this moist cloth. There now, very gently, that's it." A weak bloodstained streak appeared on the cloth. Caroline noticed. "Can you do one more thing for me Angela?" urged the nurse. "Open your mouth as wide as you can, just for one second, while I get a peep inside." As she spoke, the nurse took the tiny flashlight from her uniform pocket and directed the beam into Angela's mouth. "Perfect. All done. I can see the inside of your mouth is red and sore. That's what caused the little bit of blood on the cloth, nothing more. Tell me, does anything else hurt or feel sore?"

"My tummy is kind of twisty, and I think I need to go to the toilet," the little girl whispered, "and my mouth hurts all inside."

"Oh, it surely does and no wonder. First, let's get you to the toilet. Yellow carriage or walk?"

"I like the carriage, but maybe I should walk."

"What! And deprive me of the chance to show off my steering skills? No way."

While Angela was otherwise engaged, the nurse reassured Caroline and, in so doing, reassured Mrs. Finnerty. She left them and returned with medicine and a gargle, settled the little patient in her chaise, and placed the yellow wheelchair in its rightful spot.

Once more, the child slept.

Dublin Summons

UNA HEARD THE postman push the letters through the post slot in the door of the Bright House. Hidden among the foundation's correspondence lay a gold embossed card addressed to her. It was from St. Swithun's University in Dublin, announcing that those students who opted out of the ceremonial graduation, should present themselves between ten and two o'clock on the coming Friday to receive their certificates. She hurried along the corridor towards the sunlight workroom.

"I'm summoned to Dublin between ten and two o'clock on Friday." Anyone not in the know would be forgiven for assuming she had broken the law and was on her way to jail.

"At last," said Sammy. They had been waiting for a date for weeks. Una did not notice Charly at first and was surprised when she popped up.

"Charly are you hiding over there under that pile of stuff?" she asked.

"Not really hiding, just doing a secret project," she explained.

"You lucky girl. I never get to do a secret project," bemoaned Una.

"It's a secret for outside people but not for people inside the Bright House." Charly thought that was only fair.

"That's right, only for inside people till it's done," added Kitsy. "It's a fierce big project altogether. Loads of *components*, you might say. We're nowhere near done yet. Do you think we could do with more help, Charly?"

"Do you have a strap you could spare?" Charly asked Una.

"Maybe we should let Ms. Una in on the secret," suggested Sammy.

"Time for another huddle," said Kitsy, as they took a dive into Charly's stuff.

Detailed information was shared, and Una emerged with a clear picture of what was afoot. She did, indeed, have a strap that would work perfectly.

As Una left the house, the spare strap and other odds and ends safely tucked away in her handbag, Tony Coughlan appeared in his driveway.

"Morning, Mr. Coughlan," she said.

"Hello there Ms. Una, off to the Bright House?" He walked further down and met her as she turned onto the main footpath.

"I've been there already. Just popped back to get something for little Charly Costello. She's deep in a secret project over there and needs a few more items," explained Una.

"Oh, the girls love their secret projects all right," replied Tony.

"How is Angela doing with her treatment? I know it's tough this time."

"Yes, it is. A few more side effects than before. The worst time is right now, and then it starts to ease off. It's great both for her and Caroline to have Mrs. Finnerty there. God bless the woman."

"She is exactly where she wants to be, doing exactly what is needed in her own quiet way. I have to go to Dublin myself this Friday to finish my graduation process. Do you think I would be allowed to see Angela for a short visit by then?" Una asked.

"I think by Friday she would love to see you, and so would Caroline and Mrs. Finnerty," said Tony. "I think we should keep it as a surprise for Angela. What do you think?"

"Great idea," agreed Una. "As a matter of fact, if I play my cards right, I may have company and another surprise from across the road, owing to a certain secret project."

Tony tapped the side of his nose and watched her as she made her way towards the Bright House. Looking after her, he reflected how lucky he and his family were to have not one, but two amazing neighbours.

With an added spring in her step, Una headed up the lane. As if designed by fate itself, Charly's mother, Madge Costello, was ahead of her on the path. Just the person she needed to see.

"Mrs. Costello," she said as she fell in step with her, "going to pick Charly up?"

"Ms. Una, that's the plan, if I catch the secret project at an opportune moment. Otherwise, there's no telling."

The smile on her face showed no sign of annoyance, only amusement.

"Mrs. Costello, I have to drive up to St. Swithun's on Friday morning to finalize my graduation process and pick up my certificate. I spoke to Angela's dad on my way back who said a surprise visit to Park Edge would be perfect. Without divulging any detail of the secret project, it would be even better if Charly were there. Can you come with me on Friday? You can meet my parents and have a meal with them before heading back to Baybridge." She stopped talking as she stepped in front of Madge, halting her in her tracks.

"Well, we were supposed to pick up Justin's school blazer on Friday morning, but I suppose he can do that himself. It's all paid for. The sleeves needed lengthening, that's all."

"Good, you'll come then, really?" Nervous pause. "You'll really come?"

"Yes, we'll really come, but you will have to take care of telling Charly *and* keeping the *secret*."

"You just leave all that to me," replied Ms. Una. "You take your time getting to the house giving me a bit of a head start. Ten minutes should do it."

She raced ahead. Madge sat on the bench outside the door, enjoying the quiet moment.

"I'm back, and I brought more surprises!" shouted Una as she made her way to the workroom.

All heads looked up to see what she was pulling out of her bag. But first, Una continued with an announcement, "Charly, I invited you and your adorable mother to come to Dublin with me on Friday, and she said *yes*! I met Mr. Coughlan in the driveway as I was leaving. I asked him if **we** could visit Angela in hospital, and he said *yes!* Would you like to bring your secret project with you and surprise her there?"

Charly's eyes were wide as she digested what she heard. So too were Sammy's and Kitsy's, as they stood back from what they were doing in anticipation of the child's answer. They stared at her, thinking, *is she ever going to say something?*

"Will it be ready in time?" she asked eventually.

"Oh yes, it will," all three grown-ups assured her at once."

"Then, you're off to Dublin," added Ms. Una. A flurry of activity followed to get everything out of sight as Madge's ten minutes were up.

The flurry continued all the next day at the Bright House. Madge stayed at home. The plan was to complete the project in time for Una to take it home and stow it in the boot of her car prior to the trip to the city.

"Well done, everyone. We made it," said Sammy.

"It's almost teatime too," added Kitsy. "Couldn't have timed it better. Come on, Charly, I'll walk you home."

Madge was pretending not to be looking out the front window when they arrived. Kitsy waved as she deposited her charge in the driveway, leaving Charly to skip up the steps into her house. The project or its whereabouts did not come up during or after the tea. The conversation mainly consisted of the brothers complaining about how she got to go to Dublin, and they did not, how unfair it was on account of her being the youngest and all. Their young sister explained it had to be her as she was on a mission that none of them would be any good at on account of them having *spuds for brains*. All three brothers left the table in disgust, albeit not a scrap of food remained.

"I think it's fair to say they have finished," remarked the mother, "and we need to get you sorted out for the early start in the morning."

One by one, the brothers sauntered into her room later in the evening, each acting surprised to find the other there. They came to say they were just playing earlier and hoped she would have a good day out. She rewarded them by disclosing what the secret project was.

"Mums the word" was the parting shot.

Mixed Emotions

DESMOND AND SARA Flynn were oddly proud of their daughter, Una, for choosing to forego the theatre of a formal graduation ceremony in favour of the simpler presentation of today. Instead, she continued her work at the Bright House in Baybridge. When later they learned she planned to visit Angela in Park Edge today, they both felt an extra surge of pride.

"What time do we need to leave?" called Sara, leaning over the banister from the floor above. She knew from past experience he was a bit of a stickler for time. Over the years, she had often misjudged how much time she had before leaving, deciding to throw in a load of laundry or mop a floor, only to find herself rushing at the last minute, throwing on her coat as Desmond stood at the foot of the stairs, car keys in hand.

"Plenty of time, Sara, at least another hour, no rush," he replied.

This time, she surprised him, appearing in the doorway of the sitting room, asking, "Will this work, do you think?"

The accompanying twirl was indeed impressive. He turned his handsome head to see the woman he loved with all his soul smiling at him.

"It most certainly will. New for the occasion?" he asked.

"What, this old thing, I've had it for ages," she offered.

"Of course, you have, my darling," he accepted meekly.

"You did a lovely job at choosing the gift, Desmond. I'm sure you got the measurements right, and you will find a way to put it all together later, I know you will.

"There's always a bit of leeway with these things. We should be okay. I'm a bit excited now actually," her husband confessed.

"Me too. Let's get going."

For the first time in their lives together, she was first out the door. Desmond refrained from comment.

Their only child, Una, was at that time halfway across the country with her precious load. She was travelling east while her parents went north, a much shorter distance through County Kildare, home to the Irish National Stud with its splendid Japanese Gardens and the best racehorses in the world.

"Charly, you are going to love the village where the university is. It's very old and called Clifden. They say it has the perfect number of students and old people in it. If that's true, there will only be old people now as the school is not in full swing yet. Charly, you and I can surely liven it up, right?"

Una got no reply.

The silent child sat in the back seat of the tiny car wearing her Sunday best, a pale-lemon bolero over a floral summer dress, her feet clad in pristine tan leather sandals. To describe her as stunning would be an understatement, and the same could be said for her beautiful mother. In any other company, Una might feel dowdy or upstaged, which she wasn't by any means, but her passenger's behavior was as though they were barely put together with no idea how stunning they were. Charly liked hearing about the village, the horses, and the *big school*, but she was worried about seeing Angela in the hospital. She did not want her to be sick.

"Mammy is Angela hurting in the hospital?" her mother heard her ask.

Simultaneously, the two adults felt the assault of her words. They had utterly failed to prepare Charly for the hospital visit, instead spending all their energy safeguarding her secret project. Madge turned in her seat and read the concern and anxiety in her daughter's eyes. Una pulled over, and as luck would have it, they found themselves parked outside a small shop. Una went to get some snacks, returning only with a juice for Charly. Madge sat into the back seat and hugged her daughter.

She felt the weight of this responsibility squarely on her shoulders as she said, "Oh, pet, I'm *so sorry*. I didn't think to ask you about seeing Angela in the hospital. I was putting all my energy into keeping your project secret. How could I have overlooked what effect seeing Angela could have on you."

"I shouldn't have made it a secret, not from the start. I didn't mean for it to take over everything. From the time of the party, I wanted to do something special for Angela."

Before her mother could answer, Una returned and spoke at once. "I'm to blame for this, and I am very sorry. From the time you let me in on your generous, wonderful plan at the Bright House, I've been carried away. It's a good thing to help a little girl with a secret project. It's another thing entirely to let keeping it a secret take over good sense. Without talking it over properly with your mother, I ploughed ahead with my idea, and that was wrong. She doesn't even know yet what or where the project is. I should have done much better, and I didn't."

Charly addressed her mom, "Mammy, I thought you were pretending not to know, especially when I heard you let us go to Dublin."

"I kinda was. I knew the project would be safe and good because of the safe and good loving people who put in so much time to help you. Ms. Una, you are not to blame for any of this. You made a wish come true for my little girl, and for that, I thank you. As her mother, it was my duty to discuss the hospital visit and make that as safe and good as the project."

"It's not a secret anymore because I told the boys what it was last night," announced Charly.

"Well, that's all right then because they didn't tell me, so it's still a secret," countered Madge.

"So, you want to wait?" asked Charly.

"I certainly do as I will be the only one not to know, that's a mother's privilege."

The enthusiastic graduating social worker was far from satisfied with herself. She reflected on her doubts when first she heard she was going to St. Paul's. She had no vision of her role in a primary school. It wasn't that she thought it beneath her or that she might not be needed. Its scope simply escaped her at the time. She learned a solid lesson today, one that guided her for the rest of her career—a perfect graduation gift.

Una was surprised at the number of cars parked outside the *Spoon* in Clifden. It was raining steadily when they pulled into the only remaining spot. Though this was a favourite haunt for students during the school term, most were still at home, and most did not own a car. They made a mad dash for the entrance, Madge covering Charly with a not-too-fancy umbrella. Desmond stood up as soon as he saw their daughter, his eyes now relieved of scanning the ancient doorway for the past fifteen minutes. The interior of the café was obviously the front half of what was a room in the original house. Four small tables with seating for two met their eyes, barely three feet inside and continued to the right, coming to a halt at a bay window with a misty view of the downpour. To the left, the arrangement changed to accommodate two tables with seating for four. A stressed white door stood atop two equally stressed wooden steps, boasting a faded sign, proudly announcing *Toilets*. Good to know!

"Una, over here," mouthed Desmond.

It was a tight squeeze as they zigzagged their way to him. Once they got to the table, they noticed the space opened into an alcove, making room for an extra chair for Charly. Those assembled here were snug and cozy. The hug from her parents at this moment was all she needed, and they may never know the significance of it.

"Daddy, Mom, this is Mrs. Costello and her daughter Charlotte, known to all as Charly."

"Well, as today they thought fit to bring this fancy cushioned chair for you, we shall call you Charlotte. Come sit here by me. Mrs. Costello, it's a pleasure to meet you both," replied Una's mother.

"Madeleine, they call me Madge. I'm a bit overwhelmed to tell you the truth at being here. A day or two ago, we were sitting in the Bright House in Baybridge, keeping Charly's project a secret, and now here we are in Dublin with Una, meeting her parents and being part of this special celebration."

"Madeleine, it seems we have two pearls in our oyster today, you and your beautiful daughter, here to share in Una's graduation. She worried during her training that her impact on others might be minimal, despite her best intentions. St Paul's, Angela's Tresses and Turbans and the Bright House gifted her with opportunity. Having you here today brings the past and future together, and for that, Desmond and I thank you," Sara concluded.

"Tea please and lots of brown bread and butter—oh, and one of your special pastries" was all Desmond had to say to the approaching waitress for fear his emotions might get the better of him

The Reveal

IT WAS A short walk from the Spoon to St. Swithun's, but what a walk it was. The observant man who first made the comment "Clifden has the perfect ratio of auld ones and young ones" was obviously paying attention. A mixture of both was evident as they walked. Some were walking from the university to the village, others from the village *to* the university, and most with nothing to do with academia whatsoever, milling around even as the rain poured on their heads. All, however, were aware in their innermost selves where they were. This was sacred ground, steeped in history, culture, religion, and education to its very foundation.

It would appear from the foot traffic in and out of this prestigious place of learning, students preferred this simpler form of degree acceptance, over the more formal walking on stage system, where their certificates were presented in public. Most had already moved on, taking up positions in their chosen careers or pursuing even higher education. Signs posted at intervals led them to where the presentations were taking place. Finally, a left turn put them on a path dividing the quad in half.

Charly was the first to comment on the massive carved Victorian door ahead of them, "I've never ever seen a door that big. How do they even open it?"

"I'd say they would need a strong big fellow all right," replied Desmond.

"It's lovely, though," replied the child, "the whole place is. Ms. Una, did you really go to school here? It doesn't look like a school, more like a castle."

"Well, it does a bit, but hidden inside all these beautiful eighteenth-century buildings are the very best in modern research and teaching facilities. One day, you will go to a school like this and learn so much from these wise teachers."

"I want to go to this one."

All eyes now on Madge as she answered,

"I'll start saving straight away, pet."

They finally breached the aforementioned door as the diminutive Charly strained her little neck in an attempt to get the measure of it. By her account, she failed. The journey from there to their destination along a long corridor displayed paintings of previous noteworthy students, professors, patrons, and saints. The paint, pale green and faded yellow, surely was original. A huge sign announced they had reached their destination. This time, the wooden door to Prescott Hall, was wide open in welcome. Rising before them in tiers, they saw row after row of school desks ascending, their wood highly polished by years and years of cardigan and blazer sleeves. A table, equally polished, stood on the ground floor to their left as they entered, laden down with certificates and envelopes bearing St. Swithun's crest. A robed professor stood at the end of the ancient table, ready to bestow the coveted document on the graduated students. It was hard for the adults to take it all in. Charly, on the other hand, was already envisaging herself seated at one of those desks head down and engrossed in her study.

A voice roused them from their awe and musings. "Over here, we saved you some chairs," whispered Keely Fitzpatrick.

"Right," mouthed Desmond. They followed him to where Mrs. Finnerty and her driver of the day awaited them. Una reacted in the most unprofessional way possible given her surroundings.

"Mrs. Finnerty, how in the world are you here?" she yelped.

Nobody paid her any mind as surprises happened on these occasions all the time. Unexpected grannies, aunties, cousins and even benefactors, always elicited a similar response. As they scrunched to make space for each other, Keely pointed out the check-in desk to Una urging her to make her presence known. Una made the introductions to all in her party, as they waited and almost missed hearing her name called from the front desk. They all stood up, proud as punch, and watched their girl receive her degree. Charly's mind skipped to the future as she saw *herself* standing there. Desmond placed Una's certificate in the assigned envelope and offered to carry it when they walked out. The ladies huddled and giggled their way back across the quad, this time enjoying Una's anecdotal account of what life was really like at St. Swithun's.

They agreed to walk to the Fire House, the restaurant Desmond had chosen for lunch. Una explained that the owner was a retired fire chief and a friend of her dad. He announced that he would move his car to the Fire House and walk back to meet them.

"Don't be long, love. You will be missed!" his wife shouted at his back.

He waved without turning "Not long."

As he walked to the car, he picked up the pace to keep to that promise. He had a major task to complete before returning. He caught up with them at the start of the canal towpath. Without comment, he fell in lockstep with Sara who was sauntering along, Charly by the hand. He took the dangling hand in his as the most natural thing in the world.

"Are they swinging her?" asked Una.

"Looks like it," replied the mother, not sure when and how her duties as a parent went to the Flynn's.

"It's not clear who's having the most fun," replied the Flynn's grown-up daughter. "But I'm enjoying watching the three of them."

The rain had stopped, and the clouds obliged by dancing off stage to reveal a bright and warm sun, an often-occurring weather pattern in Ireland. They met other walkers, cyclists, and the occasional boater before arriving at the Fire House, aptly named because it was a real firehouse when it was young. It was an active emergency response centre for years, now converted to a restaurant in its old age. That's how Desmond's friend John thought of it anyway.

"I've heard a lot about this place over the years, but never been inside," Keely said to Mrs. Finnerty as their destination came into view.

"It's hard to believe it's not still functioning by the look of it. I can't wait to see the inside," answered Mrs. Finnerty.

The building was set back from the road boasting a fine courtyard out front. No Parking signs were always clearly posted and respectfully obeyed in acknowledgment of the need to keep the space clear back in the day. The exterior was painted red, of course, and the only alteration here was to convert the original bay door to a window. To the right of that enormous window, they widened the old watch room door, keeping the tall glass lookout windows intact. It now served as the main entrance to the restaurant. From the outside, everything looked as it always had. Part of the front of a fire truck had been expertly redesigned to function as the reception desk and set off at an angle as you entered. Needless to say, that was a major talking point and often caused the kids to congregate around it. Some might say that was not a smart place to put it, but it was a deliberate move on John's part, as he loved explaining all about the fire engine to the children. It took him a while however, to realize he should have dismantled the siren much earlier in the process.

"Look, Charly, it's a fire engine, and over there, look at the hoses and ladders and ropes on the walls," said Madge.

Once more, Charly was straining to see as the ceiling was so high. All about the place, the tools of the trade were displayed, flashlights, helmets, and axes with fluorescent handles adorned the walls.

"It's real, Mammy, not just a name," answered her daughter. "Look, it has the fireman's sliding pole in the middle." Sure enough, flanked by long wooden tables the polished pole stood proud as in its hay day, the turnout gear, boots and helmet all lay ready at its base.

"She's not the only one craning her neck," said Mrs. Finnerty as she too, was looking upwards, taking in this unique decor.

John, the owner, greeted them as he showed them to their table. The service here was family style, and pretty soon, large platters and bowls of food started to arrive. It was impossible to fully concentrate on the food as the longer they sat, the more there was to see. It truly was a dining experience, never to be forgotten. Desmond excused himself from the table and momentarily so did Mrs. Finnerty. She was the first to return followed by Desmond now carrying a large package. He walked to where she sat and handed it to her.

"If you please, Mrs. Finnerty," he said, "do us the honour." She reverently took the wrapped object in both her hands before saying,

"Una, your parents have asked me to present this to you today in recognition of your years of hard study and your dedication to Angela's Tresses and Turbans. Your generous devotion to the people of Baybridge is already noteworthy. We are the lucky ones as you have chosen to stay with us at the Bright House. Congratulations!"

Prompted by her dad, Una walked around to her beloved house friend who handed her the package. Without a word, she peeled back the brown paper her father skillfully applied earlier, revealing the certificate now encased in an exquisite frame. Words of thanks, congratulations, and well-wishes circulated around the table. Sara smiled a well done to her husband as somewhere along the way he managed to uncoil, frame, wrap and elicit Mrs. Finnerty's help unnoticed. *Her man was a genius.*

Una had to part with her newfound treasure as it made its way around the table. She already knew where it would hang. Quietly she asked Mrs. Finnerty's permission to add it to Madge's collection on the wall outside *Hill Hands* studio at the Bright House. The older woman, now rendered speechless, merely nodded. Charly spent the longest time scrutinizing every last detail with Madge's help. She explained the meaning of the crest and who St. Swithun was. She translated the Latin words, so expertly calligraphed. The youngster's keen interest caught everyone's attention, especially the two teachers present.

"She wants one," Keely whispered to her friend in the next chair.

"She will have more than one, I have no doubt," replied Mrs. Finnerty.

"Angela, Amy, and now Charly. Are all the kids in Baybridge this advanced?" Keely wanted to know.

"Mostly the girls."

"But why?"

"Their mothers."

No Longer a Secret

SOMETIME DURING THE excitement, it was decided that Mrs. Finnerty would go to Park Edge in Una's car.

"I don't mind at all you know. It's not that far," tried Keely but to no avail.

"It makes more sense this way as they are going there anyway. A little chat with Charly might be in order. Apparently, some misgivings about the visit have surfaced."

"Ah, on a mission then?" guessed Keely.

"Just in case" came the reply. "Una has already gone to get the car from the Spoon. Seems they walked from there to the college."

"Oh, before you go, I almost forgot to tell you. Mrs. Peterson's daughter, Rose, from across the road, you may remember her. Well, she rang to see if it were possible to meet up with you when you get back home. Seemingly, Dr. Moran is presenting part of the conference at the medical centre in Baybridge, and she will be in town for that next week. She is seriously interested in Angela's Tresses and Turbans and *deadly* serious about meeting with you and the Bright House staff."

"Seriously, Keely?"

"Seriously, my friend. So, what do you want me to tell her?"

"Yes, seriously, yes." Keely playfully pushed her towards the waiting car.

Charly walked up with Una to get the car and was now secure in the back seat as they drove back. She waved when they pulled up alongside the others. Mrs. Finnerty took the space beside Charly, who was delighted and a bit surprised, as usually older ladies were seated in the front, as a sign of respect. Aware of this, she deftly preempted her mother's possible objection when she reached the car by saying, "Look, Mrs. Finnerty, sat in with me," thus avoiding any confusion as to whose decision it was, suited her back-seat partner very well.

"What a lovely day, Una, perfect really. We are very proud of you. Your mam and dad are quietly beaming. Keely said she could hardly wait to tell her lot all about it. Of course, they have attended a few of these themselves with their own family. We might have sat there all day if she hadn't prompted you to sign in," said Madge as soon as she got settled. Herself and Una chatted away without input from the back seat for a while.

Between sentences, Madge heard her daughter whisper, "Angela would like that big university. I'm sad she wasn't able to be there today with Ms. Una, Amy too."

"It could be a sad thing, but somehow, it isn't at all. You see, Ms. Una stayed in Baybridge before to help with Amy while her mom and dad took Angela to Dublin for treatment, which made her better. Now this time, Ms. Una can visit Angela while she is getting another treatment to make sure she stays better. She takes us with her to Park Edge where she can tell her all about her graduation and you can surprise her with your own secret."

Mrs. Finnerty tilted her head back on the headrest for a second or two.

Then Charly asked, "Is she still better?"

"Absolutely, and she's in for a surprise because she has no idea about any visitors" reassured the older confidant.

They were both still whispering, and the quiet demeanor of the pair enabled Madge and Una to hear their conversation.

"Couldn't have worked out better, *two* secrets. A day to remember, I'd say."

More head resting as Charly pondered all these things in her heart, all due respects to the original source of that remark, until she saw the yellow carts, whereupon she stopped pondering. Reverting to being eight-year-old, she let out a yelp, and almost had to be restrained. Thank God for seat belts and child locks. Sean, the porter, recognized Mrs. Finnerty as soon as she stepped out of the car. "Ah, it's our special guest back to us again with more fine ladies." He selected the appropriately sized yellow cart for them. "Maybe, young lady, you would like to ride in front with me, more space for that lovely package you have there?" he suggested.

With a nod from her mother, Charly did just that. All aboard," announced their driver as they all piled into the cart. Soon they were off along the stately avenue.

"It's a secret gift for Angela," explained the child. The shoebox-sized package sat precariously on her lap as she ran her small hand back and forth on the wrapping paper, as if ironing it.

"I'd love to be you going in to give someone a surprise like that. How did you even think of it?" asked Sean.

"I didn't like it when they cut the cake with her name on it at her party. I wanted her to have something to keep instead," said Charly.

"Having something to keep is way better than cake. I have to agree with you there. I must say, in all honesty, I do like a bit of cake from time to time," offered Sean.

"Me too," she agreed as they arrived at the entrance to Park Edge. It was Una and Madge's first visit, and they were duly impressed.

Charly said to all of them, "It's like the big house on Carter Hill, not like a hospital at all."

"You're right, Charly. It does look like it, same pillars and front porch. It makes you feel as if you are entering somewhere significant, even historic." Madge was studying the architectural details. She asked Sean, "Is it okay to take a photo?" Madge had been recording the day's events as they unfolded. Now she found herself unsure of the protocol.

"Go ahead. Take a few as there are no patients or visitors about. You're right about Park Edge being historic and significant." With a tip of his gold-brimmed hat, he left them.

Mrs. Finnerty punched a sequence of numbers into the electronic pad, a buzzing sound announced the opening of the door that admitted them to Happy Street. On the way, Madge noticed the subtle transition from stately home to the hospital without alarm as Charly did not seem to notice at all. They were stunned by the clever design of the unit itself and the effect it had on them, arresting their progress and causing jaws to drop and eyes to widen. Mrs. Finnerty, remembering her reaction days before, was quite enjoying seeing the awestruck expression on the faces of the others today.

* * *

Angela was lying back on her mini chaise when she heard the gentle knock on her yellow door. As her mother went to answer, she propped herself up on the cushion and waited. Charly was the first to enter, and she came alone. With the clarity of a person on a well-planned mission, she approached Angela, smiling, balancing the gift on outstretched arms in front of her. Caroline stayed at the door. Angela sat further up on one elbow, declaring, "Charly, I never expected to see you here on Happy Street. Did you ever think you would be here?"

"No, I thought I would have to wait till you came home. Then Ms. Una had to go to her big school to get her certificate, and we got to come with her, and then Sammy and Kitsy thought if we hurried up, I could finish the secret gift they were helping me with, and I could bring it today. This is for you to keep instead of the cake that got eaten at your party."

Neither of them noticed the others slowly creeping closer, their curiosity now getting the better of them. Angela did not speak as her little friend reverently placed the box in her hands. She did cast a glance of hesitation in Charly's direction before tearing open the wrapping paper. Though shaped like a shoebox, it was far from it, with its silk-covered lid and a quilted interior. Shades of pale pink, lilac, and rose mingled to create a soft bed revealing a dainty salmon pink suede handbag nestled within, like a tiny baby in a bassinette. *Angela's Purse* embroidered on minute pieces of the material used to make the *ATT* logos at the Bright House adorned the flap. A shoulder strap, courtesy of Una, covered in matching fabric gave the owner an option as to how to wear it. The others almost gave their presence away by gasping in admiration, catching themselves just in time. Angela still did not speak, turning the purse this way and that.

"You can open it," Charly finally said. Inside lay a separate thin object loosely wrapped in a piece of tissue paper. "I thought it only fair Amy should have something too, so I put in this headband for her."

Now Angela found her voice. "Amy will love the headband, and I *love* the purse."

"Do you think you should wait till she grows her hair again before you give her the hairband?" asked Charly in all seriousness.

Without pause, Angela replied, "No. Ms. Harriet said you can create your own style, so that's what we'll do."

"I love style" was all Charly had to add to that.

For the first time this week, Angela said, "I want to show you the Pirate Ship." She stood up, tall and strong, led Charly by the hand and waved to those left behind. Her mother hesitated momentarily, then let them go

"What about us?" asked Madge and Una.

"Onwards and upwards" was all they heard as they scurried after the two. Was that Mrs. Finnerty saying that?

She was also remembering Keely's remark about the Baybridge children.

And now there were three!

137

Touch of a Cold

NEWS REACHED MRS. Walsh via the Bright House Express, a recent phenomenon, that the Twins Killfeather were getting anxious for news of Angela and Ms. Harriet was *laid up* with a slight touch of a cold. Prior to the existence of the Bright House, such things may be mentioned in muted tones in Quigley's corner shop or Grainne's hairdressers. These titbits always passed on with a concern in the voice, and on rare occasions, a little unsolicited gossipy opinion thrown in. Nowadays, if action seemed to be in order, the residents of Shadow Ridge Avenue made straight for the Bright House as if it were their community centre, a place of action, a substitute for social services or, on occasion, for the doctor's office. The person chosen to receive the news bulletin from the Bright House on this occasion, at home at the time, was Mrs. Walsh. She first stopped at Quigley's before looking into the matter.

"Kettle on by any chance?" a familiar and welcome bellow echoed along the corridor. If you were one of those poor, unfortunate souls, deprived of the friendship of the owner of the bellow, you would deem her to be sharp and impatient. Mrs. Walsh was neither. She was a woman of substance, selfless, a person of action. She was often heard to say, "I'd have it done *twice* myself while you are all talking about it." True. She advanced towards Sammy and Kitsy who were in their usual position, heads down, creative juices flowing. The aroma emanating from the Quigley's pastry bag she carried preceded her.

Sammy raised her head from the fabric before her and sniffed loudly.

"You have no manners, Sammy Garvey," rebuked Kitsy while committing the same crime.

"Scallywags the both of you, now where's me tea?"

As they settled in with their cuppa's and treats, Mrs. Walsh brought them up to date on the news from Caroline in Dublin. "Angela had a tough time as expected, but she turned the corner now, helped greatly by Charly's secret. Now I'm sworn to tell you no more as she wants to tell you herself. Suffice to say, success. The thinking is at this stage, Angela will be discharged after further test results on Monday. As school starts on Monday its best Amy stay home, go back with the rest of her class, and not go with her dad to pick her up. Una and company will be home tonight, so Amy will stay next door."

"Is Mrs. Finnerty staying on do you know?" asked Sammy.

"That's not fully decided yet. Fiona's sister in Dublin lives across the street from an elderly lady who has a daughter working in a London hospital. Currently, she is attending a conference at Park Edge. She will be coming to Baybridge Medical Centre next week for part of that conference, and there is talk of Mrs. Finnerty coming back with her," explained Mrs. Walsh.

"Monday is a big day for all the kids. Considering the trials and tribulations this summer, no doubt Amy would feel more secure having Mrs. Finnerty next door. It's still not going to be easy for her on Monday," concluded Sammy.

"I'd say she'd get a right spoiling between Una and Mrs. Finnerty," added Kitsy.

"Thank God this session is over for Angela. Though in a couple of weeks, she will have to go back again." It was difficult for Mrs. Walsh to even say those last words.

"Not to downplay it by any means, she seems to weather it all very well, the poor wee thing," said Kitsy. "Oh, speaking of poor wee things, what do you make of the news about Harriet Killfeather and her *touch of a cold?*"

"Now that's a whole different kettle of fish. I hope we are just talking about a cold, but why send word here?" wondered Mrs. Walsh.

"A young fellow came by, said he delivered something to them, and one of the ladies asked him to call here as he was passing," Kitsy explained. "He didn't know much more than that."

"How odd. Well, now I'd better go see what's going on."

As quick as she came, she was off again, a woman of action.

* * *

Ms. Eleanor Killfeather paced back and forth, wondering if her idea to send word to the Bright House was a good one. She knew wringing her hands like this was no help, and help was what she needed before deciding what to do. It escaped her mind when exactly she became the one to make the decisions, not only for herself but for her sister Harriet. Was it always that way, or when her parents got on in years? Was it after their death? She didn't know. Maybe she was always eager to put her two cents in whether needed or not. Anyway, what did it matter now? Her father's words sounded in her ears, "Keep your head and you'll get through!" The doorbell rang. "Smile a little every day," she also heard her father say as she opened the door. She did smile as she let Mrs. Walsh in. Seeing through the weakness of that smile, her visitor sensed Eleanor's anxiety at once.

Deciding to go with the good news first, she said, "Angela did very well as usual, Ms. Killfeather. She wanted you to know that she will be home Monday most likely, and she has a fresh style to discuss with you both."

"Oh, what a relief!" replied Ms. Eleanor. Before she could say more, a raspy moist cough interrupted her.

"So how is your sister doing with her cold?" asked the visitor.

"You see, Thelma is at her great-niece's wedding in Galway, just the one night. I was at a loss without her as to what to do about the cough. I hope you don't mind my sending word." For the first time, this usually robust, capable lady looked frail and, yes, scared.

Mrs. Walsh mentally jumped into action. "Would she mind if I just popped my head in?"

"She'd be pleased to see you," reassured her twin.

A slight mound in the bed was the only indication anyone was there, but the quilt shuddered with the next bout of chesty coughing.

"Harriet, my dear, Mrs. Walsh came with news of Angela."

At her sister's words and the mention of Angela, a tousled head appeared, and a pair of diminutive shoulders revealed themselves. Mrs. Walsh had no recollection of seeing such frail shoulders on this lady before. It shocked her.

"Mrs. Walsh, how nice," said a very husky whisper.

We need to get a move on was all Mrs. Walsh could think. "That's a nasty old cough you have there. Did you tell Dr. Owens about it at all?"

"Came on worse today," Eleanor reported.

"Good time to call him then." Mrs. Walsh knew from Mrs. Finnerty's stay in rehab that it was about this time of day Dr. Owens made his rounds there. "Try the rehab centre first," she suggested to Eleanor who already seemed calmer. Her neat but ancient address book in hand gave her confidence, and she was keeping her head like her father said. Turning back to the patient, Mrs. Walsh urged, "Let me help you to sit up a bit higher while I bring you up to date on Angela's plans." It wasn't hard to reposition Harriot as she was light as a feather. The shuffling did bring on another bout of coughing, and she felt clammy, which was beginning to worry Mrs. Walsh. She wanted to avoid being clinical at the bedside, more like a friend just visiting. She didn't inquire if she had taken her temperature instead turned down one of the heavy wool blankets without comment.

Before any more news of Angela was shared, Eleanor announced from the bedroom door, "the doctor is due any minute at the centre. That nice Nurse Murry promised to redirect him as soon as he arrived. She even offered to come herself at once until I told her you were here." Mrs. Walsh turned to the bed to find Harriet had dozed off. Kitty Walsh, though a highly skilled nurse, spent most of her time these days between family and balancing the budget for the foundation.

"You sit with your lovely sister, and I'll make some tea. Dr. Owens might even take a drop, and I know he likes Mrs. Quigley's scones. Two little birds, one who happens to be in Dublin told me that. Shush!"

"Can you find things, I—"

"I can always find tea things. You just rest."

She did find tea things, and whether the doctor had time for scones, she knew he would make a suitable fuss about the offer—he might even take one with him. He came quietly to the door, she let him in, and both twins were asleep when he entered the bedroom. *Typical* was Mrs. Walsh's first thought, panic before, calm as the doctor arrived. Then Harriet obliged with a further bout of coughing. He listened with a trained ear before moving to the bedside. The cough roused the patient, the doctor's presence stirred Eleanor from her light doze.

"Ladies, I've imagined coming to see you here many times. Pity it's under these circumstances. I could hear you coughing from the door Ms. Killfeather. Sounds a bit chesty. Is it okay to take a listen?"

The other Ms. Killfeather helped her sister sit up. She patted the back of her thin veiny hand as she obeyed and took the deep breaths, turned from side to side, coughed again, and tolerated her temperature being taken.

Dr Owens sat gingerly on the edge of the bed, took the other veiny hand, and watched her chest rise and fall before saying, "Ms. Killfeather, you have acute bronchitis. You have no history of lung disease and no major health issues, but we do need to treat this infection and keep a close eye on how you respond to the antibiotics. We have a few other tricks up our sleeve, but it would be better to monitor your progress over in the centre. How would you feel about moving there for a day or two and let the nurses work their magic?"

Patients of this age are often treated at home given the right conditions or admitted to a general hospital. When the county acquired the Killfeather estate to construct a rehabilitation centre, the agreement was unless their medical condition required otherwise, care would be given on-site. The discreet door leading from their quarters to the centre stayed locked until now. She nodded. He patted her hand, and she dozed off again. Smiling, he rose from the bed, beckoning her sister to follow. "Nurse Murry is at the ready. I'll just confirm with her to come over. At least one of her twin girls is volunteering today, so they can do the transfer together. As soon as she settles, we can start a breathing treatment while we wait for the antibiotic. Your sister made the right decision to transfer to the centre, Ms. Killfeather," assured the doctor.

"I'm glad she agreed. We are grateful to you for coming and to you, Mrs. Walsh, for answering my plea for help. There's just one small thing I think would help everybody. Angela and Amy asked us recently if they could call us Ms. Eleanor and Ms. Harriet so that we would know which one they were talking to. It worked very well."

"I'll see you over at the centre, Ms. Eleanor," replied Dr. Owens as Mrs. Walsh thrust the Quigley's pastry bag into the hand not holding the medical bag.

They watched him leave, a bag in each hand, one to sustain, the other to heal. The remaining two ladies had time for a cup in their hands before Nurse Murry and one of her twins arrived.

A Good Call

DR. OWENS'S NIMBLY skipped down the steps and made his way along the path towards the rehab side entrance. Though he was light of foot, his thoughts ran deep. If he himself were not a doctor, he mused, would he be aware of the extraordinary network of neighbourly kindness and generosity running through this community? Would his engineering self, teaching self, accounting self, writing self, or any other self, have allowed him to go through life oblivious to the basic goodness of the people of Baybridge? He shuddered at what he might have missed. He knew that a doctor was only as good as the nurses he left behind to care for and treat their patients. A successful outcome depended on quality nursing care. Study after study proved this. He was deep in thought when a wailing sound from his hip interrupted, and he had to orient himself to the sound of his mobile phone. Answering it, he greeted Nurse Murry.

"Dr. Owens, Carmel, and I are here with Ms. Killfeather. She is a little agitated, fussing over what she should wear of all things. It's an important thing for her to go *out in public*. I understand that. However, she has an audible wheeze. Carmel thought to bring a nebulizer with us. Do you recommend we give her a treatment here before we start to move her?"

"Good call and smart of Carmel to bring the machine. Yes, give her one dose of albuterol now," agreed Dr. Owens.

"She's already in the wheelchair by the wardrobe door. We will set up here while Carmel continues to rummage through the vast collection of clothes. Should keep her mind on styling instead of breathing." The smile could not escape her voice as she related the current scene in the Killfeather bedroom, nor did it escape the good doctor.

"Silky sailing if you please, Nurse Murry," begged Dr. Owens.

"Smooth as satin," promised Nurse Murry.

The carpeted corridor along which they travelled soon gave way to gleaming tile, a sign they had crossed the threshold.

"Killfeather Suite?" asked Carmel, referring to the private room nearest to the manor. It was an unspoken fact, if either of the twins needed a bed, this room would be theirs should it be vacant at that time, hence the name, though it was not displayed on any sign or plaque. Today, it was available.

"Almost there now," reassured Nurse Murry. She instinctively did not make mention of how much better the patient was breathing. Best not bring attention to that. "Here we are now, and there's Maura putting the finishing touches on the pillows." Harriet looked around taking in the plush Victorian decor. "Home away from home, right, Ms. Killfeather?"

"What a surprise. Neither Eleanor nor I have ever thought of visiting. It seems now that was a mistake. We thought it would be an intrusion to go traipsing about."

"Well, soon you will be right as rain, ready for your *grand tour*. Sometime during the banter, the patient was transferred from wheelchair to bed, her vital signs taken, and the nebulizer plugged in for bedside use.

"Your bed jacket is lovely, Ms. Killfeather," complimented Maura.

"Maura, I can see you're Carmel's beautiful twin sister, thank you. The jacket is almost as old as I am. Are you often here at the centre with your mother?" she asked.

"A lot of the time, back to school on Monday, though. It's leaving cert this year," explained Maura.

"We were spared that in my day," offered Harriet. "I often thought, knowing how difficult and long that exam is for you youngsters these days, we got off lightly. Even so, I must say the curriculum was loaded, and our teacher, Ms. Nelson, was no pushover." Settled in the comfortable soft bed and lulled by her reminiscences, she fell asleep.

Mrs. Walsh tidied the tea things and helped make up a fresh bed for Harriet before leaving. Thelma entered nonchalantly at first, happy to be back. She would have preferred not to have gone in the first place, but the risk of insult to her family was too high. When asked later how she knew something was amiss, she was unable to say, she just did. She threw her handbag and overnight case on the nearest chair, looked at the newly made bed, and turned on her heel.

"Rehab?" was her only word, followed by a silent nod from Eleanor. Retracing her footsteps, she raced down the stone steps from the portico, made her way along the path, and entered the centre by the side door. Inside, she walked parallel to the outside path in the opposite direction, arriving back a stone's throw from where she started. Nurse Murry met her in the hallway outside Killfeather Suite.

"Nice hat, Thelma," she commented. The fascinator she wore to the wedding was still atop her head. "You can use the private door to come and go too, much nearer."

"If you breath one word of this, Nurse Murry, I'll—"

"Ah, sure the longest way around is the shortest way home, Thelma."

She sat in the chair beside the bed long enough to take in her surroundings. Without the scrutiny of the experienced eye, the furnishings appeared authentic, every effort made to recreate the ambience of the original manor, and by all accounts, whoever the designer was achieved that. Thelma was scanning the room with interest when Harriet opened her eyes.

"Thelma, you wore your fascinator for me."

Striking a pose, Thelma asked, "How do I look?"

"Très chic" came the reply. "Moi?"

"Words fail me." Try as she must, Thelma was unable to hold back the tears. Harriet rewarded her with a faint smile about the eyes just before the sound of coughing filled the room.

Later that day, Harriet received her first antibiotic dose, long after the prayers and well wishes of the people of Shadow Ridge Avenue rippled towards her and upwards to the heavens.

Homecoming

UNA AND HER passengers arrived home safely. There was nothing significant about the journey, each of them lost in their own thoughts and reflections of the day. Madge caught a glimpse of her daughter in the rearview mirror, sketching. Earlier, she saw her rummage in her something-to-do bag. Obviously, she chose a sketch pad, and judging by the frown of concentration on the child's face, it was a matter of importance.

While she drew, Charly was anticipating the onslaught of questions from her brothers as soon as she crossed the threshold. Experience had taught her, if she were not prepared, it could be brutal. The three brothers fed off each other's lines like actors in a well-rehearsed play. She sat there, sorting, analyzing, and prioritizing, essentially writing her own script. Now armed with visual aids, she felt confident and sure it was going to be great fun.

"They're here!" shouted Kieran as Una's car pulled into the driveway.

With suppressed enthusiasm, the others filled the doorway.

"The welcome committee, I see. Were we missed?" asked their mother. Her answer came in the form of nonchalant shoulder shrugs accompanied by genuine smiles. Kieran stepped from the doorstep to the gravel driveway, saying, "Hi, Ms. Una, home safe. Mam, Mrs. Walsh asked if ye could pop over before ye get settled."

The ladies glanced at each other, recognizing this as unusual. The boys ushered Charly inside, resisting the temptation to attack the packages their mother handed them before leaving. Mrs. Walsh was not at the door, wringing her hands as they feared she might, when they got the summons. The front door was ajar as Madge called out, "Kitty, it's us."

"There you are, Madge, and you too, Una, good. I know ye're just back after a great day. Come in for a minute." She talked as they followed her into her spacious kitchen. "Harriet Killfeather was transferred over to the rehab centre today with acute bronchitis. Eleanor sent word to the Bright House asking for one of us to go over as Harriet had a cold. Anyway, when I got there, I soon realized it was more than that. They had not called Dr. Owens as yet, but as luck would have it, he was at the centre. He delayed his rounds, and he saw her straight away. As you know, they have an arrangement with the centre. Harriet agreed to moving over, and quick as a flash, Nurse Murry and Carmel came and gave her a breathing treatment before moving her. They were great, especially Carmel." Mrs. Walsh stopped to catch her breath.

"Oh my, the poor thing. Where was Thelma?" asked Madge.

"Of all the days, she was at a wedding in Galway, overnight too. I didn't want to call you as you were likely on the road by then," explained Mrs. Walsh.

"Thanks for that, Mrs. Walsh. We would have been shaken up. How is she now? Do we know?" asked Una.

"Thelma is back now, trying her best to keep Eleanor and herself together. Harriet is holding her own and between coughs, giving Thelma a good teasing about the fascinator still on her head when she went to see her. They promise to keep us posted," replied Kitty.

"She is a trooper, but she is old. There is another thing to be aware of ladies. Angela is due home probably Monday. She was saying she had a style question for Ms. Harriet when she got home. Una, maybe you could alert Mrs. Finnerty about that if it comes up and Caroline too. Do you think I should go check in on her, Kitty?" added Madge.

"No Madge, they have it in hand, and it's getting late. Let's see what the morning brings. I wanted you both to hear the news from me. The word is out, of course, and everyone is up in a heap. The Killfeather family has been a generous and fair hereabouts for a very long time. Their father employed the locals and never mentioned any help he gave over and above a fair wage. The twins are still symbols of those times in Baybridge. Off with ye now after your long day. Congratulations again, Una, you can tell us about it tomorrow and cheer us all up with the details."

As Madge entered her house, she could hear the one-act play between her children was underway. She paused. Was she eavesdropping? Probably. Still, she did not move.

"Charly, you still haven't said what was your favourite thing," prodded Justin. Sometimes a fifteen-year-old is unsure of his footing, not so the seventeen-year-old brother.

"You can't make up your mind, can you?" teased Kieran.

"I think she is holding out on us. Look at that grin," offered Michael, her youngest brother who at twelve was nearly as tall as Kieran. Finally, Charly opened her things-to-do bag and took out her sketch pad. She tore off the first page and turned it upside down on the table. She did the same with two more sheets. They lay side by side until she asked them to choose one each.

"Michael, you go first, then Justin and last Kieran. You mustn't look until I tell you, okay? One, two three, you can look now."

"Wow! You went to a fire station? Neat. Hang on, it's a restaurant!" exclaimed Michael.

"Mine is a building like a manor house or something. Did you go inside?" asked Justin.

"Another building looks like a castle. Is it a castle, Charly?" asked Kieran. "Where on earth did ye go today?"

"Do you like them? Look at each other's. What's your favourite?" she urged. They swapped them back and forth, making comments. "This is Angela's hospital, this one is an old firehouse turned into a restaurant, and this is Ms. Una's big school where I am going when I'm old enough." They stared at her.

Her mother came into the room, looked at the drawings, praised their quality, and said, "I see how it could be hard to have a favourite all right."

"Mammy, it's 'cos there isn't one. Touché!"

Then the heated debate started again between the brothers. Madge went to make the tea. A moment's quiet. At the tea table, their dad now returned from work was briefed on all things Dublin and joined the debate about the drawings. Madge and Charly sneaked away from the table, leaving the men with their varying opinions and dirty dishes.

Ms. Una was home by now. Mrs. Finnerty came home on Saturday, accompanied by Rose, and within four days, Ms. Harriet was back in her own home. Angela returned home on Monday morning.

Housekeeping

FIONA HANNON, SOCIAL worker extraordinaire, did not sit idly by while the others galivanted around Dublin. No, sir. Before the dust settled on Madge Costello's gravel driveway, she made the first call, starting the process laid out by her and Mrs. Walsh. Priority one, Coughlan's house needed thorough cleaning from top to toe and the fridge stocked prior to Angela's return. Enter Nuala's Cleaning and Catering Services, the fabulous local company who took such great care of them when Angela first went to Dublin for chemotherapy. Amy guided Mrs. Walsh through the Coughlan's house that first day, explaining whose room was whose, pointing out private and shared areas for all the family, Angela's room, and the need for loads of towels for the required frequent handwashing.

"Nuala, good morning. It's Fiona Hannon."

"Hi, we're all set. Just give us the go-ahead, and we're on it," said Nuala.

"Amy is there with her dad today but will stay with Mrs. Finnerty and Una from Saturday morning. The house is empty Saturday and Sunday. Will that work at all?" asked Fiona.

"It's grand actually. Myself and the cleaning crew can get everything in shipshape on Saturday, including the fridge. Then on Sunday, Adam and his lot can sort out the food," suggested Nuala.

"Oh, you're so flexible, Nuala. Thank you for making it easy for us," said Fiona.

"Why wouldn't we be? It's a pleasure to have a job that allows us to make a home safe and comfortable for a little girl and her family," replied Nuala.

"You're a saint, Nuala," replied Fiona.

"I wouldn't go that far now. Let me go and we'll talk soon."

Both were smiling as they ended their conversation.

The next call was more of a personal nature. The last time Fiona and Caroline spoke, she mentioned her hair and Angela's was in need of tidying, and she assumed Amy's was too. She called Grainne and got her before the first customer.

"Morning, bright and early, I see," said Grainne as she picked up the phone on its first ring.

"What, sure the day is almost gone, Grainne. It's hardly worth your while opening up at all today." Fiona was known for citing her father's recurring refrain from when they were children, shouted to them from the kitchen, especially if they had planned to cycle out to the beach on a sunny summer's morning. She could hear his voice clearly, "I thought ye were going to the beach. It's hardly worth your while now. Sure, the day is almost gone." This familiar singsong danced its way up the stairs at seven in the morning when no sane Irish person, except himself, was awake. I suppose somebody had to open the shop at eight o'clock."

"I'll go back to bed then so," quipped Grainne.

"Good idea, but before you do, Caroline wondered if you could give them all a bit of a tidying up when they get back, say Monday after you close or Tuesday?"

"No bother, I'll check with them Monday and see what they would prefer. They might be tired from the trip. Thanks, Fiona, that's me done for the day, back to bed." Grainne yawned.

"Sleep well."

Fiona arrived at Dr. Owens's office soon after. Brenda, the bubbly office manager/receptionist, greeted her. "Nice and early this morning."

"That's just what Grainne said. Am I always late?" asked Fiona with an unconvincing sad look on her face.

"Not always, only when you're not here on time" came the hoity-toity retort. Brenda was well-practiced at keeping a straight face.

"I don't suppose the two or three patients I see before I get here count." The fake hurt look on her face didn't work this time either.

"Not in the least. You are, however, in time for a cup of tea we all hope will help erase that pained look from your face," offered Brenda.

"Cured," replied Fiona as she made her way down the corridor into the cozy staff lounge off the reception area.

Brenda joined her and asked, "Fiona, do you know a Mrs. Geraldine Nolan from St. Paul's? She called late in the afternoon yesterday, inquiring about Angela and her expected return. Apparently, she is with the Convalescent Homeschooling program. Now that school is starting, she thought it would be prudent to get the plethora of forms filled out while there is time to plan the next move. She sounded very nice."

"Oh good, that was on my mind. I've dealt with their office before, but that name doesn't ring a bell," replied Fiona.

"She said if you wanted to call into the school, she would be happy to go over the forms with you, or she could post them. I got the impression they were a bit convoluted, to say the least," explained Brenda.

"Are there any official papers that are not?" replied Fiona. "I'll opt for the guided tour method and pick them up from her, what say you?"

"Safest," answered her friend.

The phone rang at the front desk. Brenda drained her mug, hoisted it over the sink with a pleading glance towards Fiona, who rinsed it with her own. The mock frown had no effect this time as Brenda was already back at the desk.

Those two!

Fiona's day turned out to be very busy. Dr. Owens had already left to make rounds at the rehab centre by the time she was ready to leave.

"I'm off to meet the nice Mrs. Nolan at St. Paul's," she said to Brenda as she passed her desk.

"Late again, I see," quipped the mischievous receptionist as they both glanced up at the enormous clock on the wall behind Brenda's head.

"Hate to disappoint." Fiona raised her briefcase above her head by way of a parting salute as she made her way out through the main entrance.

"Nice weekend, "echoed through the waiting area.

Mrs. Nolan was a much younger woman than Fiona expected, in her late twenties and, as Brenda had suggested, very nice. They sat in her office. Fiona refused the offer of tea, suggesting instead to tackle the business at hand as it was already late.

"I appreciate that, Mrs. Hannon, so let's have a look at what we need."

She produced a package and leafed through each page. "There are several sections as you can imagine," she explained, "but you will be pleased to know only one for social services and one for the doctor."

Although Fiona was familiar with the process from previous patients, she respected Mrs. Nolan's help and let her continue uninterrupted. When she finished, Fiona said, "According to the family, Angela will be discharged sometime on Monday. This is the first of two rounds of chemo post-op, and by all accounts, the delay over the weekend has to do with labs and scans rather than her current condition. She will, of course, be returning in a couple of weeks to complete this cycle. We can have the paperwork done first thing on Monday if that helps."

"There's no mad rush, but it would help things along if we got them back sooner rather than later. Sometime during her second week at home, I would like to make a home visit, a sort of meet and greet, talk a little bit about how it all works. We have found children like to have a plan, which includes things their siblings or peers are doing. Believe it or not, homework falls into that category," explained Mrs. Nolan.

"Rumour has it a bit of homework may be underway as we speak," replied Fiona.

"Music to my ears," exclaimed Mrs. Nolan.

As Fiona left the school playground, she felt calm and hopeful, imagining Angela and her family getting along just fine with this young teacher. Just about then, her mobile phone chirped. It was Dr. Owens calling from Killfeather Suite at the rehab centre.

New Curtains

THELMA SAT IN the dimly lit sitting room, sipping a mug of tea, grateful the morning was upon her as sleep had eluded her. The previous evening, once Eleanor was satisfied her sister's breathing had eased, she allowed Carmel to walk her along the corridor to her private entrance. She was visibly exhausted as she thanked her young escort. Without any urging, she went straight to bed. The sound of her light snoring was soothing, peacefully massaging the space.

This morning, as Thelma sat there in the quiet, she found herself scrutinizing her surroundings. For the longest time she thought the place was too dark, giving their rooms an undeserved grimness. Though the furnishings were elegant and well-preserved, their beauty appeared dull due to lack of light.

Her tired eyes settled on the windows as she exclaimed aloud, now wide-eyed, "*the curtains.*"

"The curtains, what about them?" asked the drowsy voice behind her.

"Good morning, you had a good sleep. You look rested." Eleanor smiled, pleased that she had slept.

"I did, and you?" asked Eleanor.

"Just fine and up in time to make the tea," replied Thelma. No need to worry the woman about her inability to sleep.

"Wonderful! Now what's this about the curtains?"

"Well, while I was relaxing here, I was wondering if this might be a good time to do a bit of a tidy up, take advantage of Ms. Harriet's absence, and surprise her when she comes home. We could start with new curtains. Maybe letting in the light to show off your beautiful things," explained Thelma.

She was not sure which way this conversation would go. Over the years, her suggestion for change was met with a kind but firm resistance. Things were a little different now. An acute chest complaint caused Harriet a stay in a medical facility. Surely, dusting and airing out the place could only be good for her breathing.

Boldly, she continued, "It might be a good time to give the place a thorough clean and have it spick-and-span before the winter sets in. A good dusting and airing will keep those chesty colds at bay." Thelma held her breath.

Eleanor sat quietly, took a dainty sip from her ancient Royal Doulton cup, sat a while longer before saying, "It's long overdue all right, Thelma." Excitement building now, she ventured, "You are the perfect person to oversee the project. Dr. Owens called Mrs. Hannon last evening to bring her up to date, saying no need to come until the morning. We'll ask her when she gets here if she can recommend someone."

If a gentle tap on the private door hadn't interrupted, Thelma would be still sitting there, slack-jawed when the cleaners arrived days later. Instead, she stood up, assumed her stance as an official door opener, and welcomed Fiona Hannon.

"Good morning, Thelma. I came here first to see how you both were doing before joining Dr. Owens at the centre in a little bit."

"Come in, Mrs. Hannon." Eleanor's voice was loud and clear from inside. "We're all fine here. Will we make fresh tea, Thelma?" Good idea, I think. You'll have a cup, Mrs. Hannon."

This was not a question. Fiona signaled *yes* with a smile. The elderly lady invited Fiona to take a seat with a sweep of her thin bony hand that belied her return to inner strength.

"Speaking of good ideas," she continued, "Thelma had a brilliant one earlier."

Grateful for the distraction of rinsing out the teapot, the owner of the brilliant idea raised her eyes to the heavens still in shock.

"Well now, so early in the morning too" was all Fiona could muster. The frail attempt at humour was lost on Eleanor as she earnestly continued her announcement. "She suggested we should spruce up the whole place while Harriet is otherwise engaged, as a homecoming surprise. Might help to keep us healthier too, she seems to think. I'm inclined to agree."

Fiona, deprived of any eye contact with Thelma, simply said, "Brilliant!"

"Would you happen to know a person or a small local business who would be suitable for the task? Thelma will oversee the project without doing any of the actual heavy work. She will be acting in my stead as I concentrate on Harriet. Now, in your professional opinion, what do you make of it?"

Thelma was forced to turn back into the room at this point, abandoning the tea making.

Fiona caught her eye before saying, "There's this lovely young couple in the area who set up their own company, Nuala's Cleaning and Catering Services. Nuala and her crew take care of the house side of things, and her husband, Adam, with his team look after the catering. In fact, Nuala is at Coughlans this morning, getting that house ready for Angela's return on Monday. Their understanding of domestic clean and medical infection control standards set them apart. Nuala is a registered nurse, and her husband is a dietitian. They also donated their services to the Bright House to get it ready for opening."

Eleanor's turn to stare! Recovering, she said, "Splendid, Thelma I told you Mrs. Hannon would know of someone. Now as soon as you are ready, get yourself down to Johnson and Burke and see what they have in the Drapery Department. They always have quality materials. Oh, it's best if you deal with Mr. Johnson himself. He will help you choose whatever else you think we need. Give him my regards. Off you go now. I'll make us fresh tea."

Fiona found herself wondering if there was much difference in age between the shop owner and Eleanor. Mr. Johnson had been in that store since she was a child and like the twins never seemed to change. His impeccable three-piece pinstriped suit with the colourful silk breast pocket square was legend hereabouts. His gracious demeanor endeared him to locals and tourists alike When the tea was finally drunk, Eleanor led Fiona to the private door and ushered her into the rehab centre with the promise to be over there herself shortly.

"Preventative medicine," said the doctor when Fiona told him the news before going to see Harriet. Though sworn to secrecy, he could not help imagining what these changes would make in the well-being of his oldest patients.

The Clean Sergeant

AS MRS. FINNERTY and Rose were leaving Dublin, Amy was making her way next door with Una. They were laden down with so many bags and hangers it looked more like a permanent move than an overnight visit.

"Are you sure you need all that, Amy?" her dad asked from his doorstep.

"Yes, Daddy, it's all the school stuff on top of all the other things. We can't be over and back when the house is getting cleaned for Angela's homecoming. We might dirty something."

"Too true, silly me," he replied. "I forgot you were the clean sergeant."

"You are silly, Daddy. You know I promised Dr. Myers."

"We're fine, Mr. Coughlan. It's not too much really. Between us, we will have it sorted in no time. Mrs. Finnerty will be here this afternoon so we will have to be tidy in here too, right Amy?"

"Of course," replied the little girl, who already had attempted to gather some of the bags into a smaller pile.

"Have a safe trip there and back, Mr. Coughlan," said Una.

"Sounds like you're very busy, so I'll get out of the way." He kissed his daughter, shook hands with Una, and thanked her.

Amy sat looking at the folded camp bed in the same room she shared with Una when Mrs. Finnerty was in the hospital and her parents were in Dublin. The bags and baggage lay haphazardly at her feet.

"Do you think we should even open it up?" asked Una as she plopped down beside her.

"We didn't use it the last time," said Amy.

"True. I think we should put it away. That will give us more room."

"I have a lot of stuff, it's because of school and everything," said Amy.

Una sensed Amy was having uncertainties, understandably so. The first day back at school is a big deal ordinarily, starting a new class, a new teacher, and making new friends. Mothers go with their children, fuss over them, and sometimes take photos to record their momentous occasion. Amy would have none of these things, and neither would she expect it. She fully understood the current circumstances. She loved her sister, missed her, and was keenly aware that she was too ill to go to school.

"Amy, for now, just hang up your school uniform and your new outfit. Leave the rest for later. I'm sure Mrs. Quigley's lunch is ready. We'll pick up something delicious and eat in the park if you like," suggested Una.

"A picnic like we did when Angela had her operation, but that was breakfast," replied Amy.

"I'd say it's high time we had lunch then. Let's go. They abandoned the camp bed, hung up the two clothes hangers, and were out the door."

Mrs. Finnerty's cat Mrs. Miller sat in her usual sunny spot on the windowsill and merely cocked one eye at the pair of them.

"Did you feed Mrs. Miller?" asked Amy.

"I did, and she ate it all. She seems to be used to all the goings and comings now, so nothing puts her off her food," answered Una.

"She wouldn't eat for me at all when Mrs. Finnerty was in the hospital. I coaxed her and coaxed, but she wouldn't," lamented the child.

"Sometimes cats pretend just to get extra attention, they love all that fuss, and she wanted more from you. You did an excellent job with her, Amy," reassured her picnic partner.

Hand in hand, they skipped to Quigley's, enticed by the aroma of her freshly made food.

* * *

Madge Costello waited until midmorning to think about visiting Harriet. She was trying to decide whether to drop in on Eleanor first when her phone rang.

"It's me," said Kitty Walsh. "Good you haven't left yet. Let's go together. I spoke briefly to Eleanor earlier. She said Fiona had already been to see her and visited Harriet with Dr. Owens, so the coast is clear for us now. Pick you at your gate in a few."

* * *

At about that time, Rose was putting her bags in the rental car outside her mother's house in Dublin across the street from Keely's. She and Mrs. Finnerty were sipping tea when they spotted her.

"Right on time. I'll give her a shout while you get your things," offered Keely.

Mrs. Finnerty was at ease as she gathered her belonging. Parting with Angela the evening before was easier than she anticipated. Though the young girl's painful mouth bothered her greatly and she was beyond tired, her spirit was alert, even with a hint of humour. She remembered with a smile their conversation when her dad arrived. "Two's company," she had said, to which Angela replied, "Three's a crowd!" Her parents were aghast at the potential rudeness of the exchange until they realized it was harmless banter between the two of them and a sign of recovery.

With a smile on her face, she left the family together having accepted Keely's generous invitation to spend the night rather than have Rose pick her up at the hospital.

"Nice morning," said Mrs. Finnerty as she put her things in Rose's car.

"I'm so jealous," wailed Keely from her driveway, hand on her heart. "Say *hi* to the ocean for me."

"Back to school for you, missy" was the wicked remark thrown at her friend and hostess.

"Mean, downright mean" was all Keely had to say as she shut her front door on both of them. They saw her waving from the window as they pulled out onto the road.

Rose seemed easy to be with, and they relaxed into each other's company as they travelled the road across the country in no particular hurry.

"What's your schedule like this coming week?" inquired Mrs. Finnerty.

"Well, as always, there's the meet and greet part, the tour, of course, various lectures, splitting into groups for specific areas of interest. Dr. Alan Moran, a very nice man by all accounts, is the principal host as it were, creating a bit of a buzz among those attending. Apparently, he has quite a reputation in his field with an innovative approach. Dr. Myers literally sent us to him."

"He's all that," confirmed her passenger.

"Actually, I'm most interested in Angela's Tresses and Turbans," continued Rose. "The beautiful turbans were very prevalent in Park Edge and seemed to be having a positive effect. Dr. Myers and I had a chat about that. She's a huge fan. For me, that's my major focus in Baybridge."

"Yes, she is, wearing one of Angela's herself. Amy had it made especially for her as she told you," said Mrs. Finnerty. "Hair is very important, historically signifying beauty, strength, wisdom, and a myriad of other characteristics."

"What is your foundation's approach to marketing the turbans? Do you advertise? Or have a slogan?" asked Rose.

The corporate tone of this question unsettled Mrs. Finnerty. Rose glanced at her once or twice before she answered.

"We don't have anything like that, Rose. I'd like you to meet some people, and you will see why we don't even use those words or think like that. Do you have any free time tomorrow?" she asked.

"I think so," muttered the confused Rose.

"Good, I will get word to you at the hotel with the details. It's the Glass Swan, right?" concluded Mrs. Finnerty.

The Milk Jug

MADGE AND KITTY were pleased to see the improvement in Harriet's condition overnight. They did not stay long as a couple of staff members were hovering outside the door, waiting to give her morning care. "She looks well, Kitty," said Madge.

"I'm pleasantly surprised," her friend answered. "It's amazing what nebulizer treatments and some fluids can do. She'll look even better after her bath and better still when the antibiotics kick in."

"I was concerned about Angela and Mrs. Finnerty, but it looks like there will be no sad news to tell," added Madge.

"Let's hope that's the case. Now that we have a bit of time on our hands, how about a quick spin out to the beach?" suggested Kitty. Charly was with Amy at Una's suggestion.

"Oh, that's a great idea. The weather is expected to be good today and tomorrow. Hope it holds till Monday at least for the first day back at school. Are ye already at your house?" asked Madge.

"No idea, Madge, not wishing to cut you short. I keep asking, they keep saying yes. I'm expecting a list of missing items and accusations from each of them on Monday afternoon. I have my speech well prepared for them."

They both laughed.

"Well, your Aiden and our Kieran are doing leaving cert this year, so there better be no shenanigans," said Madge.

"If they intend to get into the universities of their choice, they had better knuckle down. That exam is no joke," agreed Kitty.

* * *

By now, they were pulling into a parking space facing the ocean. They sat staring at it as if this wondrous miracle happened overnight and nobody told them. Eventually, they stirred themselves and got out of the car. They started to walk the familiar path through the coarse sand-strewn rushes separating the wild crashing Atlantic from the lush green of the golf course. Neither spoke. There was no need. They hoped to be back at Mrs. Finnerty's before she returned to update Una and avoid having to break unwelcome news about Harriet on her return. They made it just in time.

Rose dropped Mrs. Finnerty off at her house on Shadow Ridge Avenue, refusing an offer of a cup of tea. "I have millions of e-mails and stuff to catch up on but thanks all the same," she said. "You'll leave me a message about tomorrow?"

Mrs. Finnerty nodded a *yes* and waved.

Such excitement from within when they realized the woman of the house was home. The children rushed to the door. "A welcome committee, what a surprise! Let me have a look at you two. You grew, didn't you? I know, it's for back to school Monday and a new class. That's it."

"Did we really grow, Mammy?" asked Charly.

"Only a person who hadn't seen you for a while would notice a thing like that, so I'm sure it's true," said Madge.

"I hope my uniform fits," said Amy.

Una became aware again of the anxiety Amy was showing.

"It's more like getting older than bigger," explained the experienced older teacher. "More sophisticated for moving up a class."

The girls leaned into one another coyly and said in unison, "*Sophisticated*!" They scurried back giggling, to where they had left Una sitting on the floor surrounded by children's books.

"Does that mean you are both in the same class this year?" Una asked, half looking at a parent for the answer.

"Apparently so, Una. Charly had an early birthday, so they moved her up," answered Madge.

Una had an idea. She maneuvered the adults back towards the mini kitchen, rattled a few cups for cover, and said, "I've noticed Amy is not her usual self. She has been a bit tentative when we mention Monday. It's a big day, and neither of her parents are here to share it with her. Possibly thinking how Angela doesn't even get to go to school. It's perfect that Charly is in the same class, but I was wondering about that very first morning. Would it be possible for you, Mrs. Costello, to bring Charly here and you all walk down together with Mrs. Finnerty? I know you have the boys to see to and if—"

"Una, please, I'm ashamed. None of this crossed my mind. It is a very big thing she has to do on her own. I can't believe—"

"Shush, Madge!" interrupted Kitty Walsh. "I didn't think about that either. There's no excuse, no matter how busy we like to think we are. We are, however, a great bunch when put together. Una had the love and good sense to invite Charly to join them while we were out, spot a potential problem and come up with the solution. What do you say, Mrs. Finnerty, will we make a big splash on the first day of school?"

"We most certainly will. Before that, if you can get the word to the other board members, I want to introduce you all to Rose, our guest from London. She's wildly interested in the foundation. How does Sunday at two o'clock at the Milk Jug by the beach sound? Ice cream for everyone on the last day before school. Then Monday morning, we will all march to school. Mrs. Costello do not forget the camera. It's official business."

Una was dispatched to break the good news to the children.

Before leaving, Mrs. Walsh told Mrs. Finnerty about Harriet. At first, it upset her, wanting to go straight to the centre or at least to see Eleanor. They both agreed checking in on Eleanor was the best course of action.

"Una can drop me," she said.

"Yes, but first, you must eat and rest a while after your journey," urged Mrs. Walsh.

"Oh, I'm glad to move about after sitting all that time, and we had something to eat in Haymarket. Speaking of Haymarket, it might be necessary to take Rose over to meet Tara and see around the studio. It all depends. I'm interested to hear how you find her tomorrow. It's not clear to me what her intentions are with regards to Angela's Tresses and Turbans. The word *advertising* and *slogan* came up, quite put me ill at ease, I must say," she confided.

This amused Mrs. Walsh.

"Not to worry. She'll soften like a spoon of Milk Jug ice cream, by the time we're done with her tomorrow. I bet she doesn't know herself how to proceed. Baybridge is a far cry from London. Dublin even. She'll soon get the hang of the *Baybridge way* and be right as rain. Between us, we'll get her to the Bright House and Haymarket if need be. Aren't they all back in school next week leaving us with nothing else to do?"

"What would I do without you all? First Una, now you."

"Like you do now, everything. If anyone needs a lift tomorrow, let me know. Parking may be a problem, seeing the day that's in it and the mild weather. Charly is tagging along to keep Amy company."

With a wave, she was gone.

After dropping Mrs. Finnerty at Eleanor's, Una and Amy doubled back parked at the Bright House and walked up towards the football fields. They could tell by the silence as they neared the pitches that no matches were being played today. Still, they walked on, enjoying the sunshine. Clusters of children kicked a ball around just for the fun of it, bringing a smile to Una's eyes. She loved the rise and fall of their chatter, the soaring melody, the hushed whisperings, the chorus of laughter, and the inevitable pout or sob. It's what she most missed since leaving St. Paul's.

"Amy! Amy!" a girl's voice shouted as she scampered across the grass towards them.

"It's Cara," Amy declared, as she saw her mother, Cate, and little brother, Mathew, make a beeline for them.

"So, it is," agreed Una. "Hello there, how is everybody?"

"Fine, thank you. Can Amy play?" asked Cara.

Mathew just waited, hoping he would not be abandoned, now his sister found a friend.

"If you don't mind sharing, we just came up for a bit of a walk," explained Una. "Don't forget Mathew, Amy."

"We won't," both girls said at once as they ran to retrieve their ball.

It was a pleasant surprise meeting Fiona's daughter and the two grandchildren today. It served as a welcome distraction for Amy with Monday and Angela's return looming. "Cate, will you be glad to get back to school next week?" asked Una.

"If you promise not to broadcast it, I'll tell you the truth. I can't wait," whispered Cate.

The two sat in conversation while the kids played, and Amy was not the only one grateful for the distraction.

A Modernizing Leap

THELMA WAS IN the midst of navigating her way through the door when she spotted Mrs. Finnerty. Reaching to hold the door open, she said, "Thelma, let me help you. You're laden down there."

"Oh, thank you, I almost didn't see you there," blurted the breathless Thelma. "We're having a bit of a clear out around here. I'll get Ms. Eleanor for you. It's a danger zone in there at the minute."

The flabbergasted Mrs. Finnerty silently nodded and waited. Momentarily, Thelma reappeared accompanied by Fidelma O'Driscoll from Nuala's Cleaning Services. They met previously when they worked next door for Angela's homecoming. She was carrying a bundle of sorts, which she placed on top of Thelma's basket.

"Hello there," she said. Her warm smile spread across her pretty face as she relayed a message from Ms. Killfeather, saying she would be out in a minute. Obviously, Fidelma was not in the inner circle invited to address her as Ms. Eleanor, not yet at anyhow.

"Thank you, Fidelma," replied Mrs. Finnerty. "Giving Thelma a helping hand there, I see."

"That's right. I'm what you might call the *advance party*. Nuala and the others are over at Coughlans today."

Before she could reply, a high-pitched sound echoed across space. "Rebecca, Rebecca, of all the days to visit. I'm so sorry not to receive you properly," lamented Eleanor.

"I'm the intruder on your hive of activity. Come, let's walk down to that lovely bench of yours, and you can explain what in the world you're up to," urged her unannounced guest.

They helped each other down the stone steps, happy to find the bench in the shade and quite the place for Eleanor's announcement.

"I'm so excited to tell you what we are up to, Rebecca. I must give credit to Thelma for coming up with the idea. We are decorating. After all these years, yes, we are. Thelma has been to see the latest in curtains, cushions, carpets, and fashionable accessories at Johnson and Burke's. We will have them all here on Monday. I told Thelma to choose, and I can't wait to see what she has for us. Fidelma is here today, and Nuala and the rest of the team will come on Sunday. Her husband sent word that he could help with little touch-up paint jobs and the likes, when he finishes getting Angela's family food sorted. Fiona kindly recommended them. We must get it all done before Harriet is discharged in a few days. It's her homecoming surprise," concluded Eleanor, clapping her elegantly ancient hands like a little girl.

So taken was Mrs. Finnerty with this breaking news she forgot why she had come in the first place. She fought her way back to reality when she heard mention of Harriet, saying, "Shall we go see her then, do you think?"

"Oh yes, we must. We had better enter through the centre as it's simply impossible to get through our mess right now. Don't forget, Rebecca, not a word about our leap into the modern world."

It was an easy promise to keep because she was finding it hard to believe herself, let alone trying to convince anyone else.

Fiona Hannon was at the bedside when they arrived, their presence made known by a soft tap as Eleanor peeped around the slightly opened door.

"Someone's here. Shush, we better stop talking about the neighbours," whispered Fiona.

Harriet leaned towards her while keeping her head on the pillow and asked conspiratorially, "Do you think they heard us?"

"Nah," Fiona answered.

"Talk is cheap," commented Mrs. Finnerty as she crept up on them, delighted to hear the humour in their banter. "Look at you, they told me you were *sick*. I didn't believe a word of it."

"It's Rebecca, how lovely you're back, isn't it, Eleanor?"

"I found her wandering outside, so we both came together," replied her sister.

"I'm glad you did. Is Angela back with you?" she asked.

"More likely on Monday. They have to wait to get the results of all the usual tests following the treatment," explained Mrs. Finnerty.

"Did she do well?"

"A true trooper, and speaking of troopers, how are you?"

"Well, apparently, I can pry into other's business without coughing," she replied. "Fiona was just explaining that Dr. Owens wants to do some blood tests and a chest X-ray at the beginning of the week, while *he has me captive*, he said. So, like Angela, we will have to do as 'the good doctors' tell us." Now she did cough, thus adding, "That's my sign to be quiet."

Fiona stayed behind as the other two ladies took their leave, Eleanor promising to return later in the day.

* * *

Una and Amy were at this point loitering leisurely in the grounds, awaiting Mrs. Finnerty's appearance.

"There they are!" shouted Amy when she saw the pair appear at the side of the building. "Ms. Eleanor is with her," she added before taking off towards them. Eleanor ruffled her not so spikey hair as she greeted the child.

Amy put her hand over Eleanor's on top of her head and said, "Grainne is going to buzz us again when Angela and Mammy get back. It's a sight like this for school on Monday, isn't it?"

"Some might think that. Those who knew *why* your hair was buzzed would *admire* you and your hair," mused Eleanor.

"Anyway, Charly said we should definitely wear our turbans on Monday," remembered Amy.

"Well then, everyone will admire you both," reassured the ever-soothing Eleanor.

Una and her house friend were walking a short distance behind the two, catching the odd stray word passing between them. Mrs. Finnerty stayed Una with a tap on her arm and a finger to her lips. In fast muted tones, she brought Una up on the goings and comings with Thelma and Fidelma.

Una, unaware of the historic significance of this tidbit of information, simply said, "I've made a nice lunch already, plenty for all. We should invite Ms. Eleanor. I'm sure there won't be any cooking in the hustle of the decorating. If you agree, we can take her with us now."

"As of late, the obvious seems to escape me. I'm spoiled with so many capable people surrounding me. Yes, yes, by all means invite her," urged her friend.

Unlike Mrs. Walsh on her first visit to Mrs. Finnerty's, Eleanor stopped dead in her tracks as Amy let her in the front door. Unashamedly, she stared until Amy gently took her hand, led her to Mrs. Finnerty's carved desk, sat her down, saying, "It's a library."

A phone call to Thelma explained Eleanor's temporary absence. They ate lunch on the patio, where the goings and comings of Nuala and her crew next door in Amy's house seemed to be of no concern to them.

The child, the young lady, the older woman, and the ancient one spent a very happy afternoon in one another's company unencumbered by their generational differences. Oh, that it should always be so!

All Together Now

"WILL YOU PICK Rose up at the Glass Swan?" Mrs. Finnerty asked Una mid-morning.

"All set. I called her earlier to be on the lookout for us around quarter to two. Amy asked to come so she can have a close look at the river," explained Una.

"We should spend more time at the river, Una, so beautiful and so close. I'm as guilty as the next in that regard. When I was back and forth to the hospital and Grainne was still at Kelly's, I promised to spend more time admiring the swans. Mr. Daugherty's death put a bit of a damper on that area for me. Amy wanting to spend time there has reminded me of that urge, and I intend to honour it," disclosed the older woman.

"I've hardly seen it myself either. I'd love to walk along the banks. I bet it's amazing when the leaves turn. We should promise to see it close up, at least a couple of times each season. We still have a few days left in summer," she prompted.

"That's true, so if we are to keep to your new regiment, you'd better choose a day next week, my friend."

They were both leaning over the rail on the river side of the hotel. It was high tide. To their right, the salmon leap welcomed the rushing foaming torrent of river water, demanding its rightful path to the sea. Later, spawning salmon would successfully rid themselves of the ocean's parasites and lice, who had hitched a free ride thus far, by leaping several feet into the air, availing themselves of the shower of a lifetime. Now clean and prepared, their journey to the river of their birth continued, producing the next generation of their kind, the salmon's last act on this earth. People automatically stopped to look down from the bridge in quiet awe at the first stage of this natural wonder. Una remembered Fiona telling stories of the salmon leap, and the late evening fishermen they watched from her bedroom window when she was a child. Looking across to the far bank now, she could clearly see the back entrance to her old house and imagined what it was like for Fiona to live with such a view.

"Can you see any salmon in all that frothy water?" asked Amy on tippy toes, straining over the railing. Una took hold of her arm as they both searched the tumbling cascade of water for any sign of anything leaping.

"Not today it seems. We will have to come back again one evening, and hope we witness a beautiful salmon soaring high above on her way home to have her babies. Mrs. Finnerty wants to come too," added Una.

"Well then, we have to come," announced the child.

On the way to the Milk Jug, Amy told Rose all about the salmon leap in such informed detail Una felt she had nothing to add.

Parking was a problem as they knew it would be. The walk from the car to the beach was welcome because the sun shone high in the sky. A festive mood permeated the air about them, throwing caution to the wind.

"This is a lovely place," said Rose.

Today, she wore a colourful summer dress, open-toe sandals, and a giant sun hat in stark contrast to her more austere business attire. Her long brown hair, flowing from under her hat, swayed to the rhythm of her jaunty gait on the sandy cobbles. To her companions, this was not remarkable, but it was to Mrs. Finnerty as she saw them approach. Charly ran to meet them.

"We got here early, so we got an outside table," she announced.

"Rose, you look wonderful. I feel we are on the Riviera. Everyone, this is Rose." She hoped her enthusiastic introduction did not betray her shock at the Rose who stood before her. Where was the woman she met in Dublin and made the journey to Baybridge with?

"There's space here," a voice said, beckoning the recent arrival.

She found herself sitting between Mrs. Walsh and Sammy. "You've brought the good weather with you, Rose. It's the best day we've had all summer. I'm Sammy. I work at the Bright House in town. We make the maharaja turbans for the boys and the logos. We send some over to Haymarket where Tara Doherty and her crew artfully attach them to the female turbans. Kitsy, over there, she's the artist."

Hearing her name, Kitsy obliged with a wave and a smile.

"I'm so excited to meet you and all the others. This is a great spot to be hearing about your wonderful program. I saw samples of your work in Park Edge. They really caught my attention," said Rose.

"We have not seen any other's wearing our turbans. Of course, Amy and her family and many of the parents and schoolchildren here do. It's nice to hear about the ones we send away and what people who do not know Angela or Mrs. Finnerty think about them," confided Sammy. She called Kitsy over to share the feedback with her.

"Rest assured, your work is very visible all over the hospital. It's my hope to make that happen in my hospital in London. Then who knows?"

Mrs. Walsh was silently listening after the initial introduction.

The rest of the company sat around, confident Sammy and Kitsy had this in hand, which was a good thing, as a few had not heard tell of Rose until five minutes before she arrived. Whatever conversation was going on between them would be honest and true.

"That's the best ice-cream cone I have ever eaten in my life," Rose announced.

By now, the various groups mingled, forming others, and in no time, they all had a chance to talk with Rose.

"I'm not sure what concerns you had, Mrs. Finnerty, but it seems to me the ice cream had nothing to do with the softening of Rose. According to Sammy, she was on board from the start," reported Mrs. Walsh.

"She has shown a passionate interest, that's for sure. It's the business way she talks that has me confused," she replied.

"I hope I'm not interrupting," Rose said as she approached. "I was just talking to Fiona and her husband and hearing how social services plays a big part in identifying those interested in the turbans. It's becoming clearer to me how this foundation works. It's unusual to see an organization operate on such a personal level. It seems the driving force is the will of every person involved to do their part in easing one difficult aspect of post-chemo recovery. I don't know any other of its kind."

"There is an abundance of love amongst us., no doubt about that. But without the generosity of this lady here, none of it could come to anything," offered Mrs. Walsh.

"Nonsense" came the quick reply from Mrs. Finnerty, "what could *I* do without all of *you*?"

"I'm intrigued, and quite out of my depth to tell you the truth. There is so much I do not know," confessed Rose. "Amy mentioned the Bright House and Haymarket when we met at Fiona's sister's house in Dublin. She summed it up pretty well, in line with Sammy's account today. Would it be an imposition to ask to visit?"

Mrs. Walsh answered right on cue, "All arranged, Rose, as soon as you give us the word. Kids are back to school tomorrow, so we mammies are itching for a child-free trip. Una will be at the Bright House with Sammy and Kitsy. We can start out there anytime you're free."

Madge Costello took the last picture as Rose sat into Una's car. She would be on hand to record the rest of the visit. "See you tomorrow," said over a wave and her stunning smile.

As they headed back into town, Una found herself looking forward to Rose's visit, just something about her piqued her interest.

"What was the best part, Ms. Rose, the ice cream, or the people?" asked Amy as she sat back, waiting for the answer.

Queasy Journey

ANGELA HAD A restless night. Joyful thoughts of returning home floated across her mind—that joy diluted at times as she remembered she would be back here soon. This round of treatment was the worst yet. She understood ahead of time. She also knew the second round of this cycle would be even worse. Her parents knew she knew. Somehow, for Angela, it was the most unbearable part. She listened in the dark to the sound of their sleeping, Mammy on the hospital bed, Daddy on the disguised bed under the window. From her position on her mini chaise, she imagined the rise and fall of their chests and composed a little tune to accompany it. The lilt played in her heart silently, hoping to soothe the pain they felt on her account. Instinctively, her mother stirred and reached for her. As their hands touched, they met each other in the night.

The residents on both sides of the country woke up to vastly different weather on Monday morning. Angela looked out from her hospital room to see a bright sunrise.

* * *

Amy woke to lashing rain. Accustomed to the fragility of the elements in Ireland, it caused no surprise, just a change of clothes.

"Let me dig out that old-fashioned expandable plastic head cover thingy. It will cover your turban," Mrs. Finnerty suggested to Amy who was staring out the back window.

"We may need one for Charly too, unless her mother has an old-fashioned head thingy too," replied Amy, happy they might be able to wear the turbans after all. Una appeared with the *odds-and-ends* basket. She offered it to Mrs. Finnerty who came up trumps on the first rummage.

"There's a load of them here, Amy, come see what we can find."

She picked out a bunch for Charly to look at. She chose a clear one for herself and one for Charly. It was important to her that others could see their turbans. A shuffling at the front door caught their attention as Una went to open it. Madge refused her invitation to come in saying

"Not at all, Una, we're dripping," as she gave the umbrella a vigorous shake from the shelter of the small overhang above the door. Amy bounded towards them, basket in hand, only to find Charly was already wearing an exact replica of the one on her head.

"We have the same old-fashioned head thingies, and everyone can still see our turbans matching our uniforms," said Amy.

Charly agreed. They marched together ahead of the adults, two happy little girls off to school.

* * *

Caroline Coughlan handed her husband the last of the bags as he packed the Chariot for the home journey. Caroline went back inside the foyer to get their daughter. None of them displayed the excitement of the last time they made this trip, and no amount of effort could fake it. This child of theirs, their strong, witty, wise, and funny child was hammered by the chemo. Caroline settled her in the corner of the back seat, propping her up with cushions.

"That feels good, Mammy, I'm going to be all right now," this child of theirs said.

If only she was going to be all right now, wished Caroline, *if only*.

Angela dozed for the first hour of the journey, whereupon she sat bolt upright, covered her sore mouth with her hand, and wretched. Her dad pulled over to the side of the road and opened the sliding side door of the Chariot.

"Darling, sit on the floor and let your feet dangle out the open door. Let me help you. Good girl. Nice big deep breath. Now lean back against me and rest yourself," urged Caroline.

Tony came around to where Angela sat, went down on one knee, held his daughter's clammy hand while his wife knelt on the floor of the Chariot, simulating the back of a chair, allowing the child the opportunity to let her body go slack against her thighs.

"It's coming again," Angela moaned, leaning forward in a bout of dry heaves.

"I'm just going to hold your forehead. Let your head relax into my hand like we did at the hospital, that's it, nice slow breathing," her mother said, taking breath for breath with her heaving child.

At the mention of the hospital, Tony got up, put his hand to his ear in the universal sign for telephone, and moved out of earshot. Caroline nodded.

"It's probably delayed nausea Tony, not uncommon with her recent regimen. Give her one of the antiemetic pills you have in your home meds kit, just right for an occasion such as this. Of course, we have the added exacerbation of motion sickness. Have a look to see if there is a better spot, other than the back seat for the rest of the journey. I'll call ahead to Dr. Owens and update him since we spoke this morning. Don't hesitate to call either of us with any concern."

Dr. Myers was very reassuring, but Tony still asked, "So you don't think we should return to Park Edge then?"

"Angela will do better in Dr. Owens's care. It's what she has always asked us to do. The ducklings made it quite clear. Home is where she will thrive. Take it easy, avoid the bumps, and none of those police chasing shenanigans now, Garda Coughlan, as you go over the Curlew mountains."

Who wouldn't love a doctor like that? They followed the doctor's advice and made it to their front door without any further episodes. They did, however, encounter the Baybridge rain as soon as they left the Curlew mountains behind them. Angela was unaware of this as her father carried her exhausted sleeping body to her pristine, sanitized bedroom.

* * *

Mrs. Finnerty picked Amy up from school. Sensing something might be amiss next door, they went first to her house. Amy had bags of stuff upstairs, so it was reasonable to do so. Though the Chariot was visible in the driveway, Amy raised no objection. She had sensed something too. As soon as the key was in the door, Caroline came tearing up towards them, scooping her youngest daughter into her arms.

"We're home safe and sound. No need for worry, pet," she breathed into her child's ear.

"Angela was sick this time, Mammy, on the way home too," announced the young sister. "It won't worry Dr. Owens one bit, so don't you worry about it either Mammy. I'll keep Mrs. Finnerty company for our tea and tidy up my stuff."

Gob smacked; her mother looked to Mrs. Finnerty for inspiration. How did Amy know all this? Was she so familiar with these symptoms, she just put two and two together? Oh, my lord!

"I'm sure Amy is right about Dr. Owens. Come and find us after. We will keep some cake for you to share."

"Cake, what kind of cake?" the accommodating eight-year-old child asked in an effort to deflect further worry from her mother.

Caroline saw right through that little ploy, brokenhearted that it was offered, yet loving her for it.

Dr. Owens entered their home without fanfare or urgency.

"Thank you for coming. We didn't intend you to. All the same, it's nice to have you here," blurted Caroline when she met him on the doorstep.

His reply was a reassuring smile.

"Is she still nauseous?" he whispered as he passed the foot of the stairs. No need to announce himself from afar.

The presence of a family doctor in a house had a way of disturbing the flow, paralyzing it, allowing it to resume normality only upon their departure. It was as if the doctor merited a reverence not meted out to any other who crossed their threshold, not the plumber who could fix a leak preventing the ceiling from collapsing on their unsuspecting heads or the electrician who could save them all from death by fire or the accountant who called in to tell them their family was safe from eviction and the poor house, after all. No, only a lowly GP could impart sad news and be thanked for it. Dr. Owens spent many hours reflecting upon this and more hours rehearsing the best way to combat it. How was he doing?

They reached the kitchen before Caroline assured him there had been no other episodes, and Angela was sound asleep. He accepted the tea and the chair he was offered at their welcoming table. He remembered Eleanor Killfeather gave him a scone. Maybe he was doing okay after all.

"It seems Dr. Myers was right. The delayed nausea is not unusual even up to seventy-two hours or more. Being on the road didn't help but most likely not the main cause, as she hasn't complained of that in the past. Either way, she responded well to the medication. Now how are you two doing?" Catching himself before the answer, he added, "Amy not here?"

"To tell you the truth, Dr. Owens, we had a rude awakening this time around. We lulled ourselves into a comfortable expectation because of how well Angela did before," said Tony.

"Mrs. Finnerty was such a help the whole week, instinctively knowing the boundaries and being there when Angela needed her most. Not only that, she looked after Amy at Fiona's sister's house the first night in Dublin. Then took her to see her son Leo's horse the next morning. Of all things! Mrs. Finnerty brought her home from school today, but she made an excuse to stay and have cake instead of coming home. She said Angela was sick and that it would not worry you. She just believes in you, Dr. Owens. It's such a lot for her."

By now, Caroline's tears, held for so long, began to fill her eyes and automatically flow down her cheeks. She made no effort to find a hanky. Dr. Owens did what all good doctors do, nothing. He let her cry and waited. Tony brought the hanky.

At the moment she was about to apologize, the doctor said, "Your girls are more astute and quicker than most adults at picking up on things. We've seen it time and time again, even before Angela's leg trouble began. The two of them have straightened us adults out a time or two. Amy was right, I am not worried. All of Angela's scans and labs are as they should be, and I can dare to say, her final outcome looks very good."

Caroline's crying had subsided but started anew at the news. Tony did what all good husbands do at a time like this, soothe and keep the hankies coming. Between sobs, she mumbled, "Thank God, oh thank God." Silence before the doctor continued,

"Now it's clear to me you two need a little respite yourselves. For now, let Amy visit a while with her sister. She must see her for herself. Meanwhile, one of you ask if she can spend the night next door, certainly they will agree. Fiona and I will have a chat in the morning and see what can be arranged in a few days when Angela bounces back, and she will. Your comfort zone has taken a beating, there is more to come, and you need to prepare for it. From what I see, there is no shortage of help available to this family. Tony, can I take a quick peek at Angela if she is awake? Caroline, you sit for now. If anything is different, I'll see you on the way out."

He found the child in a relaxed, easy sleep. She, too, needed to prepare.

Rose's Faux Pas

"I'VE NEVER SEEN rain like this in my life," announced Rose when she arrived at the Bright House.

"What? Never? This is just a light shower," teased Sammy as they met at the front door.

"I'm glad it's not really raining then," replied the smiling Rose.

"Good cup of tea is all you need, then you'll be as right as *rain. Oops*, sorry." Sammy didn't appear to be sorry.

Rose lost all interest in the weather when she entered the work area. Shamelessly, she walked around, looking, touching, sniffing, listening. She came to a complete standstill at the large window, taking in the view of mountain and pasture.

Kitsy whispered, "Is she in a trance or what?"

When no answer was forthcoming, she decided to make the tea 'cos it looked like it was needed.

Breaking the spell, Rose turned into the studio and uttered, "Amazing, truly amazing. Inspirational even."

"We like it," both the girls said.

Mugs of tea hungrily consumed, they got down to the business of the day. Rose saw firsthand how the Bright House worked as Sammy and Kitsy had four new orders and three to finish since Friday. All but one, was bound for Dublin. They sat in near silence as the fabric was transformed. Rose paid close attention, confessing at some point, she was unable to sew on a button.

"That won't matter," reassured Kitsy. "We'll do all the sewing for the boys and the logos. Haymarket crew take care of the girls and the ladies if need be."

Una heard the chatter as she came in later than usual due to getting the school procession on the road. She popped into her office briefly, then made her way to the studio. If she was expecting a welcome, she was surely let down. None of them even knew she was there, so engrossed were they in their work. She thought of going back to her office when Rose sensed a presence and greeted her.

"Una, this is one special place. I'm so impressed with the quality of the work and the individual attention to each piece. I had no idea how personal it is. It's the furthest thing from mass-produced as you could find."

"Mass-produced, disgraceful," Sammy and Kitsy tutted in unison as if rehearsed.

Una shrugged with arms wide and palms up, showing she had no control over those two, also suggestive of a warning to be careful when referring to their precious product. Rose got it and would recall this moment way into the future.

"Any tea?" Una asked, grateful for the distraction.

"I'll make a fresh pot. Mrs. Walsh and Mrs. Costello will want some for sure," offered Kitsy, also grateful for the distraction.

"We're here," boomed Kitty Walsh as she and Madge joined them. Madge started clicking her camera like a pro while Mrs. Walsh said, "I see you've been introduced to our simple local enterprise, Rose."

"I have indeed, and local is what makes it unique. When I saw the turbans in Park Edge, I recognized the exquisite work, but it never occurred to me that each one had a particular person in mind. My lack of understanding may have caused offence earlier, and for that I am sorry. There is no excuse for making presumptions."

"Happens to everyone, Rose, and more than once, if truth be told," reassured Mrs. Walsh.

"Tea's up," announced. Kitsy.

"Will ye take it down to the office?"

"We will. Una, lead the way," ordered the no-nonsense Mrs. Walsh.

Allowing the others to go ahead, she lingered long enough to dig the Quigley's scones from her bag and pass them to Kitsy with a wink. She hoped the sniggers from the two left behind could not be heard up the corridor, and Madge's clicking camera was good enough cover. Una hesitated for a second when they reached her office. Casting a halting glance over her shoulder, she popped in, then out quickly, holding her framed certificate aloft. Under the astonished gaze of Mrs. Walsh and Mrs. Costello she skillfully hung it on their *Wall of fame.*

They clustered in the office until the three members of the foundation were satisfied. Rose got the gist of how it all came together and had a better understanding of the finances. Mrs. Finnerty was the sole benefactor. The Bright House was a donation from a local gentleman who supported their endeavors. It served as both the headquarters and the maharaja/logo production site. The Haymarket studio, under the guidance of Tara Doherty, produced all the female turbans. They explained how hairdressers and wig makers were also part of the foundation. The volunteers give of their time and talent, full-time staff receives a modest salary.

"We have to get you over to Haymarket," declared Mrs. Walsh.

She stood up rattling the teacups, her way of bringing the meeting to a close. You know how it is when you go to the cinema and a really captivating film ends, you just sit there in the dark, unwilling and unable to get up, breaking the spell. That was Rose. Realizing she had to get up, she staggered behind them as if adjusting to the light. "We will need a full day Rose, to get the most out of your trip. Do you have a day you can get away from the conference? You mentioned you had to be there this afternoon."

"Wednesday would be good," Rose answered, obviously recovered from her trance. "I have another staff member here with me. His name is Rafael Castillo. He is in the business office. He is from the south of Spain, been with us for a couple of years now, and has shown himself to be a stellar young man. He is very focused on patient care and an enthusiastic fan of thinking *outside the box.*"

"He must come to see how far outside the box our Tara Doherty is." At the mention of Rafael, the *stellar young man*, she added, "Una, we will need you to drive some of us on Wednesday, please."

What was she now? A matchmaker? mused Madge.

Rose departed, leaving the others congregated in the narrow hall, staring at Una's University Degree hanging proudly on the wall.

Respite

FIONA LEFT DR. Owens's office, delighted with her assignment. As she listened to the doctor's account of his visit with Coughlans the day before, her imagination ran away with itself. She passed Brenda's desk, eager to start phase one of her mission, a discussion with Mrs. Walsh. They agreed to meet in Kelly's—maybe the swans would inspire them. They came together on the town side of the promenade and walked the short distance side by side.

When they were seated, coffees chosen, Fiona said, "Tony and Caroline need a break, doctor's orders."

"I'm sure they do but did something happen?" asked Mrs. Walsh.

Early on, it had been established that Fiona could speak freely to the board members when matters of concern arose regarding the Coughlans.

"It was a tough week in Dublin and a godsend to have Mrs. Finnerty with them. Angela was nauseous on the way home, and they called Dr. Myers from the side of the road. It was a delayed reaction to the chemo, not helped by the motion of the car. They medicated her there and then, and she slept. They were both shook up by this, and then Amy sensing something was wrong stayed with Mrs. Finnerty last night."

"Did she not see Angela at all yesterday?" Mrs. Walsh was taken aback at this bit of news as it was most unlike the pair of them.

"She did see her for a while, and they spent that time talking, just the two of them," Fiona said.

"Private?"

"Uh-huh. Dr. Owens suggested she return next door for the night. All her school stuff was still there anyway. It would make its way back all in good time. He wants Tony and Caroline to get a break, as this is only going to get worse. That's where you and I come in. Can we free up money from Angela's Purse for a couple of nights away, legally I mean?" Fiona wanted to be sure of this before going any further.

"There's no problem with using those funds for respite care or anything else for that matter pertaining to family members. Remember, the original inspiration to give money was for all the extra expenses an event like this can incur. Help for the parents is at the top of that list. What did you have in mind?"

"You and I both know those parents will not leave Angela's side. I have to talk to the kids first. They may not be happy about them going anywhere either. It's tricky. You and I also know if there is an answer to this, those girls will have it."

"That's true. I'm sorry for the poor wee child. If you need me, just call. Madge too I'm sure. Otherwise, send me the bill. Don't skimp. We have to do this."

Fiona was put through her handwashing paces by Amy at Coughlan's front door.

"Did I do it to your standard?" she asked.

"Perfect, come in now. Angela is in bed, but she is getting up tomorrow. She has a surprise for me, and I am going to need my mirror, then we will go downstairs."

"Oh, that's a lot to look forward to, Amy. Lucky you." Fiona was glad to see her in good spirits. She hugged Caroline when she reached the kitchen and could at once feel her anxiousness.

"Dr. Owens said you would call in, but I expected you anyway. Fiona, I'm all upside down inside, I have to say." Caroline was close to tears again.

"Things have gotten a bit away from you, Caroline, that's all. It happens, and we are here to help. The trick is knowing when that moment has arrived and do something about it. That's where we are now. Are you up to putting the kettle on while I have a chat with the girls? I've passed the handwashing so can I go up to them."

"Of course."

Angela was propped up in bed, her pillows resting against the headboard, her sister sat sideways, legs tucked, her back against the wall. "Angela, you look good, really you do. I heard you were a bit *queasy* on the way home." Fiona's use of the word queasy caught their attention as she hoped it would.

"*Queasy*," said one then the other.

Sick or not, Angela started the giggle, which led to the other one giggling, which resulted in a good old laugh. Caroline came to the bottom of the stairs and let herself cry at the sound. She felt safe to do so now that Fiona was at hand.

"Girls, I need your help, but we have to be quiet, okay?"

"It's about Mammy and Daddy's break. We both talked about it last night. Angela said they needed a surprise too because they are sad because of her. They need to go to the beach. Mammy especially loves the beach past the rehab, with the big waves and the lovely restaurant at the top of the hill. When you look out of the big high window, you can almost see another country. Can you do that, Mrs. Hannon, can you please?" Amy looked at her sister, checking if she had said everything, they agreed on earlier. Angela's smile gave her the reassurance she needed.

"I can," answered Fiona. How would you feel if they could stay a night or two at my brother's apartment right by the water? If you wanted that extra surprise for them, who would you like to stay here with you?"

"Charly and Mrs. Costello. We love her."

Caroline had not put the kettle on when Fiona returned, and it was not mentioned.

Instead, Fiona said, "The girls are in good form, Caroline. You may have heard they're back to the giggling."

"I did, and it made me cry. What kind of a way is that, I ask you?"

"It's what we call grieving, a mother grieving for the loss of what was normally there. The everyday joy has been stolen, and you are reacting to its loss in a very common way. You feel another loss just as much, *control*. The chemo seems to be the boss, but it isn't. You are tired. Those two beautiful daughters upstairs have it all figured out because of how you and Tony raised them. Nothing is lost except sleep. The girls have a plan to rectify that. However, a few things need to be finalized. Now, Caroline, you know what they say, *ask no questions, and you'll be told no lies.*"

Fiona first checked with her brother Declan to confirm the availability of the apartment at the beach.

"It's in tip-top shape, Nona, now that school has started. You say it's the Coughlans that need a wee break. There won't be any charge for that, not at all." Her brother was adamant.

"I thought you might say that, but listen, Angela's Purse is overflowing, and it seems to me that the people who continue to give so unconditionally would love to hear they enabled such a tangible gift."

"I see. Suppose that's why you are the social worker and I am the newspaperman."

"Hold that generosity close, my brother, I may need you to do something else soon."

* * *

Madge and Charly were tickled pink at the thought of staying over with the girls. Mrs. Walsh thought it was money well spent and agreed the donors would be very happy. Caroline threw up all sorts of obstacles to the plan but lost the fight to her daughters, who asked if Grainne could come and fix their hair. She came, beautified everyone, and settled the matter of wearing the new headband for Amy, declaring it *a fashion statement.*

Mrs. Costello would take over the Coughlan household on Friday morning after she took Amy and Charly to school. Tony and Caroline would be duly dispatched. Mrs. Finnerty offered to be the relief caregiver, allowing Madge to pop home each day to make sure she still had a home. Mrs. Walsh and Una were available at a moment's notice and wondered if they could just pop in anyway.

Fiona was happy and somewhat emotional at the response. She did, however, harbor some concerns about Caroline, wondering if her current feelings ran a bit deeper. She would, of course, discuss all this with Dr. Owens in the morning.

Haymarket

HAPPY WITH HER progress, chest X-ray result, and a much-diminished cough, Dr. Owens discharged Harriet. Maura and Carmel, one pushing the wheelchair, the other carrying the bags, took her along the hall to her newly painted door. She reached to stay Carmel's hand as she knocked on what appeared to Harriet to be the wrong door. Too late, Thelma stood in the open door. Harriet refused to enter, instead, leaning forward to get a closer look at the scene beyond Thelma. This was a bright modern space, not *her* home, definitely not. Yet inside the door, a little nook just like hers greeted her, light reflecting off the white wall. A familiar antique spindle back chair boasted a dainty velvet purse dangling in contrast to the multicoloured cushion nestled on the seat.

"There's been a mistake," she said to the twins.

Eleanor's voice from within reassured her as she approached.

"Harriet, Harriet, my darling, there's no mistake. Come in, girls."

Maura wheeled her patient to the center of the new carpet, facing the large window now draped in bright light-friendly curtains, matching the cushion on the chair in the nook. Gone were the assorted rugs previously strewn at random on the wood floor. Deemed a fall hazard by Nuala, they were replaced by a much bigger carpet that covered the whole floor, leaving no unexpected edges to trip over. The walls were given a fresh coat of paint by Adam. The whole effect, though simple, was transformative. Harriet remained quiet. Thelma kept her distance, hoping she would not have to take all the blame if this went wrong. They risked wheeling her to see her bright newly decorated bedroom.

Eventually, her sister said, "Well, how do you like your *welcome home* surprise?"

The bedroom cinched the deal it seemed, as Harriet proclaimed, "I love it. Eleanor, what we have to do now is have a tea party."

"We do, a party is it, and what will the occasion be, pray tell?"

"Nurse Murry told me we would have been welcome to visit the centre all this time. You and I agreed not to trouble them and give them their privacy. Eleanor, we were mistaken. Now we will honour the staff with a tea party. You girls don't let the cat out of the bag, not yet."

Maura and Carmel promised.

Thelma appeared from the shadows.

By the time Ms. Harriet was waking up from her first night's sleep in her new bedroom, a room she did not want to leave, by the way, the excursion had begun from Baybridge to Haymarket. Conscious of the parking restraints at the studio, Rose and Madge rode with Mrs. Walsh. Kitsy, who had not yet been to Haymarket, went along in Una's car with Rafael. Sammy stayed back to *mind the house*. It was decided they would drive straight through without stopping. A late lunch after the visit sounded good to them, somewhere they could go over the day's experience.

Though they were on a common mission, the conversation in each car was quite different.

Rose said, "I'm excited to see the working relationship between Baybridge and Haymarket. It seems Haymarket is the main production site and Baybridge a smaller particular contributor."

"You could say that I suppose. Boys don't worry about their hair as much as girls. It's not the first thing that comes to mind among many other side effects. In the inpatient setting, however, they see turbans, and it piques their interest, especially the young lads. They notice and ask questions. For them, it's not a matter of vanity, but it's more like playing a character. It's a distraction, an escape."

"Gosh, how do you know these things?"

"We listen," the quiet Madge said.

A mile or so behind them, Kitsy was saying, "I'm looking forward to meeting everyone. I wonder how the logo fits on a different-shaped turban. I spoke to Dymphna, and she said it looks well. I'm anxious to see."

"Why are there two different-shaped turbans?" asked Rafael from the back seat.

Mischievously, the two girls glanced at each other.

"We'll show you," the girls said together.

"Oh, I see ganging up on me, not fair."

"Don't pout," Kitsy scolded.

Una caught his eye in the rearview mirror. He was smiling. *Oh my, he is handsome*, she found herself thinking.

The visit broke down along the same lines as in the respective cars. Mrs. Walsh and Tara spent most of their time going over the financial and logistical aspects of things with Rose. They expected Rafael to be in that camp but found him to be more interested in the artistic and social side of things. This surprised Una and Kitsy in whose company he spent most of the time. Didn't someone say he worked in the business office at the hospital?

The first words uttered on their arrival by Dymphna was, "How is Angela?"

Mrs. Walsh was the one selected to answer by the silence of the others.

"She knows you are all thinking of her, and that makes a big difference. As feared, she had a tough week, but having Mrs. Finnerty at her side made it a little easier. She's home now with Amy, and they have already taken things into their own hands. Together, the two of them have arranged haircuts, headbands, headwear, and a getaway for their parents. Fiona is in the wings, making the arrangements."

Silence while the staff digested all that.

They gathered, in what could only be described as a *group hug*, not the favoured thing among this lot. Right now, it was all they had. Mary broke loose and came forward with a basket brimming over with gifts to take back to the Coughlan family. Slowly, they separated, each to their workstations. Mrs. Shiva lingered to meet the London visitors. Kitsy followed Dymphna and Mary and was overwhelmed with how the logos fitted perfectly.

"It's how you sew them on," Kitsy offered by way of explaining how they looked so well. Rafael was deep in admiring the *other shaped turbans* when he heard Dymphna say, "No amount of sewing can make shoddy work look good, and you do brilliant work, Kitsy."

He wondered if anywhere else in the world neighbours cared enough to work together like this. Then he remembered his grandmother's village in Spain.

Rose stood still. Only now did the full spirit of Angela's Tresses and Turbans reveal itself to her. This was *it*. The question now was, did she have *it*?

Mrs. Shiva, Tara, and Rose huddled over a vibrant piece of fabric. Although well-dressed in chic outfits and often referred to as stylish, she knew very little about the origin of the material. What she recognized at a glance was the first-rate quality of what she was looking at now.

"Where on earth did you find this?" she asked.

Her despondent tone and body language unsettled Mrs. Shiva. Here was a young woman on the verge of doing something great, with no idea yet how to do it. The spark burned in her soul. She needed to light the fire.

Time to Meet Angela

BEFORE LEAVING FOR Haymarket, Mrs. Finnerty asked Kitty Walsh to take the *delegation* for a meal when they finished at the studio. She suggested the Harrington. Kitty Walsh raised an eyebrow and was duly instructed to use a specific card for the expenses, which was separate from the foundation. Mrs. Walsh had been there a few times, once to a wedding, twice to some fundraiser or other, and her fiftieth birthday. As many of the finest dining places in Ireland, it had once been a functioning castle. Unlike most, it did not suffer from the dark dank atmosphere of old. Though some of the furnishings and art did reflect its age, you did not fear being greeted by a chain-mail-clad sword-wielding foe, upon arrival. The bar and dining area leaped out at the visitor by virtue of the bright tablecloths, napkins, and upholstery. The menu as diverse and progressive as any, found its hearty stews, game pies, and carvery to be among the most popular choices.

On the hottest day of the year, the fires still burned in the massive open fireplaces. Guests cozied up, sipping their choice of beverage, and on Sundays kept watch as one of the sous-chefs baked their bread, the old-fashioned way.

Before leaving the Haymarket studio, Mrs. Shiva made arrangements to come to Baybridge the next day, bringing samples of fabric and threads for Rose to take back to London. She would meanwhile chat with some of her contacts in London and check out what fabric markets and stalls were the best these days. So, when they sat down, acclimatized themselves, and got over the unusual beauty of the place, the chatter began. Mrs. Walsh announcing that while they were all chattering, she ascertained from Angela's mother she was up to a short visit and could Rose and Rafael come for a cup of tea tomorrow evening.

The grouping on the return journey switched. Rafael wanted to tell Rose more about the sharing and generosity of the villages in Spain and no doubt throughout the world. He reminded her of several people who volunteered already at their hospital, sewing tiny hats and booties for the premature babies, crocheting lap blankets for the medical ward, and stitching duvets with matching sheets for the cots in pediatrics. Focusing on that strength and willingness was exactly what was needed to make this endeavor a success.

Mrs. Walsh was smiling and blessing the very handsome young man from Spain.

Blowing in the Wind

CAROLINE COUGHLAN WAS happy for the distraction. She put a lot of effort into not allowing herself to look forward to or, God forbid, be excited about her getaway the next morning. What right did she have to leave her girls for two nights and go galivanting off to the beach? Furthermore, who did she think she was staying in Declan's apartment, the most sought-after piece of property for miles while Angela and Amy stayed at home?

"Anybody home?" Mrs. Walsh shouted through the half-opened front door.

Amy bounded from the front-sitting room where she had been keeping watch for the last fifteen minutes.

"Mrs. Walsh, Mammy said we should go back to the kitchen."

"Good idea, Amy, closer to the tea," her visitor agreed.

Rose took a small step to the side.

"Hi, Amy, nice to see you again. At last, I get to meet your sister. You told me all about her when we met in Dublin. Now your mum kindly invited myself and my friend Rafael for a cup of tea. Rafael and I work together, and we are very interested in Angela's turbans."

Caroline beckoned them from the kitchen door, saying, "Thanks, Amy, good girl."

Mrs. Walsh led them down the hallway.

"Caroline, this is Rose from Hillgate Hospital in London and her young collogue, Rafael."

"Welcome to you both. We thought the kitchen was the best spot to sit, more room, and Angela has her comfy chair in here. Pet, these lovely people have come from London to tell you they like your turbans very much."

Before they could continue any further, Amy interrupted with an invitation for all to wash their hands before going any further.

"Amy, we could use you in our infection control department, if ever you have any spare time."

Angela and Amy stifled one of their famous giggles at the thought, which was the perfect spontaneous ice breaker.

Rafael found himself leaning against the counter just to the side of Angela's chair, a cup of tea in hand. From this vantage point, he could see the crown of her turban and how perfectly it sat there. Ah, the other turban! He crouched down beside her while the others were chatting and whispered, "How are you feeling, Angela?"

"Very tired but not sick at all. The nausea is gone now. My mouth has to get better yet, then I'll be really fine. Do you have children like me in your hospital, Rafael? I like that name."

"Well, thank you. Angela is a good name too. We have lots of girls called Angela in Spain, and we have lots of children in our hospital who are very different, with lots of lovely names. I don't know of any of them having a foundation named after them, though." Rafael waited and took a sip of his really good tea.

"They have turbans, though, if they want one, right?"

"Not that I have ever seen," he replied.

By now, their conversation had caught the attention of the others.

"Mammy, the children in Rafael's hospital don't have any turbans."

Mammy looked from Rose to Mrs. Walsh.

Rose shuffled nearer and said, "We saw them first in Park Edge, then here in Baybridge but nowhere else, Angela."

"We have to talk to Mrs. Finnerty. Somebody has to go and find a Bright House near the hospital, and people like Sammy and Kitsy and Dymphna and Mary will make them. They love doing it, don't they, Mrs. Walsh? Kitsy will show them how to make the logo. She showed Amy and me one day."

Rose and Rafael looked at each other. Rafael smiled and shrugged his shoulders. They already had their own Sammy's, Kitsy's, Mary's, and Dymphna's. All they needed now was a Bright House.

Mrs. Walsh said, "I'm sure Mrs. Finnerty will love that plan. Now we need to get out of your way, Caroline, so you can ready yourself for your getaway."

"Mammy is not sure she should go. She thinks it's selfish. Selfish is when you take something all for yourself. Going to the beach is a gift of rest and time with Daddy. Mammy is not taking it, it's being given, like the turbans."

"I suppose it is like that, a gift and a very nice one at that. So, Caroline, off you trot and pack your bag. I'll see these fine people out and then sort the girls.:

Rose and Rafael were silent all the way to the hotel.

Caroline sat on the edge of the bed and allowed her mind to imagine the beach. She felt the sea breeze sweep and brighten her face, the coarse sand spread her toes and strengthen the soles of her feet and balanced her core. Still imagining, she looked upwards towards the drifting clouds, allowing them to take her pain with them. From where she sat, she leaned over to open the top drawer of her dressing table and retrieved a gift box as yet unwrapped. Smiling now, she undid the ribbon to reveal a set of lotions and bath oil given to her by Tony at about the time of Angela's diagnosis. She popped them out of their satin cushion and put them in her carryall.

Angela was right. They had given her the gift of rest and time with their Dad. Those gifts also needed to be unpacked, just as she had done with the lotions and allowed to blow around them in the wind.

Friday

FIONA'S ACCOUNT OF Caroline's feelings would be brought into question if Dr. Owens were to see her now. She slept, folded in her husband's arms, more giving and focused than she had been in months. She left him sleeping, as she crept to the kitchen before dawn. Her newfound energy manifested itself in a mound of pancakes, fresh porridge, sausages, a choice of eggs, and a selection of bread. Tea would be made at the first sound of stirring upstairs. The smell of her creations reached her sleeping family sooner than she expected, as Amy put in an appearance.

"Early bird catches the worm," her mother said as she gave her the first hug of the day.

"Oh no, we're having worms again," wailed the child.

"Ah, but you get first choice, the wriggliest and the fattest. Wriggly, just like you."

She wriggled and squiggled as her mother tickled her. That brought Tony and Angela to the kitchen. Tony lifted the lid off a pan, the hot steam and smell of delicious food assailing his senses.

"I was about to give out to someone for waking me up, but I forgive them now that I see the sizzling reason for the fuss." He planted a kiss on his wife's cheek. "You got up early to cook all this. What do we say to Mammy, girls?"

"Thank you" came the chorus, with Amy adding, "Will there be enough for Charly and her mum?"

"Well, that depends on us lot," said Tony, rubbing his hands together in hungry glee. His wife swatted him with the tea towel. He continued, "Go on upstairs now, love, and take your time getting ready. We got this, right girls?"

Nods were all he got; mouths too full to speak. They noticed Angela was managing some creamy porridge and smiled.

Charly and her mother arrived to an over-the-top welcome and mountains of breakfast food. They brought with them an over-the-top number of books, games, and art supplies. Charly had it all planned out for the next few days. First, they had to go to school today. When Madge and the girls left, Tony went upstairs. Angela welcomed the few moments, happily sitting in her comfy new kitchen chair. She closed her eyes and listened to the sounds of her house. She relished being at home.

"Caroline, I think we are being spoiled rotten," her husband announced.

"That's what I've been saying, Tony, over and over." She stood facing him with her back to the dressing table.

"Angela's Purse is paying for our getaway, which means our neighbours, and some people who do not even know us are paying. An envelope arrived for me at the Garda Station last night from Declan. It contained the keys to the apartment and a note saying Pat, from the Seagull, has stocked the fridge in the apartment with some goodies, and we are booked with them for all our meals while we are there. We love that restaurant. Everybody does."

Tony was sitting on the bed as he told her this. She came to join him. Fear of the guilt overtaking her again rose inside as she held on to him. He understood because he felt like that himself at times. The difference was he also understood peoples need to give in practical ways.

"All those people wish they could take Angela's cancer away, make her better, stop her from having to undergo chemotherapy. But they know that is beyond their capabilities Caroline. Instead, they do what they *can* do. They make our lives easier with material things that comfort and pamper." He found himself hugging his wife even tighter.

"Then we have to have the manners to let them do it. Can you imagine their hurt if we didn't? They might never speak to us again."

"I love you. Let's go and do what the good people of Baybridge want."

When Madge returned, she and Angela shooed them out the front door. Tony drove his own car while the Chariot stayed in the driveway just in case. Madge took over as easily as if she were at home, enjoying the quiet contrast.

* * *

"Rose and Rafael are going to find a Bright House near their hospital to make turbans for the children because they don't have any," said Angela, breaking the treasured silence.

Nonplussed, Madge kept on drying a saucer.

"That's interesting news, Angela. I know they had a lot of questions about the foundation," she weakly offered.

"Yes, Rafael says they have their own Sammy and Kitsy and Dymphna, different names of course, but someone has to go and find them a Bright House."

She went back to relaxing, leaving poor Madge drying the already dry saucer.

Mrs. Finnerty was given the same news when she arrived before lunch to let Madge go home for a bit. She took it in her usual nonchalant stride. The last thing Mrs. Costello heard before she reached the front door was her, saying, "Sure Ms. Una can take care of that, no bother." She hurried away before hearing anymore. She was a busy woman.

"Will Ms. Una like to go to London?" Angela continued.

"Do you think we should ask her?"

"Oh yes. Rafael can show her where to look for their own Bright House, and then they can fix it up like ours. He needs her."

"Hm, that would probably work out quite well."

"I'm back," Madge announced as she maneuvered herself and the enormous gift basket from Haymarket down the relatively narrow hallway. "You two still in the kitchen" she commented as she heaved the basket onto the kitchen table.

"Quite cozy here, chatting away about Ms. Una going to London. Angela seems to think Rafael needs her help." Mrs. Finnerty kept her eyes averted.

Madge focused on the basket as she said, "Well, they can help each other."

Case closed.

Then Angela asked, "What's in that huge basket, Mrs. Costello? It's bulging."

"It's from the girls at Haymarket, for you Angela. Dymphna and Mary helped put it together."

"For me? It's not wrapped up or anything, but should I wait till Mammy and Daddy come home before we upset it?" Angela was very proper about this sort of thing.

"What do you think, Mrs. Finnerty?"

"As they said it was for you, Angela, without mentioning any-one else. I'd say it was okay to have a peep. We'll have to put it on the floor, though. Otherwise, you can't see inside."

All three scrutinized the contents until Angela asked if she could have a closer look at three items stacking out near the top. Mrs. Costello surgically excised the articles of interest without any evidence of looting.

"It's a book about Indian culture and history. Look, Mrs. Finnerty, you'll love it. These are sock slippers, much fancier than the ones in the hospital. Oh, this is so soft. It's a white towel dressing gown, with a *hood.*"

"They're gorgeous, Angela, really, they are," Madge commented. Then she readjusted the contents a bit revealing two separate pack-ages, one addressed to Amy and one addressed to Charly.

"How did Charly manage to get her name in there?"

"Don't you know, nothing gets past those Haymarket girls, nothing. It's a good thing we had a look, otherwise, Charly would have missed opening her package with you and Amy," offered Mrs. Finnerty.

Angela seemed to be happy with that explanation. They agreed to open them after they finished their homework.

"My feet get tingly and feel numb. Can I try the new slippers, please?"

They did help the sensation in her feet, so she suggested she walk to the sitting room and have a look at her India book. Mrs. Finnerty tagged along, saying she'd love to have a look as well.

Madge checked the previously stocked fridge with an eye to after-school snacks and tea. Realizing that was more than taken care of, she joined the others in the sitting room on their virtual trip to India and had to pry herself away to get the girls from school.

The rest of the day felt more like home to Madge as all three girls had something to say about something, sometimes at the same time. The homework was light due to the first week of school, which left time for another activity—reading. The girls took turns reading from the new India book. Angela helped when one of the others got stuck on a word. Madge jumping in as a last resort. She went back to the kitchen briefly, returning with the basket in time to hear Charly say, "We have to. We just have to."

"Have to what, pet?" her mother asked from the door.

"Go to India, of course," all three said at once.

"India? Well, now there's an interesting idea."

When the two separate packages addressed to Amy and Charly were opened later, there was no doubt left. They were definitely going to India, wearing the dazzling vibrant silk scarves sent from Haymarket.

Amy recalled how not too long ago she said in Mrs. Finnerty's guest room how the fabric she found in a drawer would make a lovely scarf. The start of it all!

Angela was delighted at finding her own scarf at the very bottom of the basket. When the time was right all three would make that trip, no doubt about it.

Saturday

SHE NEEDED TO have a word with Kitty Walsh this morning. Financial gymnastics were called for if London was to be a success. Her gut instincts told her London was the first in the bigger picture she had envisioned from the start. Mrs. Finnerty's gut instincts had a good track record. She knew Una was meeting with Rose in the afternoon at the Glass Swan. She knew Rafael was bound to be there too.

Midmorning, she telephoned Mrs. Walsh at home who immediately said, "No drama next door?"

"None at all. The gift basket from Dymphna and the others was as big a hit as it was useful," Mrs. Finnerty said.

"No surprise there. How in the world did we get so lucky as to have such genuine people with us? Look at Sammy and Kitsy and Dymphna and Mary. Not to mention Tara and Mrs. Shiva. Then there's Una."

Kitty Walsh was emotional having said all that until her caller intrigued her by saying, "Indeed, *there's Una.*"

"What? Ooooooh, I'm on my way," announced Mrs. Walsh.

"I'll put the kettle on."

Mrs. Finnerty relayed to her good friend and treasurer when she arrived what Angela had announced the day before. "How could I have failed to mention Angela earlier in my list?" her good friend asked herself.

"She has decided that both Una and Rafael need each other, that's all I'm saying," explained the other good friend.

Mrs. Walsh went next door for several reasons: one, to rinse her head of all that was swirling around in there; second, to give Angela her medication and see if Orla from paediatric oncology had drawn Angela's blood yet. She met Orla on her way out from Coughlans.

"Hello there, Mrs. Walsh, Angela is a trooper as usual. Her port-a-Cath is clear post flushing and no sign of a fever. She is in good spirits and enjoying her visitors. Noon meds were given, so I left her upstairs to have a wee rest while the others have a quiet read. I'll get these labs off directly, and she should be good to see Dr. Owens Monday morning."

"Thanks, Orla. Great care as always."

With a wave and a smile for one of the best nurses in town, Mrs. Walsh went in quietly, having first complied with the clean sergeant's hand sanitizing regimen, to see how they were at Coughlans. When she returned to Mrs. Finnerty, she was updated.

"I called Una while you were next door. She's at the gym. I think we should have a chat before she meets with the others later. What do you think? Sorry, didn't make any tea. The girl's ok?"

"I met Orla on her way out. She did an excellent job, as usual, so they are all okay. You, on the other hand, seem to have things a bit backwards. It's your call when to meet people showing an interest Angela's Tresses and Turbans. Rose and Rafael have a few more hours in Baybridge before heading off to the *Big Smoke* full of your ideas. So how did you leave it with Una?"

"I said we would meet her at the Swan for brunch. I'm calling Jimmy. We're having champagne," announced the empowered benefactor.

"We're wearing our rags," protested Mrs. Walsh.

"It's all the fashion," declared Mrs. Finnerty with a twirl.

* * *

Una saw them straight away from her vantage point facing the door. The salmon leap gushed, and the swans preened regardless, as she went to meet them. Their choice of table was simple, close to the river, and room for a few more chairs, should the need arise. Mrs. Walsh noticed a flush in Una's complexion, which of course, one would expect after the gym. Could this be something else? Definitely something else. They settled on the set brunch menu, except for the champagne. Mrs. Finnerty was particular in that regard and ordered something else entirely. The waitress took it all in her stride. Not one for small talk, Mrs. Finnerty cut straight to the point.

"Una, Angela was saying Rafael needs your help in London." At the most opportune or inopportune moment, depending on how you look at it, the waitress arrived with the champagne. "She thinks you should go." Mrs. Walsh was keeping a close eye on Una's complexion. Oh, not the gym, definitely not.

The confident young lady sitting at the table with them simply asked, "How would it work?"

"Mr. Leach, our learned solicitor and his son saw this coming, sooner or later. They already drew up the papers, short and sweet and to the point, using international foundation guidelines. Depending on local regulations, this model can be used all over the world. Find a quiet spot, Una, and look them over before Rose and Rafael arrive. We believe their hearts are in the right place. They just need a nudge. According to Angela, you are the one to do it."

Una begged to be excused, declining the offer of food. She took herself off to a more secluded nook with a view of the swans from a different perspective and began to read.

"Please." Mrs. Finnerty nodded to the patient waitress who might not have been so patient had she not known who Mrs. Finnerty was, and what she was empowering Una to do. She popped the cork with gusto.

"To us, my friend, and the power of Angela's Turbans," toasted Mrs. Walsh.

Una returned to find the bill settled, including a hefty tip and the bottle of champagne still bubbling in the ice bucket on the table. The waitress came to clear the table.

Massie Ryan from the Hill, a new graduate in social services from Galway University, now clearing away dirty dishes, introduced herself to Una, seconds before Rose and Rafael joined her.

* * *

Caroline and Tony enjoyed a splendid brunch at the Seagull. They sat looking at the wild Atlantic waves as they crashed over the enormous boulders, placed there in a sometimes-futile attempt to keep the foaming giant at bay. As with all the buildings here, a narrow road separated them from the sea. It would be impossible for any structure to survive any closer. As it was, the salt spray stripped the paint in patches to the bare wood, giving an ancient well-worn ambience to the whole village. Tony and his lovely wife sat in one of three alcoves with a bird's-eye view. The peeling paint effect, while quaint, did not extend to the interior. Here, they had a salmon pink linen tablecloth draped over a circular table with claw feet. It fitted perfectly in the space. The one shade darker napkins rested on white china. The cutlery was silver. That was all, no frills, no flounces, no flowers and certainly no drapes.

The food was another matter altogether. It wasn't so much the choice of ingredients that set it apart as it was the elegance in its preparation and presentation. All manner of fish, seafood, meat, cheese, salads, fruit, pies, and bread were displayed on silver platters, but in small amounts. The point being the food was replenished frequently ensuring every mouthful was fresh from the kitchen. No congealed remnants to be scraped from the bottom of a dish on this brunch buffet! Caroline noticed this and was duly impressed.

Fully sated and happy, they walked up a little way into the village, but soon, the call of the gulls and the crashing of the waves lured them back. They turned into the wind and braced themselves for the climb up the steepest of the dunes, all the while oblivious to the fact that in their absence, their ten-year-old daughter had just launched Angela's Tresses and Turbans onto the international stage.

Sunday

MRS. FINNERTY KNEW there was an abundance of food in Coughlans, but she couldn't stop herself from popping into Quigley's on her way home. She was up and out early and persuaded herself that Una would love something fresh from the oven, and while she was there, she might just spot something nice for the girls. So, in she went. Several customers milled about, some waiting for their orders, some getting the Sunday paper, and most getting both. Mr. Doherty crossed her mind, which caused her chest to lurch and her breath to catch for a moment. Slowly, the gentle smile of a good memory crept across her eyes.

Mrs. Quigley was at the cash register while her young helper served from the hot display case. As Mrs. Finnerty turned to greet her, the sight of brown bread, fresh from the oven, stopped her. *That's it—that's what we need!* She scanned the nearby display. *Yes, the home- made blackberry jam was right there.*

She trotted off home, happy as Larry.

"It's me, Una, and you'll never guess what I've got."

Una knew she had made a stop at Quigley's and would be equally happy no matter what she had with her.

"Yea, Mrs. Quigley's brown bread and jam. I made a pot of tea, but you might prefer coffee."

"Tea is what's called for here, Una, definitely tea."

"Delicious together," said Una between mouthfuls.

The mumbling sound and licking of jam-smeared fingers and lips were way beyond poor table manners. Neither of them cared.

"What time are you meeting Rose and Rafael?" Mrs. Finnerty stood at the sink, her back to Una as she asked.

"They need to get on the road, so we said at eleven o'clock. Rafael is flying back tonight. Rose is staying with her mother for a little while longer. She hasn't finished at Park Edge, still trying to finalize the yellow cart transaction. Today, she can bring us up to date on what the hospital board's preliminary decision is. Rose made several calls yesterday and finally got in touch with the key players."

She abandoned the dishes while still clutching the tea towel. Taking a seat opposite, she knew she was probably sending Una away, and it hurt. She briefly studied the young woman sitting before her, confirming her to be the most loyal, caring, and honest of people. Una was beautiful, talented, and dedicated to the foundation, and despite her feelings, Mrs. Finnerty knew her future lay elsewhere. London was where she would flourish using her love, training, and experience to add one positive little gift to a sick child.

She said, "If they want to proceed, Una, do you think that would suit you in your heart?"

"Oh yes, Mrs. Finnerty, I think it would."

"Right then, meet me at Pepper with your news. We'll get Laddu for the girls, maybe some of Mr. Shiva's creamy rice pudding for Angela, as her poor mouth is still sore. Later, we will go next door together and tell Angela and her family the news."

* * *

Tony and Caroline slept late having no appetite for a big breakfast. They lolled about the places still in their dressing gowns. The Sunday paper was squeezed expertly through the letter box earlier, and they split it, each taking their favourite section once Tony had brought her up to date on the headlines, none of which was of interest to them today.

Caroline looked up from her crossword and said, "Tony, do you know what I'd love to do today?"

"I don't, but whatever it is, we will do it."

He put the paper down and gave her his full attention. As a police officer, he was very good at paying attention, or so he'd been told.

"How about we drive over to Ewing's Point? I'd love to walk along the strand and maybe get my feet wet, paddle a bit. It's grand here, and the dunes are amazing, but it's too dangerous to go into the water. At Ewing's Point, there are miles of strand close to the water. We could stop in the village first, get a sandwich or something, and eat it on the beach."

He stood up, kissed the top of her head, saying, "So what's keeping you, missus?"

They had to pass close to their house to get there but resisted the temptation to stop. They were still on their break. In a few miles, the first of the village houses came into view. They parked and walked along the road, buildings to their right, calm ocean to the left, framed by a low stone wall. They were on a gradual incline, giving the impression of going *up* to the sea, as a mere slice of blue water separated earth from sky. They walked on, obeying the curve of the road, until it now ran parallel to the shore. Then the miracle of sand and sea came into view way below them. The reaction was universal, even to those who lived in the village. They stopped, stared, wondered, incredulous at its presence.

Tony and Caroline stood and stared. The breeze was gentle, the sun shone, as they dallied in the glory of it all. There was no hurry. Reluctantly, they went in search of lunch. They walked back towards the village along the low stone wall on the shore side of the road.

Spotting a set of ancient salt worn steps, Caroline asked, "Is that a café or deli down by the water?"

"There's a sign above the door. Let's go down and see," answered Tony.

The descent was magical as they got closer and closer to the stony shore. Yachts were dotted about the water, each boasting a sail of vivid colour. The mast stood erect like a ballet dancer on point, as the wind whipped the sail as in a pirouette. One fishing boat was anchored alongside.

"Look, the sign says *Taste*. What a great name for a restaurant. Hope they serve food to go," Caroline wondered.

They did, and as elegant as the food was at the Seagull, *Taste* matched it with its rustic approach. It would be hard to find bad bread in Ireland. Simple fact. However, the bread used to make their sandwiches surpassed all. Tony opted for a roast chicken salad, while Caroline settled on the smoked salmon. Their choices were presented on doorstep thick slices of brown, nutty, grainy, seedy bread, slathered in locally made butter. Then they were wrapped in sturdy greaseproof parchment paper so tightly, the chance of them falling apart before being eaten was slim. Into a bag of similar strength, they went, fit for a journey anywhere, but mostly to withstand the abuse it might get on the strand.

They stood a while outside to recover from the experience of the food and the friendliness of the woman, whose name was Delores, who served them. The few fishermen thereabouts were busy; nevertheless, their greeting and salutes were genuine and added to the memory.

They drove back up the incline, parked, and attacked part of their lunch without being hungry. They couldn't wait to taste what *Taste* had to offer.

They walked down the set of steep steps that led to the second strand, challenged themselves by scrambling over some rocks at the bottom and made a beeline for the water's edge. Now barefoot, Caroline took her first step into the ocean this season without acknowledging the cold sting. She picked up the pace and, without realizing, found herself running, splashes of seawater and sand clinging to the hem of her skirt, and still, she ran. Her husband let her go and walked casually in her wake. Her pace gradually slowed until Tony caught up with her. Hand in hand, they walked and talked for the next hour. They surprised each other when they revealed their private fears for the first time. They confessed their silence was to protect the other and vowed to stop that right now. They would protect each other. They shared their thoughts until their spirit was restored, leaving all the doubts and fears in the magnificent Atlantic Ocean.

Sitting on the top of a dune, they ate the rest of the gigantic sandwich from *Taste*. Now they were ready to go home.

* * *

Mrs. Finnerty and Una dropped in later in the afternoon, and as usual, Amy met them at the door with the hand sanitizing basket, Mrs. Walsh coincidently arrived minutes before them. Madge was about to leave. After the usual exchange of pleasantries and the usual squeal about the Laddu, Mrs. Finnerty asked for a bit of quiet as Una had some news.

Ms. Una said, "Rose's hospital in London has agreed to open a branch of Angela's Tresses and Turbans. Rafael has been authorized to find a suitable location, and the sooner, the better. They have asked me to help set it up. I'll be going to London in a week or two. Congratulations, Angela, you've gone global!"

Angela's parents stared first at Mrs. Finnerty, who was grinning from ear to ear, then Una, finally their daughter. Then everyone clapped and hugged everyone, hugging the same person more than once as the significance of the announcement sank in. Amy made sure Angela remained slightly apart from the others, no hugging. Madge sent Charly to get the camera from the other room.

"It's okay now Mammy, the children will get their turbans. Anyway, Rafael needs Ms. Una," declared Angela

"Can I have a taste of your rice pudding, Angela, on a separate spoon, before you start?" Amy wanted to know. Tony and Caroline exchanged a guilty grin at the word *taste*. That was their little secret.

Madge took some of the best pictures then, unaware of the effect any of her photos would have in the future.

House Calls

BRENDA CALLED DR. Owens at home. "Good morning, Brenda, good weekend?"

"Don't be silly," she quickly replied.

"Not true now, Brenda, and you know it."

"'Tis too, and you know it. Anyway, now that I have escaped the domestic mayhem, I am at my desk and about to forward Angela's results."

"Good, they're back. Is Fiona in yet by any chance?" the doctor asked. It was way too early, but he asked anyway, just to hear the answer.

"Not at all, late as usual" came the long-standing expected reply. "Late for the coffee, late for the tea, late for the lunch, and even late home. She's probably late getting away from the care plan meeting at the centre. I'll page her and tell her not to be late calling you."

"Don't *you* be late home to the family tonight, Brenda. Give them my regards."

"Too late for that, Dr. Owens."

His phone pinged immediately. "Good morning, Fiona. I've just been talking to Brenda. Not keeping you late for anything, am I?"

"I'll kill her!"

"Did you say something, Fiona?" he asked. He was having too much fun to stop.

"Nothing of importance, Doctor, nothing at all."

"Well, that's good, and what's also good are Angela's labs. I'd like to pop in to see her before going in for my ten o'clock. Do you know if her parents got away for a break as we suggested?"

"Yes, they did. They went to the beach. They came back yesterday afternoon. I have them on my schedule for a visit later on this morning. Unless you need me to be there now, I would like you to see them first and assess Caroline. I wanted to discuss her further with you today. She had a bit of a meltdown on Thursday," explained Fiona.

"It's best this way 'round then. See you when you get in. Don't be late." *Click.*

That's the way to start a Monday morning was Dr. Owens's thought as he chuckled to himself. He looked over Angela's results and put them in his bag. He hand carried a manila envelope containing another document, lest he'd forget. Satisfied, he bade his beautiful wife and children farewell and headed for Coughlans. He knew no matter what their state of readiness, he would be welcome. Knowing that made him feel good as did recalling the banter between himself, Brenda and Fiona. Just as he had realized early in his career the importance of the nursing staff, he understood as a G.P. he would be useless without the office staff and social services. They were comfortable with one another and thus had become friends, each knowing their own scope of practice.

"Amy, not time for school yet. Good, I wanted to see you," the doctor said as Amy opened the front door, presenting him with the hand sanitizing basket.

"Good morning, Dr. Owens, don't forget between your fingers."

Satisfied with the procedure, she led him to the kitchen.

"Morning all, hope I'm not too early, thought I might cadge a cup of tea."

"You're welcome any time of the day or night, Dr. Owens, you know that. I was about to make a fresh pot anyway. Tony is getting Angela ready to come down. See, she has a new comfy spot in the kitchen, so that's where she will land." She nodded towards the new chair.

"Perfect, right in the middle of all the action, but first, can I have a word with Amy?"

She was quite comfortably sitting beside him at the table. Caroline turned from the stove, wiping her hands on a towel. Angela and her dad could be heard coming down the stairs. He waited till Angela was settled, greeted them both, and asked Amy to please go stand beside Angela. The twinkle in his eye reassured the parents.

He stood up and formally walked to where the girls were, cleared his throat with melodramatic effect, and said, "Amy Marie Coughlan, on behalf of Dr. Myers and the Infection Control Committee of Park Edge Hospital, I present you with this certificate of excellence, signed by Dr. Gwendoline Myers."

"What?" She lowered it in front of her seated sister to confirm what it said then read it aloud for further confirmation.

"Congratulations, Amy. It's well-deserved. Word reached Dr. Myers on the amazing job you were doing. Ms. Rose Peterson and Rafael were full of praise."

Tony and Caroline were speechless.

Angela said, "You are the best clean sergeant ever. Thank you."

The sideways hug they exchanged was a testament to that.

"Any sign of that cup of tea, Caroline?" the doctor asked over Tony's shoulder as he was being squeezed in a manly backslapping bear hug.

During the scrutinizing of the certificate, Angela said, "Should she take it to school to show the teacher Mammy? They should see it at school."

All eyes on Angela as they once more witnessed her generosity towards her young sister, wanting to boast about her to everyone.

"What a grand idea, pet. Let's put it back in the envelope so it doesn't get creased. Daddy is taking you to school today 'cos Dr. Owens and I are going to have that cup of tea." She placed a slow deliberate kiss on the top of both her daughters' heads. Amy was almost out the front door then stayed her dad with a touch on his arm. She ran back to the kitchen, book bag bobbing up and down on her slender back. Throwing her arms awkwardly around the seated doctor's neck, he heard her whisper *thank you.* "That's one happy little girl," stated her mother.

Once they had been reassured that all the labs looked very good, with no sign of anything abnormal, including kidney function, Angela asked to be excused. "My India book is in the front room, so I'll try out my new walking socks and go sit there for a while. See you soon, Dr. Owens, and thanks for Amy's certificate."

"No bother. See you on my way out."

"That's okay. I'll be stuck in the book by then."

"I suppose she's onto us Caroline, so tell me about your getaway."

"Two things to report. Even before leaving here, Tony and I started to open up to each other, and that got easier and easier. We discovered we were keeping things in to spare each other, often the same doubts and fears. We vowed to stop that right now. I ran as fast as I could in the sea, unaware of its cold, and I left my pain and smothered anguish in the Atlantic. Thank you for sending us."

He noticed she was smiling through tear-filled eyes. As he left, he bade farewell to Angela sitting behind the front room's closed door. Angela, too, was smiling.

* * *

Fiona was delighted when she heard the doctor's account on his return to the office. She told him of her conversation with Caroline. He paused, taking his time before answering.

"Fiona, I have firsthand knowledge of the power of the Atlantic in these matters, believe me. But as powerful as it is, I agree something else might be going on here, something the ocean might need a little help with. Dr. Myers is the right person to go forward with this, casually introducing Caroline to the family counselling services as a matter of course. I'll put her in the picture. If need be, she can continue here in Baybridge. There's a way to go yet."

"Isn't that the truth. Caroline knows that too. I'm sure she will not reject the help. I'll update my notes then. Thanks, Doctor." As she reached the door, she heard him call her name.

"Fiona, thank you. Don't be late writing those notes now." He ducked under his modest desk, the one he had since medical school. It was his father's.

* * *

Caroline was barely back in the kitchen when the phone rang. *Busy morning at the Coughlans!* "Good morning," said a youthful voice. My name is Geraldine Nolan, and I'm calling from the home-school program at St. Paul's. I hope this is a good time to catch you."

"Good morning. Dr. Owens just left, so it's just Angela and me for the minute. Fiona Hannon said you would be calling."

"Routine visit from the doctor, I hope?"

"Oh yes, just routine."

"Glad to hear that. Is there a chance I could come by today? I won't keep you very long. I would like to meet you and Angela and tell you a wee bit as to how the program works. If Angela is up to it."

"I think she would like to meet you. She and our next-door neighbour, a retired teacher and good friend, have been doing some journal work and other little projects all along. We would like her to be here when you come."

"That's the sort of thing we love to hear around here. Mrs. Hannon hinted at some work being done all right."

"Around here, there is always some kind of *work*, as you call it, being done. You'll see."

"Intrigued," said Mrs. Nolan.

"We get a lot of that too," replied Caroline. They settled on half past three when Amy would be home from school.

As Brenda had previously said, Mrs. Nolan was indeed a nice lady. Her purpose today was to meet the family, learn the medical condition of the child and their tolerance for a learning program. Modifications were common, allowing for a wide variety of capabilities. The main thrust at the beginning was to keep the child's interest in learning and avoid a complete start over after recovery. Well, she needn't have worried about any of that in this household.

"Good afternoon Mrs. Nolan, I'm Caroline. Come on back. They're all here in the kitchen."

The sight that met her eyes was not one she had expected. Hitherto, she met her pupils in their bedrooms or propped up, convalescent style in an armchair.

"Girls, this is Mrs. Nolan from St. Paul's. Here is Mrs. Finnerty from next door, and that's Amy, Angela's sister."

"Then this must be Angela."

By now, Amy was on her feet, whispering to her mother, "Did you use the sanitizing basket?"

"No, here it is. You're much better than I am."

Amy went straight into action, giving strict instructions to the newcomer. All that done, she was invited to join them at the table.

"It's nice to see you all at work. What are you having them do, Mrs. Finnerty?"

"Oh, I'm here in case a pencil needs sharpening or something. Amy is doing her homework for today. Angela, why don't you tell Mrs. Nolan about the project we started in Park Edge? I'm afraid it's spread all over the table at the minute."

"Hello, Mrs. Nolan, We went to Haymarket where they make the turbans, on our way to the hospital in Dublin. They gathered samples of receipts, invoices, fabric, cost of transportation. Lots of things to put in my report for school. The Twins Killfeather gave me a very old velvet journal to write it all down. Mammy and Mrs. Finnerty said it was too precious for school, so we got a jotter instead. Amy got a certificate from Dr. Myers for how well she makes people wash their hands. Show Mrs. Nolan, Amy."

Mrs. Finnerty observed the skilled home tutor navigate the condensed version of events and bring it all together by saying, "Amy, I can see why you got an *excellence* judging by the lesson you gave me today on the proper way to clean *my* hands. Well done. I can see Angela; your standards are equally high to have put that report together. I'll leave you to continue the work in your own good time. Then we can send it into the program. I brought some suggestions for homework with me today, but I can see that won't be necessary. Do you mind if I take a peek at that colourful book beside you?"

"Certainly. It's about India where Mrs. Finnerty used to teach and where all the fabric for the turbans comes from. Dymphna and Mary in Haymarket sent it with these scarves," explained Angela.

"They are beautiful, Angela," remarked Mrs. Nolan.

"Yes, they are. Amy and Charly got one too. We were just working on the plan for our trip to India before you came in. We are too young now, but it's good to plan anyway."

"It certainly is, Angela," replied the young tutor, thinking, *So much for my plan.*

"Would it still be all right to leave the homework you brought?"

"I can do that, certainly," replied Mrs. Nolan.

"*Education is not the filling of a pail but rather the lighting of a fire,*" said Mrs. Finnerty, quoting W. B. Yeats.

As Mrs. Nolan left the Coughlan's house, her thought was how bright that fire burned therein.

Swan Lake

UNA AND MRS. Finnerty were having a bit of breakfast together on the patio. It was a lovely morning. It didn't feel a bit like autumn. The sun was warm, the absence of a breeze was noteworthy, and the birds chirping reminded one of spring. As with all the weather patterns in Ireland, ten minutes was all it took to move from one season to another. For now, they enjoyed what they had. Mrs. Miller, the windowsill cat, on hearing voices, sauntered around the side of the house, checking if there was anything that needed her attention. Satisfied all was in order, she sneaked off, unobserved, to her usual perch in the warm early morning sun.

While polishing off the last of the brown bread and blackberry jam, Una said, "Mrs. Finnerty, you have been kind and generous to me since we met. I am so grateful for all you have given me. What I really want you to know is how you changed my life. Before Angela's Tresses and Turbans, I had no idea what my place in the world was. I doubted my ability to be effective in the way I have always wanted to. You have given my life purpose, and I have no way of showing you what that means."

Neither did she have any way to stop the tears. Her experienced house friend knew the tears would stop themselves. She waited.

"Una, you are a smart, intelligent young woman with so much to give. We are the lucky ones to have you with us. You are perfect for the London project. You also need to be aware that this is the start of something much bigger. You have a bright future ahead, which you must pursue wherever it leads. I will miss you, nevertheless. Now let's eat the jam before we both cry and salt it with our tears."

They eased into silence, broken eventually by Una. "Remember the waitress at the Glass Swan who waited so patiently to open the champagne?"

"We were a long time, weren't we? She was patient and very polite."

"She spoke to me when she was clearing the table. Turns out she knew who you were and the work of the foundation. She didn't mind waiting. She just finished her degree in social science at Galway. Her name is Maisy Ryan, and she is from the Hill."

"That's very interesting. Do you think Sammy knows her?"

"Would it be okay to ask?"

"I think you must, in the next day or two, don't you think? I'm thinking you have something in mind, Una."

"Far be it from me to overstep, but I liked her while she was serving the table. Something about her caught my attention. After she spoke, I thought of my leaving and what an excellent opportunity I was given as a new grad. I think it's worth looking into."

"I see. Talk with Sammy, Kitsy too. If Sammy thinks she might suit us, then it will be time to bring in Fiona. Look at you, spotting a potential replacement in the most unlikely of places. London has no idea what's coming their way."

Another comfortable silence.

"There are certain things I will miss there. I know that for sure. Remember how we said we should go see the swans more often. Do you think we could round the girls up after school one day? I can drive to the slope at the far end of the park. It's very close, so not much of a walk for Angela. Rose and Rafael are more than keen to find a Bright House or a Haymarket of their own. They want me to come in the next few days. Is that an unreasonable request, do you think?"

"Una, did Fiona or Sammy or Tara think they were being *unreasonable* when we first started? I would say warp speed best describes the pace. When an idea such as this matures in the soul, there is no waiting. Fear it might not come to pass is the driving force. That you might miss an opportunity to brighten one child's life if you delay is not an option. Go to them and allay their fears. Be prepared because you will be doing this a lot in the future and not only in the UK."

"Can we go to Swan Lake tomorrow? Angela will be returning to Park Edge in a few days, and I think I should spend a couple of nights with my parents before flying out. Mrs. Finnerty, it's going to be a shock to them."

"My dear, Una, not a bit of it, believe me."

* * *

The excursion to the lake generated much excitement. It was as much about the preparation as it was about feeding a duck or any waterbird. Normally, you gather the food in a plastic bag, go to where you know the birds are, call to them, throw the food, and watch them eat. That was the usual course of events—not today. As the children approached the slipway bags of food at the ready, all seemed well. Mayhem ensued when the first morsel hit the water. Two massive swans appeared from a bend in the river, wings spread like parachutes. They literally attacked the ducks. Every bit of food was brutally scavenged almost before it hit the water. Now you would expect the girls to retreat in fear for their lives, but not this lot. They stepped closer, shooing the big birds away in favour of the ducks. That was a waste of time as the battle raged on.

"I've never seen anything like this. Don't get any closer girls."

Una took a few steps back, holding Angela's hand. They could hardly hear each other over the quacking of the ducks and the trumpet cry of the swans.

"Don't throw any more food, girls," instructed Mrs. Finnerty.

"But we want to feed them."

Reluctantly, they stopped. Una asked for some of the food and moved further along the lakeshore to lure one or other of the species to another spot. Only one young duck took the bait. More earsplitting ructions as the swans spat at their food rivals.

Then Angela, who by now was sitting further back on a low wall, shouted, "Look, look, the swans have babies over there in the rushes! They're trying to get the food for the babies!"

Now what was a person supposed to do?

Sure enough, that's what that was all about. On the way home in the car, the ethical dilemma remained. This story would be hashed and rehashed whenever they were together for years to come, still unable to decide which side was more deserving, always ending with what Angela said aloud that day to nobody in particular, "Well, that's what *we* do. We fight to get the turbans to the children."

Una's Plans

MADGE WENT STRAIGHT to the Bright House after she dropped Charly at school. Much as she welcomed her daughter's passion, she had about enough of the duck/swan story. She popped her head around Una's open door as she passed. Finding her on the phone, she made her way to the studio.

"Morning, Sammy," she greeted, plopping down on Kitsy's empty stool.

"All alone this morning? Will I make the tea?"

"Would you mind? I have to finish this piece in a hurry. Fiona called to say our young Marty McKenna has been touting our business, showing off his turban all about the place. I finished one yesterday, but this one needs a bit more work," explained Sammy.

"No Kitsy today?"

"Not till later. She's away off to see her young sister receive an award at some literary club. She has a few already. It seems this is a big one, though." Sammy offered, the head down, engrossed in the sewing, without looking up.

"Literary award, that's something to be proud of." The more Madge was exposed to the power of thought and word, the more her photographic acumen developed.

Una appeared. Noticing Kitsy's absence, she casually mentioned Maisy from the Hill. Now hearing the familiar name, Sammy took a break from her stitching and looked up.

"Maisy Ryan, is it? Lovely girl, smart as a whip without being smart. Her dad is a dab hand with woodwork, works in the college with Fiona's husband. Her mother works up the back hill at the hospital, catering department I believe. Lovely family." Madge went about her business, unaware of what was afoot.

"Mrs. Finnerty and I met her at the Glass Swan on Sunday. She and I got talking while I was waiting for Rose and Rafael. She just graduated from Galway with a similar degree to mine. She's waiting tables in the meantime, hoping for an opportunity in her field. It turns out I must leave for London by the end of the week. Mrs. Finnerty agreed that Rose should push ahead like we did at the beginning."

"That's very sudden all right Una, but it's not goodbye. Sure you'll be back and forth all the time. Are ye thinking to give Maisy that opportunity?"

"Your opinion is important, Kitsy too, if you think she would fit in here at the Bright House."

"There is only one Una, never be another. From what I know of the Ryans, they are a great family. As I said, Maisy is a dedicated girl who worked hard to put herself through school, even contributed at times to help her mam. You know how the Hill families are. Kitsy may know her from a different viewpoint as they are closer in age. Let's see what she thinks when she gets in." Sammy went back to her stitching. Madge elbowed her way back with three mugs of tea. Una took her mug to her office.

Kitsy arrived just before lunch, proud as punch of her younger sister. "Aw, Sammy, you should have seen her. She sat on a stool and read from her short story to a room full of mostly strangers. They all stood up and clapped when she finished."

"Was she nervous? I'd be shaking in my boots," said Sammy.

"Not at all. She took her award and some lovely flowers, gave a little bow, and walked off with the chairlady of the Baybridge Writers Guild, Junior. Cool as a cucumber she was."

"Imagine that, at her age, the wee dote. What's the story called?"

"'Marty,'" said Kitsy and waited for the penny to drop.

"'Marty'? Our Marty? *Maharaja Marty?*"

"The very one."

Up until now, Madge was sitting at the little out of the way table, which was affectionally known as the news desk, on the fringes of the conversation. Now she sat bolt upright.

"Madge, did you hear that?" asked Sammy. The use of first names had long replaced the formal use of missus, except in the case of Mrs. Finnerty. That would never change, and she no longer protested. "The real story or based on him? Does he know?"

"His real story. Of course, he knows. He was there with his mam and dad."

"Kitsy, I'm sitting here finishing off one of the turbans right now. Look."

"I know you are, and they are the bones of the story. Before the two of you ask, I did not know myself until today. She tells it in a lovely way. You'll be very proud. Madge, time to catch up with them, don't you think?" prompted Kitsy. "I might happen to know where they are headed, near swans I believe."

"What a scoop!" She slung her camera bag over her shoulder and almost collided with Una in the doorway.

"Breaking news?" Una asked.

"Huge," both the girls said at once. They brought Una up to speed who agreed this was huge.

"Something else that could be huge is Una heading off to London sooner than we thought. Mrs. Finnerty and Ms. Una here, were wondering if young Maisy Ryan, who graduated from Galway with a degree in social science, might fit in here with us when Una goes off galivanting. What do you think, Kitsy?" asked Sammy.

"Are you serious about this? We walked down the town together only the other day. She's working at the Glass Swan at the minute. She's always working somewhere, but she mentioned she was worried about finding something in her field locally. She likes to be near her family. I said something was bound to turn up. Una, could this be it?"

"Looks more and more like it now, Kitsy. Sammy already thought she would be good here. Can you get hold of her and ask her to contact me. I don't want to go barging into her current place of work. Then if she wants to, I'll set up an interview with Fiona."

* * *

Maisy Ryan joined Sammy and Kitsy on the following Monday under Fiona's supervision. In truth, she was well up to the task, and in no time at all, she was flying solo.

Somehow, Una asked Angela if it was okay to break out the cake they were saving, thinking it was a suitable time to share it. So, to celebrate Angela nearing the end of her treatments, Una moving to London, Maisy starting at the Bright House, and Marty's short story, they gathered together in the Bright House, and Ms. Una and Angela cut the cake together, hand over hand. Madge stopped randomly clicking, put her camera aside, and asked for everyone's attention. She had in her hand a colourful brochure, held aloft.

"I have here a prototype of Angela's Tresses and Turbans news-letter. The hope is to publish monthly with input from the children we serve, their families, staff, various experts and local contributors, or anything else inspiring that comes along. This month's features excerpts from 'Marty,' the award-winning short story written by Kitsy's young sister, Colette Ryan. In acknowledgment of the exqui-site fabric sent to us from India and the influence of our dear bene-factor Mrs. Finnerty, we call our publication *Indigo Crown*. Feel free to look through it at your leisure. I left a plethora of photos out for you all to go through and select a few to include. I can't wait for your feedback, and don't be shy, it's your news we are sharing, so everyone has a say. It's a way to keep the community informed and involved in what we passionately do at the foundation."

Mrs. Finnerty, standing at the back of the group, caught Madge's eye and surreptitiously nodded her approval, while the others exam-ined the document in awe. Squeals from the photograph table light-ened the mood. While they were excited and proud of their progress, the response to the newsletter was somewhat muted. It worried some of them that this could be seen as bragging, a quality totally alien to them.

Kitty Walsh put it best when she said, "Every organization worth its salt communicates with its clients. We don't have clients. We are a family. Una is about to take us overseas. No matter how far and wide Angela's Tresses and Turbans reaches, *Indigo Crown* will always trace it back to Baybridge. That's all of us. It's good to be quiet. I see you all reflecting inwardly on the enormity of what you have taken on and the difference you are making, each little stitch at a time. It's the little things that count."

Mrs. Finnerty's voice reached the crowd, saying, "Let them eat cake," causing peals of laughter and relaxation around the room.

St. Margaret's

HILLGATE HOSPITAL ENCOMPASSED three wings divided by main roads. St. Margaret's wing sat in the centre, forming three sides of a quad. The classrooms and faculty offices lay straight ahead as you approached, flanked on the right by the residences for nurses and doctors and on the left by administration. A large manicured lawn dotted with well-tended flower beds and filigree iron benches, carpeted the green space, replacing the fourth side of the quad. St. Margaret looked down from atop her marble plinth in the center, watching over them all. A bank of popular tennis courts snuggled behind the residential area. To the left of St. Margaret's wing, through an ancient wrought-iron gate and across the road, sat Hillgate Wing, the oldest of the three, home to paediatric oncology and orthopaedics. From the right side, a concrete path led to the busiest and widest of the dividing main road across which Ridgewood Wing, where the medical and general surgical patients were cared for, loomed above the city.

"Una, Una, over here" were the first words she heard on English soil.

She traced their source, finding Rafael waving furiously to attract her attention at the arrival gate. They spoke little while they navigated their way through the airport. She hardly noticed when he took her hand as they stepped off the escalator or before stepping onto the moving walkway. Soon, they were in the London

Underground, awaiting the first of two tubes that would take them north to Hillgate. They went straight to St. Margaret's wing, where Rose and another lady awaited them in her office.

"You made it, Una. How was the flight?" greeted Rose.

"Short and sweet, you might say. Without Rafael though, the tube journey would have been a whole other story. I'd still be wandering around underground, trying to make sense of the convoluted map."

"Oh, you'll get the hang of it in no time. Come and meet Monica Williams. She is our director of social services. Monica, this is the wonderful Una Flynn I've been raving about."

"Finally. It's good to meet you." Monica Williams was a woman in her late thirties, early forties. She wore a lightweight navy suit, a hint of lavender showing at the neck. Her loose brown curls bobbed a bit as she spoke, adding emphasis to her words.

"Tea or coffee anyone?" Rafael asked.

Rose answered for them, saying, "I think a pot of tea would be lovely, right girls?"

As if the choice was expected, a young girl arrived almost immediately with a tray. While they sipped their tea, Una explained the key role social services played in the organization.

"We like to respond to a particular child's request. The turbans are their own promoters. A child sees another wearing one, which piques their interest. One thing leads to another, and before you know it, instead of one, you might need four."

"I love that concept," said Monica, scooting forward in her chair.

"Let me show you one, and you will see the vibrancy and feel the texture of the fabric for yourself."

As Una spoke, she produced the sample package sent by Mrs. Shiva from her bag. She gently unwrapped it, allowing the magic of the contents to speak for itself. The deal was sealed there and then without a single word.

Monica offered to take their guest to the residence where a room was made ready for her. "If you would prefer to be off campus, that can also be arranged," added Monica.

"Not at all. I'd much prefer to be in the residence. I'm looking forward to exploring the grounds later," replied Una.

Rose, caught up in the excitement of the moment, realized she had not told Una what she had planned for the remainder of the day. She jumped in saying, "Una, before you go with Monica, we should go over the plans for the day, so you know what you are doing. We thought you would like to meet Ruth Anderson, chairwoman of St. Margaret's Ladies Guild, a lovely lady and leader of the artistic group who are chomping at the bit to see one of Angela's turbans. She's joining us for lunch. That will give you time to relax a bit beforehand."

So, the two set off, along a path leading to the entrance to the residence.

"Mrs. Williams, the quad reminds me of St. Swithun's, my university in Dublin," commented Una.

"Not nearly as old or historic I fear, and call me Monica, please."

This was a much older section of the wing than the one they had just left. They pushed through a heavy wooden door that opened in the center, one half of its gleaming brass knocker going in the opposite direction to the other. A fixed stained-glass half-moon panel spanned the width at its top. To the right immediately inside the door, a bank of well-used wood pigeonhole mail/message boxes completely covered the wall. Various pieces of paper, envelopes, and small packages stuck out at odd angles.

"Archaic, but surprisingly, it works," said Monica, unable to stop her eyebrows from rising.

"Just like home," added Una, allowing her eyebrows to do as they pleased. To the left, an unoccupied office with a laden-down sturdy desk could be seen through its open door. Pile upon pile of paper material covered its entire surface.

Una cast a questioning glance at Monica who shrugged, saying, "Sorting office maybe."

Una was not sure if she should believe that or not.

They took the curved stairs to the third floor and turned left. Her room was basic but large, with its own bathroom. A desk with a matching chair and a small floral upholstered two-seater sofa sat against one wall. A TV with its remote control and all such gadgets seemed at odds with the room, standing there on a very modern metal perch. A freestanding wardrobe and a tiny chest of drawers adorned the other wall. The view from the large sash window delighted and surprised as it framed the quad below and a picture of the spires, rooftops, and distant parks of North London. She had no idea the hospital was located on such a high hill.

"We thought you'd appreciate the vantage point. Settle in, and I'll come and fetch you for lunch."

Monica left her, turning this way and that as she tried to map out her new surroundings from above.

* * *

Ruth Anderson arrived as they were orienting themselves to the bustle of a large hospital cafeteria. All manner of uniformed staff milled about with trays held at odd angles as they sought friends, coworkers, and some, just an empty chair. She spotted Rose at once, seated at her usual table, her confidence conveying she had every right to be there.

"Here comes Ruth now," said Monica, "fashionably late."

Una watched her approach, thinking her to be in her mid-fifties, a little on the chubby side. She wore a black knit calf-length dress that even from a distance screamed *designer*. A multicoloured silk scarf hung from neck to hem, as elegantly casual as Una had ever seen. Her hair was cut as short as it could be and still maintain the spike It was platinum blond. Gold-stud earrings adorned each lobe, a bracelet similarly studded hung on her right wrist. Her feet were nestled in burgundy suede pumps with the thinnest of gold rims outlining the heel.

"I'm late, again aren't I?" she said in a surprisingly soft voice. "Is this the lovely Una? I'm Ruth from the Guild. We're all on tenterhooks waiting to see our first turban." Though her voice was almost sultry, it was not affected. The woman was genuinely emotional.

"It's a pleasure to meet you. Rose and Monica have been telling me about how artistic your group is. I can see from your dress and scarf they were not exaggerating."

236

"Oh, don't pay them any heed. They know I've had this dress for years. I used to work as a cutter for Yves Saint Laurent in town, made this from some leftover scraps one day. I wear it a lot. I do have to give him full credit for the scarf though, gorgeous, isn't it?"

"We have had the pleasure of seeing the turbans and some fabric samples," cut in Monica, giving poor Una a chance to recover from that bit of disclosure. She remembered how flabbergasted she was on first hearing that story.

"Yes, and I can assure you they will blow your socks off," added Rose.

"So, what are we doing sitting here then?"

"Getting lunch. Una has travelled and must be hungry. All in good time, Ruth."

"That was thoughtless of me, Una. I can…"

"I'm okay really. Maybe we can get a sandwich or something to go," suggested Una.

"If you're sure, we could ask Janet Keating to meet us in Hillgate. Janet is the director of nursing services for the wing. She is very keen to get this show on the road. You have everything with you, Una?"

"All here," she said, patting her leather bag.

Gate House

THE BUILDING WAS indeed old, but the interior certainly had a makeover. The original long narrow corridors appeared wider and more welcoming due to the strategic placement of a mural and artwork, no doubt courtesy of the children. The ward had been reconfigured to allow for single rooms, private treatment areas, and a smattering of small lounge chairs, randomly placed. The ambience was one of devil-may-care untidiness while the infection control precautions were evident. There was no sign of a nurses' station or a uniformed staff person. Janet Keating, wearing casual street clothes, was much younger than Una expected, especially holding the position of director of nursing services.

It pleased Una to see that, noticing her voice was light and jovial as she said, "Welcome, ladies, come on in here and eat your lunch while I return a phone call." She opened a door to what was probably the staff lounge/meeting room. Things were very casual here.

"There goes our Janet, always on the go," said Monica. It turned out they were hungry after all and polished off their sandwiches seconds before Janet returned.

"Monica, can you spare a minute before you leave?" she asked before sitting down.

The social worker understood it was in connection with the phone call and merely nodded. Rose introduced Una.

Ruth, unable to contain herself further, cut in, saying, "Oh, please, please, can you just show us."

"Well, that's the ice broken I suppose," said Rose. "Go ahead, Una, put her out of her misery."

Una placed her precious parcel on the table. Both Janet and Ruth slid their chairs forward. Tissue paper yielded to Una's fingers, crinkling its way flat enough to expose two girls' turbans, two maharaja turbans, each with distinct colours, two logos, and several folded swaths of fabric. An envelope from Mrs. Shiva was enclosed. It took a while for anyone to speak, and then they couldn't be stopped.

"What's in the envelope?" asked Ruth.

"Go ahead, open it," urged Una.

"It's a greeting from the designer, a Mrs. Shiva in Haymarket, Ireland. Look, she sent drawings, patterns, and notes of well wishes from all the staff. Sammy and Kitsy also sent their best from Baybridge. There's a list of fabric vendors and loads of other info. I can't believe it. It's all so beautiful." She rewrapped the package as best she could and slid it across the table to Rose.

"Ruth, you need to keep that. No doubt you will need it."

"I will, won't I? Oh my gosh, wait till the ladies see this. They will be blown over by the quality. I hope we can measure up."

Una was getting to like these ladies more and more and found herself saying, "When Mrs. Shiva and the girls at home realize a Yves Saint Laurent cutter is leading the pack, I think they will be the ones blown over."

All present had to agree. Janet Keating, who until now was an observer said, "We will all be overcome when we see our first little girl wearing her turban. Thank you, Una and Angela's Tresses and Turbans. That phone call confirmed our beauty shop has already styled her hair. Anita is seven years old and very excited."

"Time's a-wasting," Ruth announced as she rose from her chair and gathered her parcel. "I need to get hold of Florence so she can summon the girls. We have work to do."

Rose and Monica stayed behind on the ward while Una and Ruth headed back towards St. Margaret's. They parted ways, leaving Una to her own devices for the afternoon. She welcomed the chance to be alone, to wander the area and explore her surroundings from the ground rather than from her room. She was looking up at the building, trying to find her window when she almost bumped into a man sharing the same narrow path.

"I beg your pardon," said a voice with a trace of an accent. "I honestly did not see you there. Are you okay?"

"It's my fault entirely. I just got in from Ireland this morning, and I was trying to locate my window with the splendid view. I should watch where I'm going."

"Ireland! Why would you do such a thing as that?" he asked in earnest.

"Leave Ireland or look for my window?"

"You're teasing me now. Why *did* you leave Ireland?" They were close to one of the benches, so he indicated they should sit. "By the way, my name is Amir. I'm one of the doctors."

"My name is Una, and I'm a social worker here from Ireland to launch Angela's Tresses and Turbans." She continued to tell him the whole story, including Ruth and the Yves Saint Laurent connection. She failed to notice how much he was enjoying her telling of things and how much he was smiling until she had almost finished.

"Are you making fun of me?" she asked.

"Not at all. It's the way you tell it. Now I must tell you something. I'm an oncology dermatologist on the team with David Brown, orthopaedics, and Garry Evans Oncology. It seems we will be working together. Appearances matter to these children and to me. Rumour had it, something was afoot with turbans, and nothing could please me more."

"Yes, we have seen that time after time. We also have a line for the little boys. That's all very well, but we must find a suitable place to make them," Una explained, "preferably on the premises."

He jumped up, saying, "Come and take a look at this."

She followed him along the path, retracing her steps until they turned left just before the gate and up a slight knoll. There, overrun by brambles and bushes, sat the quaintest of structures.

"It's the old gatehouse," Amir explained. "Let's get a closer look, but be careful, these bushes might be thorny."

They peered in the windows but could see very little. The front door was locked, so they walked around the side gable. Then she saw it. Beyond the wilderness stood a one-story long building with windows everywhere.

"Look, what's that building back there?" she asked as she made her way through the brush.

Dr. Amir followed equally intrigued.

"What's this?" he asked himself. "I haven't noticed this before. I take pictures of all sorts of odd things in case you were wondering," he added for Una's benefit.

She looked over her shoulder and smiled. They traipsed all over the place and found it to be a one-room building with a long wooden structure, akin to a thin butcher's block, running down the center, parallel to the windows. They couldn't see much more. Una thought she was dreaming. She could not help thinking how much it reminded her of the Bright House. As they made their way back to the quad, they speculated as to what its original use could possibly have been. They went from the ridiculous to the sublime with no solution. She had to get hold of Rose.

"Thank you so much for finding it no matter what it used to be. Really, Thank you."

"Actually, it was you who found it. It may not be your Bright House, but it is the Gate House." Amir was very pleased with the discovery as he made his way back to the oncology wing to check in on his seven-year-old patient.

* * *

Lionel Pinkerton, a kind man and chief administration officer, was approached by Rose about the gatehouse and its other structure. He had to make inquiries about the single-story building. As far as anyone could tell, it was a receiving depot for deliveries when the gatehouse was a barrier to the outside world. Anyhow, he authorized the maintenance department to check out the condition of both and report back. He said time was of the essence. Within a day, the long building, which was a more modern but simple construction, was declared safe, and the crew began clearing the ground around both. The gatehouse assessment would take a lot longer.

Una invited Dr. Amir to come with them when Rose, Ruth, Monica, and Florence went to inspect the place. He brought his camera. Was he to be their Madge, always with the camera at the ready? Mr. Lionel Pinkerton and his secretary surprised them, arriving minutes later. Rafael was beaming, standing beside Una. Ruth laid a linen cloth on the wooden workbench that had not yet been smoothed. Florence stood beside her as together they unfurled another cloth wrapper. That was when the first of Angela's Tresses and Turbans outside Ireland was shown. Florence gently handed it to Monica.

"It's for Anita."

Dr. Amir stepped forward under the guise of a photographer. His interest was much more than that. Anita was his patient!

Baybridge

AMY STAYED WITH Mrs. Finnerty while her dad took Angela back to Dublin. She was quite happy for him to stay the whole week or whatever time it took, but they settled on him coming back on Monday. As a family, they thought Amy needed a parent home this time around. Their neighbour agreed with them. All the same, she planned a bit of spoiling of her own for Amy and rejoiced in the fact she got to do one school pickup and one drop-off with two whole days in between. She hoped and prayed that one more chemo cycle would bring an end to these ordeals.

"We can go to the admissions office and take a weight off our feet while we finish this paperwork. Angela can show Muriel where everything goes, right Angela?" Dr. Myers introduced Muriel to Caroline and Tony when they arrived. "This is one of our students from St. Swithun's. Muriel, meet the Coughlans."

She had grey eyes set in a heavily freckled face, crowned by a mop of wild red curls and a smile that could crack a stone. Right away, they were taken with her.

"What a lovely girl," Caroline said as they crossed the hall to the office. Caroline and Tony recalled the first time they sat in this same place with fear in their hearts. They wondered if it was any less now.

"She is lovely and a great student. I'm glad you like her because she is all yours for the remainder of Angela's treatments, this cycle and the next. There is no indication that further chemo will be appropriate after that," explained the doctor. Caroline grabbed her husband and burst into tears. Giving her a moment or two, she continued, "You both have travelled this road with stellar bravery and courage. You have been the least demanding parents in our history, in fact never demanding anything. The wonderful community support you have at home is amazing, but the burden has been yours, and that takes its toll. Caroline, Muriel will share that burden with you while Angela is here, and she will follow up with you both while you are at home." Angela's parents looked at each other and, without a hint of resistance, accepted the presence of the beautiful Muriel. Dr. Myers could see their bodies unfurl as their shoulders separated from their ears for the first time in months. "You have been keeping up appearances for your good neighbours too, which is an added stressor. All that help will still keep coming because they really care for you, but now you have Muriel, and you can speak openly and frankly to her at any time. One more thing, Caroline, I would like you to join the group we have here in house. Take a break, mix with other family members, and freely express your feelings in confidence. Muriel and Angela will be fine. Both of you can give it a try together before you go home Tony."

This was a game changer for the family as they flourished and healed. Muriel stayed in touch long after the last chemo cycle ended.

* * *

Madge was adamant about getting input from everyone involved before she went any further with the newsletter. Did they like the title, was the layout okay, was the content relevant and should they have one at all? She got a resounding *yes* from all before she told them her plan. She approached her photographer friend who helped put Mrs. Finnerty's album together. He was most helpful and commended her on her idea, asking her to give him a week or two.

Sammy and Kitsy were happy to have Maisy on board. She settled in well, and Fiona was surprised at her knowledge. One morning at the Bright House, while they were discussing a new referral, Maisy asked, "Does anyone from here visit our little customers while they are in the hospital?"

Sammy and Kitsy, needles paused in mid stitch, looked up. Madge leaned back in her chair at the news desk. She had no idea that's what editors did in movies.

"Grainne and the other hairstylist see them if they visit them in their homes," answered Fiona.

"I see," was all Maisy had to say.

She seemed disappointed as she continued reviewing the new request with Fiona. Sensing this, Fiona was prompted to ask, "Did you have something in mind?"

"I just had this notion how nice it would be for one of us to meet with the little ones in person from time to time. I understand the need for limiting their exposure to all in sundry. It was just a thought. I was trying to imagine our newest referral wearing her turban and if she wondered who made it." An introspective silence fell upon them. Maisy, her half-baked interest in the papers in front of her waning said, "What about a video of Sammy and Kitsy at work?"

It didn't take much down Baybridge way to spur the folks into action. Madge went straight home without a word and fumbled with the many settings on her camera. Without doing a hands turn in the house, she waited for her eldest son, Kieran, to come home from school. He was first in every day, so she assailed him on the back doorstep.

"Mam, are you, all right?" Noticing the camera in her hand, he felt sure he had broken it. "What, is it broken?"

"No, no, not at all. Show me how to use the video."

Relieved to hear he was not guilty of misappropriation of his mother's prized possession, he resisted the urge to say, "Jeez, Mam, it's not hard."

Breathless, she arrived back at the Bright House, brandishing the camera on high, announcing, "I've got it, Maisy. Look, I've got it!"

"*By gosh, I think she's got it,*" someone lightheartedly said, borrowing a quote from *My Fair Lady*. It was the last time anyone took Madge Costello or her work for granted.

The kind man in the photography shop had everything ready when she called in to check some days later.

Angela was finally home, recovering from her last cycle of chemo and doing well. Her next appointment was in six months. She continued with the homeschool program and was due back in the classroom in the New Year. The previous week, Mrs. Finnerty took Angela, Amy, and Charly to *Pepper* for dessert. They ordered Laddu of course, delighted to see them served on the tiny gold-rimmed plates and some of that creamy rice pudding Amy so coveted in matching little bowls.

Finally, Madge was excited to show Mrs. Finnerty the projects they had been working on, so they all agreed to meet on a Wednesday morning. Sammy promised to make the tea. Mrs. Walsh would bring the usual scones.

"It's not like Mrs. Finnerty to be late. Do we have the right day?" someone asked as they were all milling about.

Madge knew she had the right day. With her heart pounding in her chest, she casually offered to go check. She walked steadily down the path and along Shadow Ridge Avenue. Her pace did not quicken as she approached the house. Both cars were parked in Coughlan's driveway. Madge made a mental note of that. Mrs. Miller, the cat, was not in her usual spot. As Madge tentatively placed her foot on the front step of Mrs. Finnerty's house, someone came out of Coughlans. It was Tony. For some reason, he did not speak but went back into his house, returning with a key. Together, they found Mrs. Finnerty lying on her back, one arm by her side, the other under the pillow with the corner of a book firmly in her dead hand. Silently, they stayed there together, God only knows for how long. Gradually, Police Sergeant Coughlan recovered and did what he had to do.

When the linchpin of their community was no longer with them, their generous, easygoing nature gave way to an artificial robotic existence. After the initial shock and disbelief, avoidance was their only escape. The path they had walked so easily with Mrs. Finnerty cracked, splintered, and became dangerous. They tiptoed across its sharp edges, sidestepped its gaping chasms, tossed its sandy gravel aside with their unsteady gait, and often did not venture forth at all.

Eventually, as human nature has a way of doing, it restored in them the love, commitment, and resilience they shared. Realizing that much work awaited, they forged a new path. Mrs. Finnerty would never leave them. A surge of energy burst forth, each one tripping over the other to get things done.

Oh, Mrs. Finnerty was with them all right in the thick of it—*onwards* and *upwards*.

Madge

THE EARLY MORNING bedlam gave way to silence as the last of her family shut the back door behind them. Madge made her way to her tiny office, which the boys called the "broom cupboard," it's only redeeming feature being a good-sized window with a view of the back garden. A copy of *The Baybridge Star* newspaper lay open on the little desk as it had since the day Declan wrote the article. She read it again for the umpteenth time.

"*A heavy police presence was visible yesterday in Baybridge as they redirected traffic in anticipation of Mrs. Rebecca Finnerty's unprecedented funeral procession. Hundreds lined the streets, many falling in behind the police honour guard, two on either side of the hearse, and the lone officer in dress uniform walking behind. Twenty cars followed those walking at a slow pace. When the procession reached the outskirts of Baybridge, it paused to allow the honour guard to fall away, and Sergeant Coughlan, the lone guard, to join his family in the lead car. The motorcade then picked up speed until slowing down in Haymarket, to allow six more vehicles to ease in behind, finally arriving at the family plot in Mrs. Finnerty's hometown in County Wicklow. Following a brief ceremony, she was laid to rest beside her loving parents.*

Mr. Shiva, a good friend of the deceased and owner of Pepper, the Indian restaurant where she ate lunch every Sunday since moving to Baybridge, invited anyone who wished to an open house lunch, sensing there would be a great void after the motorcade left. The response was phenomenal as the need to exchange stories of this woman's quiet generosity was great, as was their shared sadness and sense of loss at her passing. May she rest in peace."

Madge closed the paper, folded it, and placed it in her satchel. She, too, shut the back door and walked to her real desk in her new place of work. When it became known that Mrs. Finnerty deemed Angela and Amy her heirs and the shock waned a little, Tony and Caroline had a lot of thinking to do. The girls spent time together, trying to figure out what it all really meant.

Amy said one day as they finished their after-school snack, "Mrs. Finnerty's house is always going to be a library, isn't it, Mammy?"

"Is that what you would like, pet?" asked Caroline.

"Oh yes, always, I wouldn't want it to be a house to live in, only to read in."

"I think we should move Mr. Doherty's mobile bookcase over to the children's corner. He would like it to be over there, I'm sure," suggested Angela.

"I'm sure he would. What great ideas you both have."

Caroline and Tony had their answer about next door. They consulted with Mr. Leach, who explained the property would remain Amy's with no binding restrictions on its use. That same week, he informed Charly and her parents that Mrs. Finnerty had set up a college fund for her.

The young girl simply said, "I will make her very proud."

Her mother's heart ached.

In due course, it came to pass that Madge Costello became the director of the Rebecca Finnerty Library and Resource Centre. Overnight, it seemed she had turned a corner. Today was *her* new beginning. She sat where Mrs. Finnerty always sat, at the huge desk facing the road, opened its slender pencil drawer, slid the newspaper article inside, and closed it tight.

At ten o'clock sharp, the workmen came to convert the bedrooms into reading rooms. The earlier shipment of books lay on the floor still in the boxes, awaiting the installation of more bookshelves on the top floor. Here, people would have access to inspirational literature and current management of cancers among other diseases, which they could browse at their leisure. While pondering all this, Madge's gaze fell upon the framed object on the desk to her right. To avoid the sun glare now resting upon it, she turned it slightly towards her. She recalled with a smile how it got to be there. The day Mrs. Finnerty died, she had brought it to the Bright House, intending to share it with the others before giving it to Angela. When eventually she did show it to her, she was more than amazed that the foundation had such a thing.

"A newsletter," she exclaimed, "the first one ever. Amy, Mammy, look, *Indigo Crown!*"

"We all decided you should have the first one. It's in a hinged frame so it can stand up like an open book. Do you like it?"

She liked it very much, so much so that when the library idea came to pass, she asked Maude, "Can you please put it on Mrs. Finnerty's big desk so that everyone can see it?"

There it remained.

Both Madge and the library flourished. The children's section expanded. Visiting children loved wheeling Mr. Doherty's mobile bookshelves about the place, intrigued it could move. Any child who wished to write a story could do so and place it on the mobile cart for anyone to read. "*Marty,*" by Colette Ryan, was the first to land there. Soon, it was overflowing. Amy and Angela read them every Sunday afternoon at about the time they would be having laddu and book club with their sorely missed friend. The publicity and PR for the foundation remained in Madge's hands. As more and more branches opened, she had cause to travel. Her first trip took her to England, where she recorded the launch of three new centres. As the children got older and more independent, she undertook projects further afield.

Maisy's suggestion of making a video of Sammy and Kitsy at work took off like wildfire. Mr. Leach, the solicitor, reviewed the appropriate privacy regulations and parental permission require-ments finding everything in order. The children also enjoyed being recorded, modeling their turbans. Some even took to making their own videos, sharing their stories with simplicity, humour, and inspiration. Maisy's casual remark reminded her of a casual remark of her own when she first heard of Angela Coughlan's illness. She, Mrs. Walsh, and hundreds of others stood outside the cathedral during Angela's mass. The whisper between herself and Mrs. Walsh got around to the extra expense all the back and forth to Dublin would incur on the family. She asked her friend, "Are you thinking what I'm thinking?" And at that moment, the tote bag receiving the first donation became known as Angela's Purse.

That day, a new Madge Costello began her journey, transforming the unassuming, tentative, beautiful housewife and mother into the artistic leader she was today. In her mind, the confidence to do any of this lay squarely at the feet of Mrs. Finnerty.

The finest woman she had ever known!

Mrs. Walsh

WHAT YOU SAW was what you got with Kitty Walsh. Her direct approach launched the biggest and most successful fundraiser on record in Ireland. When she and her neighbour Madge Costello passed her tote bag around the congregation, she had no idea where it would lead. That the Baybridge people were generous was not news to her—she had seen it before. This was something else entirely. The amount raised at the church was such that she and Madge, unsure of the next step, sought legal advice as to how to proceed. The money kept coming at every turn, long after Angela's chemo finished. When she protested to anyone stopping her in the street or Quigley's offering her money, the answer was always the same.

"Sure doesn't she have to go back and forth for scans every few months and as she gets older there are all those adjustments to be done. Please take it."

That much was true, but Angela's Purse outlasted all that. Two years after that first euro was discreetly slipped into her tote bag, it was registered as a charity. Mrs. Walsh held a meeting at St. Paul's school, where the numerous donors voted on three causes, they would champion. The Rebecca Finnerty Library and Resource Centre was their top priority. Dr. Allan Moran's unit at Baybridge Medical Centre and Park Edge Hospital in Dublin followed closely behind.

Personally, she was beyond grief when word reached her of the sudden death of Mrs. Finnerty. Added to that was her guilt that *she* had not gone to check that day rather than Madge. How could she be so selfish? Oh, poor Madge. For days, she told her family her mind was in fuzz, and she couldn't get a picture of herself. Her boys thought her words funny but understood what she meant. Then one day, she said, "I have to go out."

She didn't need to knock on Madge's door. She saw her looking out her front window. Kitty imagined her sitting there for days, waiting. Why had she not come sooner?

"Oh, Madge, Madge," and "Oh, Kitty, Kitty," could be heard throughout the house. They spent ages apologizing to each other until exhaustion silenced them.

It was time to get back to work!

The Twins Killfeather

HARRIET AND ELEANOR were old enough to have seen many of their friends die. They were always mindful of how fortunate they were to be in such good health at this stage of their lives. Their visits with Madge and Kitty after Mrs. Finnerty's death was a comfort to them, and as sad as they were at her passing, it served to lighten their view of their own lives. Together, they decided to make changes to their will and summoned their solicitor.

In appreciation of the constant care given from the heart by Nurse Murry and her daughters, they set up an education fund for Maura and Carmel, enabling them to go to nursing school. They left the money previously designated for the rehab centre unchanged, with the remainder of their estate going to their lifelong friend Thelma. Outliving Mrs. Finnerty by four years, they continued the relationship with Angela and Amy who brought Charly into the fold. At times, it was hard to determine who was at fault when they were all together, the kids or the twins when the shenanigans were heard down the hall. Dressing up in Ms. Harriet's clothes was usually at the root of the ruckus.

Finally, they moved to the centre, taking up permanent residence in the suite occupied by Harriet when she had her bronchitis under the watchful eye of Mrs. Murry and her daughters, who continued to volunteer during their nurse training. They peacefully passed away within days of each other, wearing their colourful turbans as they said goodbye to this wonderful world.

That's the beauty of good style—you can show it off anytime, anywhere.

Fiona

SOCIAL WORKERS, BY the nature of their work, have a built-in resilience. When Mr. Doherty first came to tell her of Mrs. Finnerty's fear of having cancer, Fiona's skills kicked in naturally. Again, after her stroke, those skills enabled her to deal with the situation. Angela's diagnosis of osteosarcoma tested her professionally and personally, causing her real physical pain. But she got through that, and all seemed well. The sudden death of Mrs. Finnerty called upon her to support an entire community, a task that stretched her to the limit.

The blanket of bleak sadness hovering over their earth was smothering. She was in mourning and shared that fact with those who came to her for help. She set up shop in the Bright House, making herself available to whoever cared to drop in. Sammy and Kitsy continued their work, constantly telling and retelling little things that had transpired between them and Mrs. Finnerty.

Maisy had no such history but said one day, "I know one thing for sure, she was a great friend to the people from the Hill. Look at us three here, doing this kind of work. Nobody else would have given us this chance, nobody."

Sammy understood that from personal experience. Mrs. Finnerty gave her the chance before ever meeting her. Maisy went back to her office and allowed herself to cry for all those shunned because of where they lived. She lamented the lost opportunity to get to know this great woman.

Caroline asked Fiona to be there when they told Angela and Amy. The old nagging, gnawing pressure under her ribs came back with a vengeance. It was the hardest thing she had to do in her career, and she was terrified. She arrived as the girls got in from school. They sat around the kitchen table. Their dad told them. No reaction at first.

"She was thinking of you girls because she was holding the photo album when she just went to sleep." Tony was doing his best.

"Did she just stay asleep, Daddy?" asked Amy.

"She did, Amy. That's what she did," answered their heartbroken Dad.

"Did a stroke make her sleepy so she couldn't wake up like before?" asked the older sister.

"It seems that way all right," he answered.

Fiona and Caroline sat transfixed. Tony was managing this.

"Will they keep the album with her, do you think?" asked Angela.

She got up and went to sit on her mum's lap.

"I expect you will get it since she told you she will always be with you."

Well done, Tony! Amy hugged her dad and moved closer to Fiona. Silence followed. Tony took his leave while he still appeared to be in control—far from it!

"When Mr. Doherty died, Mrs. Finnerty was very sad. She was in the hospital and tried to hide it. She wasn't able to talk about it much because of me." Tears stung Angela's young eyes as she spoke. She tightened her arms around her mother's neck. Caroline and Fiona were shocked. Amy was quiet, moving closer to Fiona. Seems like the girls had talked about this together before today. "She will be able to check on him now, and I'm glad. He was a nice man." A silence fell upon them again, as they each reflected on the child's words.

Fiona spoke, "He was a nice man and cared about you. He also cared about Mrs. Finnerty. It's possible to care for more than one person, worry about more than one person, and be sad about more than one person all at the same time. That's how we get by because we can do all that for each other. We always hope the other person is better because of us. They both hoped that for you, Angela." Fiona was holding on by a thread. Then Angela said, "It's a good thing they don't have any more worries." As Mrs. Finnerty often quoted,

Out of the mouths of babes

They should have known the children would have the answers.

Hill Hands woke up one morning full of energy. Inspired by Maisy's remarks, they had a powwow amongst themselves. They asked Fiona and Mrs. Walsh to join them whatever day they could manage. Two days later, they met. Sammy spoke.

"It's great the success Una had achieved in England. We hear she is off to Spain to look at some of the work already going on there in the local villages. Rafael has some ideas for those communities. Kitsy, Maisy, and I were thinking we have kinda stood still here in Baybridge, Haymarket too. The videos are great for the kids, and *Indigo Crown* is awesome, no doubt about it, but we need to expand in Ireland. It's not a criticism, not by any means, we just want to do more." As nobody spoke, she added, "I'll put the kettle on."

"I'll get the biscuits," Sammy said, hot on her heels.

Fiona and Mrs. Walsh were at a loss as to what Hill Hands wanted to do. When they returned with the tea, Maisy got the nod to present the plan.

"It occurred to us that a lot of time could be saved if we held designer workshops in strategic locations. We have a wealth of talent in our midst as things stand. Mrs. Shiva can source fabric and make a turban in her sleep. Sammy here is a genius with the boys' turbans, custom making each one. Without Kitsy's logo, there would be no message from Angela. The turbans could have been made anywhere and by anyone. We need to pass on this knowledge on a grand scale." Pause for a sip of tea. "Social workers need to be exposed while they are students to the significance of hair loss to these children and what a difference a simple thing like a turban can make in their lives. The distraction is therapeutic and has a positive effect on their everyday lives. Look how the London hospital wasn't aware of that. Speaking at college campuses, in hospitals and community centres would accomplish that." She finished her tea.

All eyes on Fiona and Mrs. Walsh. By the following Tuesday, Maisy had an appointment with the dean of social studies, at Fiona's husband's college. A week later, Mrs. Shiva was addressing a class of students at the Haymarket School of Art and Design. Sammy and Kitsy held evening workshops. The response was such they had a waiting list. Fiona's brother Declan ran excerpts from *Indigo Crown* and missed no opportunity to promote the cause. Within eighteen months, five more Angela's Tresses and Turban centres opened across Ireland. Dr. Owens feared he might lose Fiona. Not a chance, she told him.

Well done, *Hill Hands*!

The Children

CHARLY AND MRS. Finnerty got to know each other in Dublin when Una picked up her certificate from St. Swithun's. They had lunch in the converted Fire House afterwards, where the framed certificate being passed around caught Charly's attention. Mrs. Finnerty knew when the child entered the university that day, she made up her mind this was where she would go when she was old enough. At lunch, she scrutinized Una's certificate, seeking out every little detail, imagining it was her own.

When word reached her of Mrs. Finnerty's death, she felt a bit of that hope slip away. She did not talk about her feelings with anyone but fell silent and aloof. She spent all her energy searching for something or someone to replace her new missing friend, she could not. Instead, she dedicated a tiny space in her brain to Mrs. Finnerty, working hard at school and telling her about it at night before sleep. Gradually, her old self returned, much to the relief of her family. When her parents told her about the college fund, she smiled. Mrs. Finnerty had not left her after all.

She continued her drawing as she grew, spending extended periods sketching the magnificent bank designed by Vincent Craig overlooking Swan River. She had admired it since she was very little. She travelled to County Down to sketch the Royal Ulster Yacht Club by the same man and went on to study architecture at St Swithun's, graduating with Honours. When she took her certificate in her hands, she clutched it to her heart as she and her mother made their way from St. Swithun's to County Wicklow to show it to Mrs. Finnerty before returning home. She sat on the ground at the graveside and brought her up to date. Madge walked around, giving her space. That night, she opened herself to the future assured that Mrs. Finnerty would always be with her.

* * *

Similarly, Amy felt Mrs. Finnerty's influence, remembering how she told her she would make a great reporter. While still quite young, she wrote short articles for Mr. Doherty's cart, but soon, she found herself asking the other contributors about their work, and how they came to write their articles. One of the visiting mothers, whose child was in Baybridge Medical Centre and awaiting his turban, asked, "Do you write down these interviews and put them on the cart? You should, you know." That's what she did, and they grew in popularity as her skill improved. She followed Charly to St. Swithun's, studying journalism.

She became the editor of the *Student Gazette*, an in-house publication with controversial commentary on occasion. After graduation, she accepted a junior position and eventually a staff writer's post with a major Dublin paper. She worked hard, was not picky about assignments, put in the hard graft, and soon had name recognition. Her phone rang one day.

"Hi Amy," said Declan from the *Baybridge Star*, "how are things?"

"Just put the paper to bed, so quiet at the minute. How about you?"

"Not so quiet, but I thought *you* might have a minute. I've been mulling an idea over in my head for a while now. I would like to do a special edition or a separate glossy on the history of the paper for the upcoming anniversary." He took a breath.

Amy jumped in, "Wow, Declan, that's a monumental task."

"It's rattling around loosely in my head at this point, but what do you think?" he asked.

"I think it would be awesome," she replied.

"Okay, it's yours."

"What, are you kidding me? Me?"

"Oh, you'll have staff."

She moved back to Baybridge, a house owner without anywhere to live. She camped out in one of the upstairs rooms in the Bright House, relishing the view and the company downstairs. She sank her teeth into the project, got involved in Mrs. Finnerty's Library and Resource Centre again, and loved being near her parents. She forgot she owned the house next door. They did too!

She barely had her meager belongings put away when she was summoned to Wicklow for Una and Rafael's wedding. The wedding was some reunion but no surprise.

None of this was a surprise to their departed friend!

Angela

THE GENTLE GLIDING of the pocket door to the conservatory roused her from her thoughts. A handsome face, crowned with jet-black silky hair, peered around the corner. His smile caused her heart to dance a little in her chest. She loved him from the first moment they met.

"Remembering?" Previn asked.

"Yes, but happily," his wife answered. It wasn't always that way, but now Angela could sit in this lovely, peaceful space and recall to her heart's content without pain.

"I brought you a cup of tea, but you need to eat something, Doctor."

"Don't pull that one on me, Doctor. I bet you haven't eaten either," she teased.

"I picked off Finn's plate, nothing like dribble garnished toast in the morning. He's out for the count now, dribble and all."

"You did not put him down like that, did you?"

"You know what they say, 'Never poke a sleeping bear'."

"Some kind of a pediatrician you are." She patted the space beside her.

Taking the cue, he sat down as he passed her the tea. "All sorts of things went through my mind sitting here. How long have I been in here?"

"Long enough for Finn to destroy the kitchen."

"Not long then. I was thinking about the scarves sent to us girls from Haymarket, the ones we all wore when we went to India that first time. I was waiting to start med school in the spring. Amy and Charly were on Christmas break."

"Mom said it was the best time to go as the weather would be perfect. It was snowing when we stopped outside to pick you all up, and Madge was fussing about our clothes," said Previn.

"It was chilly in New Delhi, but once we moved south, it warmed up, so we could wear our summer clothes," recalled Angela. She sipped some more tea.

He was staring at her, drinking her in before asking, "Did you know then that I loved you and wanted to marry you?"

"I knew the day you helped me out of the Chariot in Haymarket," she whispered. She kissed him. "I'll be out in a minute."

She had been back to India three times since that first visit, one to visit Previn's family and twice for the foundation, but that first trip stood out, for two reasons. First, the visit to Mother Theresa's convent, orphanage, and leprosy hospital. The absolute pervasive poverty and the throngs of people in need, brought her to her knees. She knew, however much she would like to, she could not touch on the work these nuns and their volunteers did, day in and day out. In the leprosy hospital, those that could, worked on looms, making the fabulous fabric she and the girls had become so familiar with, standing for long hours on withered limbs. The happy, smiling faces of the people at every turn amazed her, despite their plight. It was a life-changing experience. Then the visit to the village where Mrs. Finnerty had lived and taught, which was the main reason for the trip. They received a royal welcome, with firecrackers lighting the sky, announcing their arrival. Every household prepared food in huge caldrons as surrounding villages joined to share in the festivities. Every single person they spoke to praised Mrs. Finnerty and attributed their children's success to her. Amy, Charly and herself fell squarely into that category.

All this shaped what kind of doctor she was today. She had seen it before up close with Dr. Owens, Moran and Dr. Myers. From them, she learned how to speak directly and honestly to the patient regardless of their age. Allowing the children to contribute to their own care, listening to them was the key. They were also open to any opportunity to see the funny side of things, no matter how dire. But of course, the Coughlans knew that already.

When Finn tried to get to her through the glass door, she was brought back to the present once more. His little palm prints all over the glass were proof his father had put him down for his nap straight from the mess he had made of the toast. She swept him up in her arms, mumbling something to her son about how Granny and Auntie Amy better not see him in this state. As she neared where Previn was standing, grinning from ear to ear, she said, "If I didn't know better, I'd say your father was useless with children."

Finn chuckled; a sound that made her heart swell every single time.

Gratitude, joy, and peace hailed down on Caroline Coughlan as she read to her grandson Finn before bed,

And when night falls, they swim to their little island and go to sleep

About the Author

EILEEN FINN LOVING was born in Sligo, Ireland, a place she returns too often. She moved to London to pursue a career in nursing. She worked there as a registered nurse until Paul, a young man in the United States Navy, swept her off her feet. After their marriage, they were deployed to the San Francisco area, where their two sons were born, then to Rota, Spain, back to London, and finally to the Pentagon. They settled in Northern Virginia, where four lively young grandsons keep them on their toes.

To Nicole

Eileen Finn

Lou in

CPSIA information can be obtained
at www.ICGtesting.com
Printed in the USA
FSHW012337201021
85595FS

9 781662 438363